THE FINAL BATTLE

ELIZABETH KNIGHT

CREATIVE WONDER PUBLISHING

Knight, Elizabeth

The Final Battle

Editing: Swish Editing & Design

Cover artist: Malice and Mayhem Book Covers

Formatting: Creative Wonder Publishing

This is for all of you who made it through to the end of this slow
burn series.
RIP your panties.

CONTENTS

One

Izel

"**E**verybody out!" Cassarah bellowed. "Get out of here, now!"

My gaze snapped to the windows, where I was greeted with the sight of flames coming straight for us. Grabbing Phillip, I yanked him up and out of the chair he'd been sitting in and ran toward the door. The air exploded with heat and glass as the odd-looking dragon burst into the dining hall. Thank God the ceilings were so high, or else I'd have been worried he'd knock the roof down, crushing us before his flames could do the job. Shoving the crown prince out into the hall, I turned to head back in to get the others out.

Abbott was hurrying past me with Queen Catharine's daughter, Princess Amelia, in his arms. "Help Cassarah. She was closest to the attack," he ordered.

Slipping past him, I tried to find out who was where in the utter chaos of the space. Milky white wings filled the space, crashing into everything, smashing it to the floor, making it dangerous to venture farther. That didn't matter—finding Cassarah was what mattered. Without her to lead the battle for our kingdom, all would be lost, and the Lost King would never be stopped.

Finally, I caught sight of her hiding under the stone table with Dayson as another blast of fire was shot their way. As soon as it was over, I motioned to Day for him to send Cassarah my way. Grabbing her arm, he surged forward, moving quickly for a man of his bulk. I took a step closer when I saw the dragon I could only guess to be Xotha, pair-bond to Henry, the Lost King, driven mad from dark magic. It was the only explanation for the lack of color in his scales, the solid black eyes, and the acid that seemed to be leaking from him.

"Watch out!" I yelled when I saw Xotha whip his tail out toward Cassarah.

It wrapped around her waist, dragging her back toward the window. Leaping over the stone table, I chased after them, watching as Cassarah stabbed the dragon with an arrow created from her Birthright. It pierced through the armored scales, loosening its grip, but not enough for her to get free. As if the next sequence of events happened in slow motion, I watched as Cassarah was dragged out the window and plummeted down the cliffside.

The Dragon Castle was built into the side of a mountain high in the air with a wooden bridge connecting it to the main road to the village. Sharp rocks and a swiftly running river would greet her at the bottom. No one could survive a fall like that, but that didn't stop me from reaching out to my dragon, who'd been guarding the area and diving off the ledge to follow her. Cassarah's black dragon, Vasin, battled with Xotha, doing everything he could to keep him away from her. While strong and king among dragons, Vasin was still young, and his scales weren't as thick as they needed to be, nor had he been able to breathe fire yet.

Dragging my gaze away from the fighting dragons, I searched for Cassarah, my little warrior, the woman who had appeared out of nowhere to claim my heart—the Dragon Queen and leader of the mercenaries, with blazing amber eyes that captivated you and wild mahogany curls to frame her proud jaw. She wasn't a woman who needed to tell you she was in charge or even wanted to be our leader, but her presence alone had you stand up and take notice. Then you caught a glimpse of her incredible intelligence, which should scare you far more than us with our swords and arrows. My little warrior could crush you without even lifting a finger if she put her mind to it, and that was far more dangerous than any dragon or warrior.

A roar filled the night air, followed by a burst of flame as Vasin lit Xotha up before slamming him into the mountainside. It gave me enough light to see by, and I spotted Cassarah's form below me, her skirts billowing in the wind. In the brief moment I saw her clearly, my heart seized in fear. Her eyes were closed, and she looked resigned to her fate as she hurtled toward the ground.

No! Cassarah wouldn't give up, not her, not like this. She's fought too hard to get to where she is now to throw it all away.

Another roar, closer this time, alerted me to Shanshen, my blue dragon, arriving. Swooping under me, I latched onto his neck and clung to him as his massive wings thrust downward, shooting us in the opposite direction I wanted to go. As swiftly as I could, I got myself settled in the saddle-like harness all our dragons were wearing so they were ready in case we needed them—it seemed it was a wise choice.

"We need to get to Cassarah before it's too late," I ordered Shanshen.

With a growl of understanding, he tucked his wings to his side and dove. The wind streaked past us, pulling at my clothes and hair tied up of my head. My knuckles turned white as I kept myself steady, not wanting to risk falling off and creating more problems. The deeper we went into the canyon below, the darker it got, making it hard to see her, but I'd heard Cassarah tell us that dragons had far better night vision than humans, so all I could do was trust my dragon.

A blinding blue light burst into existence, blinding me to the point I had to close my eyes and tuck my head under Shanshen's wing. Once the light dimmed, I whipped my head back up, searching for the source of the light. There, floating in the air with a pair of ethereal blue dragon wings, was Cassarah. Shanshen snapped his wings out, slowing us so abruptly that I was almost thrown from his back as I focused on the most beautiful sight I'd ever seen. The wings shimmered with power, making me wonder if they were created from her Birthright. Once she'd marked all of us as her consorts and the castle's magic accepted her, I'd seen a change in her power. It was stronger and acted unlike any Birthright I'd ever seen.

The look on her face told me she was just as shocked as I was, but it quickly morphed into a look of determination. My brows furrowed as I watched what was happening above me—her wings propelled her upward like a streak of lightning. It was as if she was there in front of me, and in the blink of an eye, she was soaring toward Xotha, who was still locked in a fierce battle with Vasin. Blood streaked down Xotha's side, but the dragon didn't even seem to notice.

Shanshen chased after our queen, hot on her heels without me even needing to ask. Cassarah's bow, the typical form her Birthright took, appeared in her hands. Without slowing down, she drew the string back and let loose an arrow, hitting Xotha right in the eye. The dragon let out a scream that chilled me to my bones, green bubbling liquid gushing out of where his eye had once been. With one final swipe at Vasin, the wounded dragon broke away and shimmered slightly before disappearing into the night sky.

What the hell did I just witness? How could a dragon vanish into thin air with the snap of a finger? Clearly, there was more going on with the Lost King and his dragon than we realized or were prepared for.

Vasin shoved off the craggy cliffside he'd been tossed into and followed after his pair-bond, and they headed for the main roost. I wasn't sure if I should follow or go back and tell the others she was okay. In her mind, the most important thing right now would be to look after Vasin and ensure he was all right. Depending on how bad his wounds were, she could be there all night—best to tell the others she was okay.

"Take me back to the castle, then we'll meet up with Cassarah and see if she needs anything," I instructed Shanshen.

With a snort as my only acknowledgment, he turned us toward the castle. While I thought he would take us to the dragon perch near the previous king's quarters or even the one near our space, he decided to go right to the source—the dining hall. Digging his talons into the stone, he clung to the outside of what had once been a wall of windows, tucking his wings in to make himself smaller. Now, here I was again hanging off the edge I'd just jumped from.

"Izel!" Gavin called, rushing over to me. "Where is she? I saw her get pulled over the edge. Why isn't she with you?"

"Cassarah is fine. She is with Vasin at the roost. He was injured fighting Xotha. To what extent, I don't know, but I figured I should come tell you all is well. Where are the others?" I asked, surprised he would be the only one here.

Gavin gave me a disbelieving look. "On their dragons looking for Cassarah. Where else would they be once they got things settled here? I stayed behind to deal with my aunt and uncle, not trusting to leave them alone with only the newly created castle guard."

Of course, they went after Cassarah. If I'd been willing to leap off a cliff to follow after her, why wouldn't they do the same? "I'll see if I can find the others and make sure to keep you informed. Thank you for staying here. I know it will ease her mind once she can process all this."

"It's a small thing, but it's what I can do right now for her," Gavin agreed as he started to back up, waving me off. "Go find the others so they don't think she's dead at the bottom of the ravine."

Nodding, I patted Shanshen's neck, and he shoved away from the ledge and back out into the open air. I was quickly learning how much trust you needed to have in your dragon when they pulled moves like this. I would have been terrified if I didn't believe he would make sure I was all right.. Even though I couldn't talk to Shanshen like Cassarah could to Vasin, we found a way to understand each other.

"Let's find our brothers and get back to the roost. I don't like leaving her alone right now. Xotha could come back any second." Shanshen let out a snarl, followed by a blast of flames lighting up the sky. It was almost as if he were signaling to the others our location.

A roar sounded in the distance, echoed by two others, giving me hope they would be heading back in this direction. Sure enough, I saw Tahir, Jade's red dragon, first, with his vibrant scales being easier to see in the dark. The others were right behind him and proceeded to circle me, each looking to see if I had Cassarah with me.

"She went with Vasin back to the roost. He was wounded, and she needed to check on him first," I hollered at them. "Gavin knows and is staying at the castle while we guard Cassarah."

Cole, not even waiting for me to finish talking, sped off on his dragon, with the rest quickly following. I couldn't really blame them. Cassarah was our whole world, even before she officially claimed us as consorts. The moment that mark appeared on my forearm, giving me the title of guardian, there was no turning back. Watching her grow into the queen she was becoming made me love her even more. Being her consort just meant I could finally do something about it.

Shanshen didn't linger and chased after the others, soon overtaking them as he flew higher to pass them all, only to dive down when we reached the plateau where the roost entrance was. When he landed, dust billowed around us as he flared his wings to slow us down enough that we didn't crash.

"Oomph, was it really necessary to make such an entrance?" My dragon turned his one good silver eye at me, letting out a snort of smoke. "All right then, seems you have quite the competitive streak in you now, doesn't it?" I chuckled as I slid off his back and rubbed his neck. In answer, I got what I would consider a smile of sorts as he bared his teeth at me, bobbing his head.

Being the show-off he was, Paxton dropped out of the sky to land in a crouch beside me, popping back up with a grin. "Man, that move never gets old."

Abbott walked up behind him and cuffed him on the back of the head. "Now is not the time to be acting like a child. We almost lost Cassarah tonight because we acted overconfident."

"Fuck off, would you? I know what happened tonight. I have the singed clothes to prove it," Paxton shot back. "Take the stick out of your ass and acknowledge that we now know the Lost King's dragon is real and our plan worked... kind of."

"You wouldn't be acting that way if you saw what I did," I stated, crossing my arms and glaring at him. "That dragon is not something we can underestimate. He took tons of damage and shrugged it off. It wasn't until Cassarah shot him in the eye that he decided to give up on the fight. Then the bastard vanished right before my eyes... *poof*, gone."

Paxton narrowed his icy blue eyes at me. "What do you mean vanished?"

"How many other ways can something vanish?" I challenged, not feeling up to dealing with his attitude. He'd been getting better, with Cassarah always putting him in his place and learning to trust the rest of us more. Yet moments like this still happened, and his stubbornness made him act like an asshole.

"Do we know if that is some sort of dragon magic, or are we dealing with something else?" Abbott asked, frowning.

Relaxing my arms, I motioned to the roost. "The one we need to ask is in there. Vasin is the only one that knows what any dragon could be capable of. Personally, I don't think it was natural dragon magic but has to do with whatever spell brought the thing back to life. Did you see the acid seeping out of it?"

"Fucking hurts, I'll tell you that," Cole announced as he joined us, followed by Zan and Dayson. "Some of that shit landed on my arm and ate right through my shirt sleeve, so I had to rip it off."

Glancing around, I noticed we were missing one. "Where's Jade?"

"Oh, you think that protective asshole was going to wait for us to go in?" Dayson grumbled. "Nah, that man had his dragon fly right into the roost from the top."

Dayson was right. Jade was obsessive when it came to Cassarah's safety, even to the point of making her angry on several occasions. "Maybe if he's had a moment with her all to himself, he'll let the rest of us close enough to check on her."

The men around me muttered their agreement as we headed in. I hoped Vasin hadn't taken any severe damage because I wasn't sure we would have much time left after this stunt. The Lost King was gearing up for battle, but I'm afraid that now our time to prepare was gone, and the element of surprise was lost.

TWO

CASSARAH

As I stood in the cave that had been hollowed out by dragons centuries ago to be used as a roost, my body hummed with power. It felt like when you stood outside in a thunderstorm and could feel the energy right before the lightning struck. My heart pounded as my mind wrapped around everything that just happened. I thought I was going to die, splattered on the rocks below the castle as I watched the twisted white dragon fighting with Vasin. Then, in that split second, I chose to believe my life wasn't going to end that way, and my Birthright burst from me, creating wings. *Wings!*

I caught sight of Izel and his blue dragon coming for me, but I wasn't sure they would have made it if I didn't have my magic save me. The world glowed in an electric blue haze from my wings, illuminating the battle.

"Cass, I need you!" Vasin roared, fire shooting out of his mouth.

It didn't seem to be doing much against Xotha, though, and in seconds, my wings responded to my need to protect my dragon. My bow materialized in my hand, and I hit true right into the black, soulless eye of the creature that once had been a living dragon. Now, here we are in the dimly lit roost, alive and safe for now. Vasin was laid out on the sandy floor, shredded wings spread out, showing the damage from the fight. Tears threatened to spill over as I took in the sight of him, but that wouldn't help either of us.

"*Don't cry, Cass. All will be well. The healer will be able to help, and I will be all right in a few days.*"

Hearing Vasin sound as calm and assured as always moved me to action.

"I need the healer in here now!" I commanded loudly, letting my voice echo off the walls.

An attendant walking out of one of the tunnels, heard me and dropped what he was carrying to hurry off. In moments like this, I didn't mind that I had the power to halt everything to have my needs met first. Vasin was half of my soul, and I couldn't let him lay there in pain. That thought finally got my body moving, and I walked right up to his head. There was a gaping wound on his snout, so I ripped off a large section of my underskirt and pressed it to the wound.

"*Xotha's blood is poison. The healer will need to create some kind of antitoxin to combat it. I can feel it burning through my veins, trying to thin my blood so I bleed out faster,*" Vasin informed me.

"*Please tell me we can save you.*" I sobbed, unable to keep the emotion out of my words. "*If this plan I came up with ends up killing you, I will hate myself forever.*"

"*Cass...*"

"Little bird, there will be none of that fucking nonsense coming out of your mouth ever again," Jade snapped, cutting off whatever Vasin was about to say as he marched up to me.

His seafoam green eyes were alight with rage. In contradiction to his visible anger, he swept me up in his arms and kissed me soundly, his fingers sliding through my hair before gripping it tight enough to make me moan. I wrapped an arm around his neck while the other went around his back, holding him close to me and allowing myself to let him hold me up. As if my magic sensed I was now completely out of danger, it subsided, leaving me drained. If Jade hadn't held me so tightly, my legs would have crumpled under me.

"Whoa there, I got you, little bird," Jade assured me as he scooped me up into a bridal hold. "Trust me, I'm never letting you go, not after watching you get dragged out that window. If I hadn't had to worry about keeping King Thomas alive, I would've leaped out that window right after Izel."

That bit of information caught my attention. "Izel what?"

"The crazy bastard charged right after you out that window as if he were diving into a pond. Good thing we all got dragons now, or his ass would have been strewn across the valley," he muttered as he nuzzled his head against my neck before lifting it to meet my gaze. "Thank God they got to you in time."

"He didn't... my Birthright saved me," I said, and before I could explain further, the dragon healer came running across the sands with his kit.

The boy who'd run to get him was carrying even more items, struggling under the weight. We'd given the healer a heads-up there might be a dragon fight tonight and to have whatever he needed ready and on hand. Thankfully, Zan had suggested that, so we didn't run the risk of the healer not being here. Jade set me down but didn't let me go farther than his arms could extend from where they rested on my hips. I gave him a scolding look over my shoulder, but he just cocked a brow at me.

"Is there anything I should know before I start treatment?" Peder, the healer, asked me.

"Vasin said that the dragon's blood was poison, a type that's thinning his blood. It also looked like that vile creature was leaking an acid of some sort out of his mouth," I informed.

Peder nodded and mumbled to himself as he grabbed supplies and started to mix things.

"Will you be able to save him?" I pressed, needing that hope to cling to.

Peder looked at Vasin and then back to me. "Your dragon is young, healthy, and strong. If we can neutralize the poison, then I don't see why he won't make a full recovery. He'll have some scars, and his wings will take some time to repair themselves, but things are looking good. I only wish we had some of the toxin to test on, but I'm going to start with my general antitoxin and work my way from there."

"Thank you, Peder. Please do whatever it takes to ensure he'll be okay. I won't stand in your way," I said as I sank next to Vasin's head, running a hand over his cheek.

"YOUR OTHER MEN HAVE ARRIVED. GO TO THEM… THEY ARE WORRIED. I'M NOT GOING ANYWHERE. I'LL BE HERE FOR SOME TIME, RESTING AS THE HEALER WORKS. REMEMBER, YOU HAVE A KINGDOM TO RUN AND AN ENEMY WHO IS ONLY GROWING STRONGER. NOW WE KNOW WHAT WE ARE DEALING WITH WHEN IT COMES TO HIS DRAGON. EVEN THOUGH THIS BATTLE DIDN'T GO AS WE PLANNED, WE STILL LEARNED THINGS."

"I'm not going to leave you! How can I walk away when you're hurt? I did that once, and it didn't turn out well for either of us, now did it?"

"CASS, THEY NEED YOU JUST AS MUCH AS I DO. GO TO THEM AND AT LEAST LET THEM SEE YOU ARE WELL. THE LAST THING THEY SAW WAS YOU FALLING. SET THEM AT EASE, THEN YOU CAN COME BACK TO ME."

I could tell by his tone he wouldn't let me brush this off, and as he chided me, I understood his point. When it came to Vasin, I had tunnel vision, and this was one of those moments. I was still learning to be a good partner to my men. Vasin was right to tell me to go to them. He was in good hands, and I couldn't abandon everything to sit here with him, even though I wanted to.

"You're right, as always. I will be back later to check on you after I've assured my men and checked in on things at the castle."

"THE LIFE OF QUEEN IS ONE OF COMPLETE SELFLESSNESS. THANKFULLY, YOU HAVE A LARGE HEART AND CAN MANAGE WITH THE GRACE BEFITTING YOUR ROLE."

Placing a kiss on Vasin's nose, I reached up and let Jade pull me to my feet. "Vasin said the others are here."

"About time they caught up," Jade commented as he tucked my arm through his, and we walked to the entrance.

When my other men spotted me, relief seemed to hit them at once, their pace quickening until Jade was yanked away from me. I was passed from one lover to another, each smothering me. I couldn't help but laugh as I was covered in kisses and sweet words as they checked me over.

"Don't ever do something like that to me ever again, mouse," Cole scolded me as he peppered kisses over my face. "I thought I was going to have a heart attack where I stood."

Dayson stole me away and caught me up, spinning in a circle as he growled with joy before setting me on my feet. Cupping my face in his hands, I got a sound kiss on the lips. "How the hell did you survive that?"

"My Birthright. It seems it can manifest itself into more things than just a bow," I shared.

Izel let out a sharp bark of laughter, drawing everyone's attention. "Yeah, like dragon wings that she could manipulate as if she'd had them all her life."

"What! You got *wings*? How cool is that," Pax exclaimed, pulling me from Dayson and grabbing my shoulders. "Let's see them."

Cole started to approach like he was going to smack Paxton, but I shook my head at him. "Using that much magic has left me drained. To be honest, I'm surprised I'm still standing."

Pax's face morphed into a worried expression. "Why didn't you say something sooner? We need to get you back to the castle so you can eat and rest. I know you hardly managed to get anything down at dinner."

"Yes, rest and food would be good, but I think I need to check in with Queen Catharine and King Thomas first," I answered, my shoulders slumping at the thought.

"Don't worry about them... Gavin is handling the situation. I'm sure their royal highnesses will be able to manage until the morning," Izel countered. "You and Vasin are our priority right now. Seeing we have Vasin settled and being looked after, that just leaves you."

"Are you sure you can't talk to Vasin?" I teased, letting Pax tuck me under his arm and lead me to the entrance. "He said pretty much the same thing."

Pax handed me off to Zan, who was already on Ifra's back, reaching for me. Climbing, Zan placed me in front of himself so his arms were wrapped around me, holding me securely. Zan and I hadn't been as physically close as I was with the others, but I knew I wanted him in my life and by my side. Our bond was more emotional, understanding what it meant to be underestimated and defying all the odds. Who would have ever thought a blind man could be a strong warrior and dragon rider? Of course, he had the help of Ezzu, his little dragonette female, who was his eyes when he needed them.

"I'm so glad you're safe. I've just found you, and I couldn't bear the thought of losing you before we got the chance to really begin," Zan whispered, his lips brushing the shell of my ear.

Shifting, I turned to face him and searched his cloudy silver eyes. "I couldn't agree more. This is just the start for us," I answered and quickly kissed his lips, startling him.

He recovered quickly enough as a smirk bloomed on his face. "Come on, Ifra... let's head back. I think we've all had enough excitement for the day."

The flight back to the castle was quick, and Zan had Ifra drop us off at the access point to our chambers on the fourth floor. The last king of the castle had known I would be coming and had the insight to understand I would have eight lovers and two other female guardians, Becka and May, who kept an eye on me when the men couldn't. Without me even having to say anything, Zan handed me off to Abbott, who led me to the bathing chamber, where the steam from the pool of water curled around me, pulling me to indulge myself.

Becka had to help me into the dress I'd been wearing, but Abbott anticipated my needs just as he always has, offering me his support and calming nature without ever needing to ask. Feeling his fingers releasing the laces down my spine ignited my body with desire. Ever since Jade and I slept together, it was like my body had awakened to a new world, and it craved to explore it further. Over the years of listening to our maids talking about their conquests, I always thought they were exaggerating their experiences. However, now I knew I'd been so sheltered from the truth I just hadn't been prepared for what had actually happened. The dress fell around my feet, leaving me in a simple white floor-length chemise you could definitely see through. Turning, I faced Abbott, and being the gallant man he was, his eyes never strayed from mine.

"Will you join me?" I asked, my voice unsure even to my own ears.

Abbott raised a hand, letting his fingers trail down my neck to my shoulder. He let his finger trace the edge of my chemise until it came to the tie in the front held tight with a simple bow. Tugging on the end of one of those strings, he unwound the bow, stepping closer until his lips brushed my ear. "Do you really mean that invitation, little phoenix?"

I shivered, reaching out to place my hands on his chest, pulling at the ties on his leather, jerking until I could shove it off him. "Every word of it."

Without further hesitation, Abbott seared his lips to mine, hooking his fingers on the chemise and tugging it off my shoulders until it joined my dress. His calloused hands from training with his sword as much as he did, scuffed along my skin, making me suck in a breath. Trying to catch up, I tugged his shirt out of his pants and slipped my hands under it to shove it out of my way. We broke the kiss long enough for him to tug off the shirt and toss it somewhere to be forgotten. Over the year I've known Abbott, I never allowed myself to dream about touching him like this. He'd been someone I leaned on and trusted with my whole being. As I traced the mark over his heart, claiming him as mine, I smiled, knowing I didn't have to hold back any longer.

Abbott pulled back and tucked a finger under my chin, raising my head so I looked him in the eyes. "You are one of the most stunning women I've ever laid eyes on. To be chosen as one of your guardians and now your consort, I couldn't think of something that brings me more joy. I'd been struggling to keep my feelings for you to myself, unsure if you'd allow yourself to choose more than one of us. I prayed you would, but hope is such a double-edged sword when it comes to love."

"Funny, I was thinking something similar, only I was reveling in knowing I don't ever have to hold back how I feel about you or any of the others. I know I was scared and wanted to wait for the right time to make things happen between us, but if tonight showed me anything, it's that you never know how much time you have," I shared as my hands worked at his pants. "Now, as your queen and lover, it's not nice to leave me as the only one standing here naked."

"My apologies. I shall remedy that immediately," Abbott teased, pressing a quick kiss to my lips before he kicked off his boots and yanked down his pants, revealing himself to me.

Seeing him, I couldn't help but lick my lips. This time, I wanted to give as much pleasure as I was given. Becka and May had explained how it worked for a woman to take a man into her mouth, but I still wasn't sure what the appeal was. They made it seem as if it was as enjoyable for the woman as it was for the man. I guess the only way to find out was to do it. Slowly, I sank to my knees before one of the men I loved with all my heart and looked up at him as I reached out and placed a hand on his dick, gently stroking it from the tip to the base. I didn't want to hurt him, and when he hissed, I yanked my hand back, scared I'd done something wrong.

Abbott took my hand and returned it to where it'd been. "Please don't stop. I love that you want to touch me so badly. I wasn't hissing in pain but pleasure, little phoenix... you could never hurt me."

I wasn't so sure about that, but I appreciated his confidence in me as I slowly stroked him up and down, making him toss his head back and moan.

THREE

ABBOTT

My brain couldn't comprehend that the woman's hand wrapped around my cock, stroking it like it was her beloved pet, was Cassarah. The shy, noble lady I'd met when she first came to the clan was gone. Now, kneeling before me was one of the most powerful queens that had ever existed. Of course, Cassarah didn't see herself that way, but that's what she had us for, to remind her every day what her value was in the world.

This outcome hadn't even been on my mind when I'd escorted her to the bathing chamber. After almost losing her, I couldn't stand to let her be anywhere without one of us close by, and I knew Zan wasn't ready to be alone with her in this setting. They were working on their relationship, just as she was with Pax, each trying to figure out where they fit in the relationship as a whole.

Her tongue flicked over the tip of my cock, making me grunt as I thrust into her hand, completely caught off guard by the action. *How did she even know about something like that?* It must have been Becka or May because I don't think any of the guys would have had the balls to explain it to her. Jade hadn't mentioned anything about her going down on him, so I don't think she's done it before, and the hesitation before she decided to take me fully into her mouth told me this was all new.

"Little phoenix, that feels so good," I managed to voice somewhat coherently as the feel of her hot mouth wrapping around me caused my mind to go blank.

I slid my hand into her hair and helped her find a rhythm that worked for us. Leaving my hand there more to feel connected to her than to control her reminded me this wasn't a dream. It didn't take her long to gain confidence, letting her hand rest on my hip while the other wrapped around the base, keeping it steady for her. Much to my disgrace, I had reached my limit far too quickly than I would have liked. While I was no virgin, it had been many years since I'd had any physical intimacy with anyone. That, combined with the skill she shouldn't have with this being her first time, I couldn't fight the inevitable.

"Cassarah, if you don't stop, I'm going to finish in your mouth," I warned, but she ignored me and proceeded to move faster and suck deeper.

Mere moments later, I exploded, gripping her hair tightly as I thrust deep into her mouth, making her gag, but I couldn't stop what was happening. Cum shot down her throat, and she swallowed every drop of it, along with my soul, leaving me a panting mess as I pulled her off me and dropped to my knees in front of her. Before she could say whatever it was she wanted, I slammed my lips to hers, letting my tongue delve where my cock had just been, unphased as I could taste myself as I tasted her. She met me with the same energy, not even pausing as I scooped her up and carried us into the pool, hot water enveloping us as I seated myself on the ledge.

As we kissed and explored each other, I leaned her back to feast on her perfect breasts that had taunted me for so long. Licking up the column of her throat, I felt the primal need to leave my claiming mark on her, just as she had done to us. Dropping to the swell of her breast over her heart, I nibbled, licked, and sucked the flesh until my mark was clearly visible. Male pride rose in me seeing it there, knowing each of the guys would know what we'd done here. Not once had I been insecure about the others. I'd always sensed that I'd have to share her with at least Cole. What's the difference in sharing her with one or seven other men? If she was happy, safe, and looked after, then I didn't care how it happened as long as I got to be a part of it.

"I love you, Cassarah, my little phoenix," I murmured as I worked my way back to her lips, my hand sliding between us. "A day will never go by that you don't hear me say this to you. I never want you to doubt my feelings."

Gently, I eased in one finger, stroking slowly, letting her adjust to the sensation. I'd known Jade was her first, but I don't think she and Cole went that far, so her body was still learning to accept us. Once my finger started to slide easily, I slipped a second in alongside it, making her breath catch and her nails dig into my shoulders as I distracted her with my lips. Feeling she was ready enough, I shifted her up only to let her slide down on me. Her channel was so tight I feared I might come right then and there. Gritting my teeth, I held myself together and wrapped her up in a hug, letting us both take a moment before I started moving.

Her hands slid into my hair, pulling it back from my face. "I love you, Abbott, but if you don't hurry up and take me, I'm going to find one of the others who will," she demanded, swirling her hips to add to her point.

I couldn't help but chuckle at her desperation. No doubt her body was craving sex now that it'd gotten a taste of it. "You're not going anywhere until I'm done with you."

Pulling out, I placed her to the side as I stood and pointed. "Face that way with your ass up in the air. You want me to fuck you, then I'll fuck you good and proper."

Excitement flared in her eyes as she turned, resting her arms on the pool's edge, knees bent and ass up in the air like I'd asked. My hands settled on her hips, holding her steady as I thrust into her as deep as she could take me, forcing a scream out of her mouth. The others no doubt heard us, but I wasn't sure if any of them would check on us. If they did, I wasn't sure if I was willing to share this moment or not. Pushing away all those thoughts, I focused on the woman whose back was bowed in pleasure as I rammed into her.

"That's a good little phoenix, taking my dick nice and deep," I praised, stroking her ass as I moved. "Is this what you wanted?"

"Yes," she panted. "This is exactly what I wanted… a reminder that I am alive and still with you all."

"Oh, we would never let you go that easily," I growled out, furious that we'd almost failed her. "You. Are. Ours," I stated, pounding each word home, causing waves in the pool to crest around us.

Cassarah had to shift, pushing back on the edge so I wouldn't thrust her right up and out of the water onto the cobblestone floor. Not that I would stop if that happened, but this was more comfortable for us and warmer. Feeling she was too far away from me, I reached up and curled my arm just under her bust, pulling her back so she was flush against me. Nipping at her ear, I picked up my pace, not going quite as deep as I played with the nipple in my hand.

"Oh my God, I think I'm going to explode!" Cassarah cried, her hands gripping my arm as if holding onto me would keep her grounded.

"Fly, My Queen, let go and just feel," I whispered into her ear as my other hand found her clit and started to work it.

If I'd thought she was tight before, it was nothing compared to her now that she was on the verge of climaxing. Thankfully, she was so close because I don't think a man in this world wouldn't be swept right along with her as she shattered in my arms. I knew the second it happened. Everything in her locked up and just as quickly turned into a shuddering mess as she cried out. The sound of her voice, husky and broken with pleasure, was the final straw, and the next thing I knew, I was shooting off deep inside her, clutching her as close as I could.

"Fuck, she sounds amazing when she comes," Dayson rumbled as Cassarah and I sank back into the pool.

I had no idea when he entered the room, but I was thankful he let us be and didn't join in like Cole would have. With Cassarah cradled in my arms, her face nestled in my neck, sweat coating both our bodies, I gave him a dopey smile. "It's way better to feel it."

"Of that, I have no doubt," he grunted as he set a tray of light finger foods and a goblet of something down next to the pool. "Didn't want to interrupt but figured you'd want this after, and by the looks of it, you won't have the energy to eat once you get out."

Cassarah reached out for him. "Thank you, Day, always looking out for me."

"You sure make it a full-time job," he teased, kissing her palm. "Now get cleaned up this time and don't take too long. Can't have you passing out in the water because you're overheated."

I cocked a brow at him. "Has that happened one too many times?"

"What can I say? I'm a man who likes a good long soak," Dayson answered with a shrug. "Our dragons keep these pools far hotter than any I've ever experienced, and she's been through enough today without that."

Nodding, I shifted Cassarah to sit next to me as I grabbed a cloth and bar of soap. When I turned around, I found her kissing Dayson in a cute, sleepy kind of way that wasn't hurried in the slightest. "Now, what were you saying about making sure we stick to getting clean?"

"Like you could say no to our woman naked, freshly fucked, and cuddly as a kitten?" Dayson retorted, not taking his eyes off her. "Now, Cassy-bear, I need you to try and focus so we can get you to bed before you fall asleep on your feet."

"You could come in here and do it yourself..." Cassarah challenged.

We looked at her wide-eyed, shocked at her words. "Cassy-bear," Dayson warned, tapping her on the nose with his finger. "None of that. When I get my time with you, no one will see us for a few hours. I'm talking about bringing the snacks with you because I'm not letting you leave the bed until we know how many freckles we each have on our bodies. Don't think I'm not tempted, but I'm also a man who can be patient when the reward will be well worth the wait."

"All right, you make a fair point," Cassarah agreed, giving in to his demands and dunked her head below the water.

"You're a better man than me. I don't think I could have said no," I commented as I started to wash up.

Dayson shoved to his feet and shook his head, muttering as he left the bathing chamber. "I must have lost my mind to turn her down."

My laughter echoed about the room as Cassarah emerged to grab the bottle of cleansing oil for her hair. "What's so funny?" she asked.

"Nothing, little phoenix, just a moment between men is all," I answered, waving off her question as I snagged the bottle and took over the work.

"I can wash it myself, you know. Becka doesn't do it all the time," she argued.

Pressing a kiss to her temple, I ignored her protests. "It has nothing to do with you not being able to do this. I just want the excuse to keep touching you."

"You and your honeyed words." She smiled, looking at me over her shoulder. "Fine, I'll let you this time, but only if I can return the favor. You're not the only one who hasn't had enough of the other just yet."

When it came time for her to wash my hair, I won't deny I was easily swayed into round two as she sat in my lap. Finally, we managed to get ourselves clean, and she ate while I brushed out her hair and braided it before we headed back to our rooms. Entering her space, we found Dayson snoring, sprawled out on the bed in nothing but a pair of loose pants.

"Do you want me to kick him out?" I asked, running a hand down her back.

"No, let him be. I'm glad he's going to join us," she answered with a sweet smile.

Each of us men decided to have a drawer of clothes in her room, knowing the reality of us being in here needing to change or something to sleep in would be a thing. While she pulled on something to sleep in, I did the same, again thankful for Zan and his forethought. When she climbed into bed, Dayson woke up enough to pull her to his chest and toss a leg over her hip before resuming his snoring. I couldn't help but thank the previous king who designed the rooms and ensured we had a bed big enough for us to fit easily. Dayson was a beast of a man, and I wasn't much smaller, but even with both of us in the bed wrapped around our queen, there was room for more. I guess we'll have to see how long it takes the others to learn from Dayson and claim their spot in her bed. I had a feeling it wouldn't take long, but that was tomorrow's problem. Right now, I wanted nothing more than to fall asleep to the sound of her heartbeat in my ear, letting me know she was safe.

Four

Cassarah

The next morning, I didn't get much time to enjoy being wrapped up by two burly men. Instead, I had Becka bursting in, whisking me to get ready for the day.

"Cass, you need to wear a dress. It's your coronation day. I know it's not happening until later, but still," Becka argued as I pulled on britches.

Ignoring her, I continued to dress in the clothes I'd become accustomed to wearing since I came to the clans. "There is too much to be done, and I don't have time to deal with a skirt getting in my way."

"I'm sorry. Did the leap out the window rattle your brain, making you forget you're the *queen* in this castle?" Becka grumbled as she handed me a nicer leather vest that had to be laced up in the back.

Giving in, I turned, letting her lace it up so the high and mighty Queen Catharine knew I didn't get dressed by myself. "No, I'm fully aware of that, which is why I want to see what's happening with the dining hall. Last night was a disaster, and while I need to deal with our guests, they are not at the top of my list. Ensuring the castle is sound and my people are all right is what I care about most. I know there were other guards in the room with us. Do you know if any of them were hurt?"

"One got a cut on his scalp from some debris, but other than that, a few minor bumps and bruises. Cole is the one with the worst injury from whatever nasty poison was seeping out of the monster," Becka informed me. "The dragon healer also reached out, letting us know he was able to neutralize the poison, and Vasin is resting soundly. Peder gave him something that would put him in a healing sleep, so if you can't reach him through your mental connection, that's why."

The tension I was holding in my shoulders relaxed as I sighed. "That's excellent news. While I'm sad he won't be with me today while I do this coronation thing, I'll survive, and so will he."

"Can I talk you into eating something before you get swept up in being the world's most perfect saint?" Becka asked, arms crossed, blocking the way out of the dressing room.

"Let me guess, you already had food sent up for me, didn't you?"

Becka gave me a bright smile, telling me everything I needed to know. "Dearest May is waiting for you in the common room with your tray, Your Majesty."

"Don't call me that," I muttered as I glared at my best friend, following her to the center of our rooms.

Sure enough, there was May, standing sentry over a meal laid out on the table. Paxton lounged in one of the chairs, looking put out and cradling one of his hands. Walking over to him, I combed my fingers through his soft white-blond hair, drawing his attention. "What happened to you?"

"I tried to take the bowl of pickled eggs because I know you don't like them and wouldn't want them to go to waste. The evil henchmen over there decided to attack me by stabbing the back of my hand with a fork," Paxton explained, showing me the five small marks the utensil left behind. "Will you kiss it and make it better?"

"Don't you dare. He needs to know he can't do things like that just because he's one of your consorts," May challenged. "It's not proper unless you want to become the queen's taste-tester. Then feel free to eat all you want before it reaches her plate."

"All right, you two," I said, cutting in before Paxton could respond. "I have plenty to do today without dealing with this. He's not wrong, May. I hate pickled eggs and typically give them to him because he's the only one who enjoys the awful things. Pax, next time, just wait until I'm here, and I will gladly hand them over. Problem solved."

Neither of them looked happy with that response, but that was what I had to offer. The nutty smell of the kavat waiting for me gave me hope I could make it through this day with its help. Gulping down half the mug was my first step in getting this day under control before I moved on to the porridge. I'd refused to let them make me extravagant meals just because I was now living in the castle and officially going to be crowned their queen. If it was good enough for me before I took the throne, it was fine after.

"Has anyone checked in with the king and queen?" I asked, looking up to find most of my men now at the table. Gavin and Jade were the only two missing.

Izel answered as he grabbed an apple from the fruit bowl on the table. "Gavin stayed on the third floor with them. As your consort and ambassador, he felt it was his place to make sure they were settled and didn't cause any trouble."

"Then where's Jade?" I questioned, knowing it was unlike him not to check in with me first thing in the morning.

"Oh, he's been up for a few hours, already working with the crew to clean up the mess in the dining hall and ensuring there are double patrols out in case Xotha returned. He thinks they will try and stop the coronation from happening. Clearly, the Lost King doesn't realize you already have access to the castle's magic, and this is just a formality for the public," Zan said as he fed a piece of meat to Ezzu, who was perched on his shoulder watching me.

I slammed my spoon to the table, drawing all their attention. "This wasn't something you felt I needed to know?"

"Mouse, you were completely drained last night," Cole pointed out. "Even if we did tell you, what would have changed? This is why you have guardians to look after you when you can't look after your-self. None of us were going to keep this from you and always planned to share our thoughts as we are now. But I'll remind you that while you are our queen and lover, you are also our responsibility. We were called to you to ensure we keep you safe, no matter how you feel about it."

Closing my eyes, I took a deep breath, knowing he was right. My emotions were all over the place from the events of last night, and I was lashing out at them because I was shaken at how badly things turned out. No one was killed, and only minor injuries were being taken care of. It could have been so much worse. The dragon had gone after me and left the rest of the village alone. I would never put it past the Lost King to do something drastic to ensure his victory. If I were to beat him, I needed to start thinking like him, which scared me even more. Using his own tactics against him would be so easy, but how many innocent lives would be lost in the process? Shaking my head, I shoved those thoughts to the side to deal with later. Today would be enough to get through without adding all that into the mess.

"You're right, Cole. It's not fair for me to be upset when you're doing exactly what you should be doing," I apologized. "Clearly, what happened last night has shaken me more than I thought."

"If we could push off this coronation, we would, but this needs to happen so that in the eyes of the world, you have full power as the Dragon Queen. The stories might have been suppressed, but the people who fear it coming to pass are well aware of what today means," May explained.

It seems everyone felt the need to give me some tough love today. Picking up my bowl, I slurped the rest down, wiped my mouth, and stood, squaring my shoulders. "Am I allowed to check in with what's happening in the castle, or do you have other plans for me?"

Dayson snorted at my comment but looked at May for the answer. It appeared they'd put her in charge of me today, knowing I wouldn't ever be able to say no or talk my way out of things.

"I think it would be good for you to check in with the Creisal royalty. After the events of last night, they might have reconsidered their position on an alliance," May said with a smirk. "Gavin might have also mentioned that they sent one of their guards back with one of our dragon riders to ensure their army was on alert."

My brows shot up at this. "Seems they weren't just listening to their own voices. Come on, let's deal with them first, and then we can attend to the things that really matter."

Cole and Izel shoved back their chairs as they finished their breakfast, following us as we left our chambers to head down to the third floor. I opened my mouth to comment on them joining us, but one look from May had me shutting it, accepting that she had asked them to join us. It seems Jade wasn't the only one up at the crack of dawn making plans for my day. They all seemed far too prepared to manage me for them to have just woken when I did.

I picked up my pace when I heard raised voices coming from one of the sitting rooms. Arriving, I hurried through the door that was ajar to find Gavin red-faced, glaring down at shattered dishes on the ground next to where his aunt was sitting.

"There was absolutely no need for you to act like a child if what they brought you didn't appear to be appetizing to you," Gavin bit out through a clenched jaw. "All you had to do was tell me, and I would have had them make you something different."

Queen Catharine sniffed at him. "They served me porridge like a commoner. It's an insult, and I will not be treated this way after all that's happened to us here. We came in good faith that your alliance with this *whore* was something we should support. Now I see she is nothing but trouble and chooses to slight us at every turn."

So much for May's assessment of them changing their minds on the alliance.

"Catharine, enough!" King Thomas barked, glaring at his wife. "We are guests in this palace, and I would warn you against speaking ill of Queen Cassarah, especially when she is standing in the room."

Catharine's head snapped to the doorway where I stood, trying to figure out the best way to handle her. Clearly, the king and queen didn't agree on how they wanted to handle their next move. My guess was King Thomas was seeing the error of his ways while Queen Catharine was far from agreeing with him. Clasping my hands behind my back, I walked up to stand beside Gavin, letting my shoulder brush against his in solidarity.

"Good morning. I hope you both got some rest last night after everything that happened?" I inquired, keeping my face neutral as I spoke.

Catharine scoffed and started to speak, but King Thomas cut her off. "You are kind to ask after us, but we weren't the ones who were tossed off a cliff by a dragon. We are overjoyed to see that you are well. It's a miracle to see you completely unscathed. Your dragon, he fought gallantly. Tell me, is he all right?"

"It is thanks to my dragon and consorts that everyone made it out alive and mostly unharmed. My pair-bond didn't fare as well as I did, but the healers tell me he will recover in a few days," I shared, smiling at him, pleased that he asked after Vasin. Turning to the queen, I looked down at the mess on the floor. "Did you not find the food to your liking? I just finished a bowl of our porridge and found it quite tasty. You'll have to forgive the simple meal, but since we have the feast and other coronation preparations today, I didn't want the staff to do anything too lavish. They have so many other more important things to do that having a normal, everyday bowl of porridge isn't a hardship. As queens, it's our duty to look after those under our care in the castle, don't you agree?"

Her eyes narrowed at me, knowing full well I cornered her into sounding like an ungrateful bitch if she disagreed with me. "That is rather forward-thinking of you, Your Majesty. While I see your point and support it, I do believe that since you have guests, it might have been wise for your staff to inform us of your request. That way, we did not perceive it as a slight when it arrived."

"You do make a good point, and I apologize for that oversight. I guess it was too much of me to assume that guests in my home would be grateful for the food and protection I'm offering after they made it clear they didn't support me or my kingdom. In fact, if I'm not mistaken, there was absolutely no desire to combine our two kingdoms in the slightest. Any other ruler would have just sent you and your family on their way, danger or no danger, seeing as we didn't have any responsibility to look after your safety," I paused, turning to King Thomas. "If that is still the sentiment of Creisal, then I believe it would be best for your family to leave before the coronation takes place. We wouldn't want to give the Lost King any room to misunderstand."

King Thomas rose from his seat and walked over to face me, holding my gaze for a moment before bowing his head. "Queen Cassarah, I would like to formally apologize for my wife's and my behavior for how we spoke to you last night. It was short-sighted and unnecessary on many levels to treat you in such a manner when you've done nothing to warrant it. Gavin and Phillip took the time to walk me through what happened with their father and letting

Queen Mary live when it would have been in your rights to behead her as well. You are a truly honorable queen, and Creisal would like to formally declare an alliance with you and fight alongside you as you face the Lost King. His blight on this world needs to be put to an end to ensure the safety of all."

Even though my plan didn't go how I'd hoped, it seemed that the threat of almost losing his or his family's lives was enough to make him see reason. I would have led our people into battle no matter the outcome of this meeting, but knowing I would have their army to back us up gave me hope. This battle was going to be one for the history books, and I'm glad it will show we didn't have to do this on our own.

"It is my honor to accept your alliance. We will draft a contract of terms once the coronation is finished and make this official along with Crown Prince Phillip," I answered, bobbing my head in return. "If you'll excuse me for now, I have other things I must attend to before things are set in motion. Oh, and I'll have the staff send up another bowl of porridge, Your Majesty. I would hate for you to go hungry until the feast tonight."

Queen Catharine didn't say a word as I took Gavin's hand, tugging it for him to follow me out of the room.

"Love, you are a queen among queens. Never forget that, no matter what," Gavin whispered as he squeezed my hand, laughter in his eyes.

FIVE

CASSARAH

Knowing I wouldn't have much time before I had to prepare for the coronation, I headed straight for the stairs to the second level, where the dining hall was. Once we reached the stairwell, Gavin pulled me to a stop and pressed me against the wall, his hands firm on my waist. Before I could ask him what was happening, he cut me off with a kiss, letting his entire body press into mine, showing more physical attention to me than he'd ever done before. Feeling no need to fight, I let him deepen the kiss when he nibbled on my lower lip, my hands running up his arms to slide into his thick, curly hair. His moan encouraged me to do something else to get a reaction like that out of him again, so I slipped a leg between his so I could press my core against his hardening cock.

"Don't you ever put me through something like that again," Gavin whispered against my lips as he pulled back. "Losing my father was hard, but if I lost you too, I'm not sure what I would do. You, my love, give me purpose and meaning in life. Without you, I'm not sure I'd be able to go on living."

I didn't know how to reassure him, so instead of words, I pulled him back down for another kiss, letting my emotions bleed into it. I'm not sure how long we would have stayed there in the stairwell, but someone cleared their throat, and I knew our time had come to an end for now. We were panting at the flurry of emotions and how fast our hearts were beating. With one more lingering caress of my cheek, Gavin released me, only to take my hand again, leading me the rest of the way down. None of the others said a thing, for which I was grateful. If all of them were going to be intimate with me, then they needed to be all right with seeing stolen moments like this.

The flurry of activity on the second floor when we stepped out was overwhelming. Men carried tools and lumber into the dining hall while others carried debris out in large baskets strapped to their backs. Ballard was directing people coming and going, making me smile that he was so willing to jump into things after all that had happened with the previous clan leaders. Thankfully, this level of the castle was still intended for the royal family and guests and wasn't meant to be used for anything related to the coronation.

"Good morning," I called once I got close enough to Ballard.

He looked over his shoulder, and a smile flashed across his face when he saw it was me. "Your Majesty, I'm so glad to see you looking so well after what happened last night."

Coming to a stop beside him, I peered into the room they were working on framing the gaping void where the wall had once been. Thankfully, only the lower half of the wall took the brunt of the attack, leaving the third and fourth floors stable. "So, I'm guessing everyone knows what happened?"

"That the Lost King's dragon attacked you while the Creisal royalty was visiting... yes. That you almost died in the mix of the attack... no. I advised your guardians there was no need for more people to know than those who already did. The shock of the attack was enough to unsettle many of the people in the village." Ballard grabbed my arm to halt me as I started toward the stairs. "Don't, Cassarah. The viceroys are already taking care of things. If you go down there, they will feel like there is something more to worry about. It's why none of us have suggested postponing the coronation. Your people *need* you to be fine and put on the illusion the war hasn't started yet."

I held Ballard's gaze as he pleaded for me to listen to him, which I did. He's been the one looking after everyone as the clan leader of the Raven Rose clan, and I needed to trust the judgment of the one man, other than my consorts, who has believed in me since day one. Ballard was almost a surrogate father to me since I started this journey, and he wouldn't steer me wrong. "I will trust your judgment in this, but I won't make a habit of keeping things like this from my people."

"That's not what I'm asking you to do. All I'm saying is that they don't need to know this moment. Give them this victory, bringing our people back together under the rule of the Dragon Queen. Then tell them that the time of war is upon us," Ballard explained. "Use the passion your people have for this land and our people to fuel their anger for the battle to come."

He was absolutely right, and I'd almost missed this opportunity because my head wasn't focused on the target. If the Lost King had hoped to rattle me with this attack, then he'd done it. The woman I was now had so much to fight for but also so much to lose, and I was playing it safe, trying to conduct damage control when I should be sharpening my sword. "Thank you, Ballard, for not letting me act like a loose cannon. Everything you've just said is true, and we can do far better for our people waiting to tell them what's really going on. The plan I made blew up in my face, and I think because of it, I've started to second-guess myself."

Ballard pulled me into a side hug. "Oh, my dear girl, all leaders make mistakes and need to learn from them. The testament of a true ruler is how fast they can adjust and ensure it doesn't happen the same way twice. The Lost King's dark and twisted mind leaves us at a disadvantage when dealing with our morals."

"I've had that same thought as well," I said, pulling away from him to enter the dining hall with Ballard following me. "What I keep coming back to is why didn't he have his dragon do more damage? Was he just trying to cause chaos and kill me before I came into the throne? Or was it to find out if Creisal's royalty was really here? Something about it doesn't add up, and that makes me more worried than anything."

"If there is anyone who can figure out what he might be up to, it would be you, Cassarah. Your mind is unlike any I've ever had the privilege of knowing," Ballard shared, gripping my shoulder before he walked off to talk to a man waving him over.

The massive stone table that had once been the main focus of the space was now gone, leaving the room feeling far too large. I walked over to the wall they were working on and stood at the edge, looking down at the ground I almost found myself leaving my mark on. Part of me thought I would feel something standing here, but all I felt was anger starting to bubble up inside. Henry, the man who calls himself the Lost King, felt so confident that he could send his dragon after me because I wasn't worthy enough for him to deal with personally. By the end of this, I would prove to him how that had been his biggest mistake.

Spinning on my heel, I turned to head out of the room, only to come face to chest with Jade. I gasped and involuntarily took a step back, but he caught my arm and tugged me to his chest. "Let's not tempt fate quite so soon, little bird. I know you got your wings, but I don't think you've gotten enough rest to pull that off again so soon."

"Then you shouldn't sneak up on someone when they're standing near a cliff," I snapped back, my adrenaline pumping through my veins.

Jade gave me a bemused look as he led me away from the edge. "Having a bit of a rough start, I see. I told them it was a bad idea to put May in charge of you today, but I was outvoted."

"No, it was the right call. If it were anyone else, I wouldn't have listened as easily. May doesn't give a damn that I'm the queen or not... she's doing what she needs to do to keep me safe," I relented as I leaned into Jade's body. "I'm just so angry, and the last thing I want to do is deal with this coronation or our guests. Vasin isn't here to take me flying and talk things through like normal, so I'm floundering a little on how to manage."

"Little bird, I swear I was put on this earth to remind you that you don't have to shoulder it all. The fates gave you eight men and two women who want nothing more than to help you shoulder the weight. Now leave us here to work so we can get this sealed up before everyone leaves for the coronation," Jade ordered, brushing a kiss against my lips before shoving me in Cole's direction, who'd been coming over to collect me.

"Sorry, mouse, but if you want to see Vasin before Becka demands you start getting ready, now would be the time to do it," Cole pointed out.

"Yes, I need to see him. I think that will help make the rest of the day easier to manage," I agreed and let him lead me out of the room.

May let me visit Vasin with just Cole on the promise I would be back in a timely manner, or she would hunt me down. That was threatening enough that I didn't even consider pushing the limits. As it turned out, when Cole and I arrived at the roost, Vasin was still in a deep sleep but appeared to be healing wonderfully.

"Putting him in a healing sleep wasn't what I wanted to do, Your Majesty, but it was the only thing I could think of to help him heal the fastest that he could. After the events of last night, I got the feeling we don't have much time before we will be leaving Sheca to wage war," Peder shared when he greeted us. "I'll make sure to send out all the staff I have to gather what herbs and other items we need from the valley so that we will be well-stocked to manage whatever comes our way. Also, I hoped to ask your pardon on going to the coronation so that I might keep watch over Vasin as he sleeps?"

"Granted, without question," I answered quickly. "Caring for Vasin is the same as caring for me. If anything were to ever happen to him, I would soon follow, but besides that, he is an extension of my soul, and I appreciate you for understanding that."

Peder placed his hand over his heart and bowed. "It is my honor to work alongside the Dragon Queen and her pair-bond. Long live Queen Cassarah!"

"Long live the queen!" Echoed through the roost as Peder's staff called out in response.

"Go with peace and strength, My Queen, and we will be here making sure Vasin has everything he needs," Peder added, all but dismissing me back to the castle.

Cole and I headed out to where Jovid, Cole's purple dragon, waited for us. Stopping, I turned to the man, who was also one of my best friends, and pleaded my case. "Do we have to go back right now? The coronation isn't until sunset, and it's hardly close to midday. Couldn't we just go fly around for a bit? I feel like I just need a moment to forget everything because the moment I'm crowned queen, there is no going back. Cassarah, the person who used to sneak into the library and read books about war late at night and beg her father to teach her just one more word in the language he was teaching me, will be gone."

"Cassarah, no matter what title you hold, you are still you," Cole argued. "Every time I call you little mouse, I remember when I saw you curled up in the corner, trying not to be noticed as we talked to your father. The amazing woman you are now is all because of who you were growing up."

"My brain understands all that, but my heart is the one that's slow to catch up. I placed my hand on his chest, hoping he would feel my need. "Please."

Cole groaned, letting me know he was going to give in to my request. "May never should have let you be alone with one of us… we're just putty in your hands," he grumbled and waved for me to climb up. "I was waiting to show you this place until after all the coronation nonsense, but it seems like you're gonna need this now."

Jovid launched himself into the air, and we were off heading in the opposite direction of the castle, toward the coastline and a breath of fresh air.

SIX

COLE

W e all knew Cassarah was struggling today—it was written all over her face. It hadn't taken me long to learn to read her subtle expressions, helping me get a feel for her mood, but she wasn't hiding anything right now. Other than when we met with King Thomas and Queen Catharine, all her worries had been fully displayed for everyone to see. I'm sure she feels like we are being harsh on her, but she refused to admit that almost dying last night was a major event. After all she's been through, I knew she would reach a breaking point, and it seems today would be that day.

She's been able to roll with the hits every time something got thrown her way, but even the strongest of people have that one event that pushes you too far. While I supported May's plan of just getting her through the day and letting her fall apart once it was over, I didn't think we had that much time. The rest of them might be upset that I was stealing her away without a word, but I was her guardian and, above all, her friend. Hell, she was my best friend. We had a connection to each other I didn't understand, and when I first met her, she scared me. I'd been an asshole, pushing her away solely because I knew if I let her too close, I would fall head over heels with no chance of turning back.

That first month, as we fought and snarled at each other, created a kinship where we could be honest with each other. I'd gotten her so angry during a training session that she called me a bastard. The woman who hardly ever uses curse words flat-out told me I was being a right bastard, and she was right—I was. How she could think that who she'd been would ever be forgotten is ridiculous. The timid woman standing up to me in her nightgown was forever etched into my brain. Lady Cassarah was just the foundation to create Queen Cassarah, ruler of the mercenaries. It was now my job to remind her of that after I'd given her a safe place to fight it out with her feelings. She'd been trapped away in a room without an outlet for far too long, so I was going to give her one.

Jovid and I found this place while we'd been scouting, and I'd known right away I wanted to bring her here. Having never seen the sea before made me feel so small in the world with how it stretched farther than my eyes could see. One of these days, after the battle was over, I'd love to fly out there and see if more land existed or if this was the end of the world.

Then, a little farther down the coastline, I spotted this inlet with a small beach and a cave for shelter, almost as if a dragon had created it at one point for its home. I could hear her gasp as we crested the mountain range and caught the first glimpse of the Caleden Sea. Jovid took his time and even skimmed the water's surface, dragging his claw and creating a spray of water around us. The sound of Cassarah's laugh told me I'd done the right thing bringing her here.

When we reached the beach and landed, the first thing she did was run to the water's edge. "Have you ever seen anything like it before? It goes on forever!"

"I was hoping you might know with all the studying you did with your father," I commented. "We didn't know about Sheca, but Creisal butts up to the same body of water, so I wasn't sure if it had come up."

She shook her head, her curls wild from the flight. "No, Creisal, as a whole, has kept to themselves since the last Battle of the Kingdoms.

They built up their army to ensure they would never be a weaker power, and with the sea at their back, it was easy to do. I only know that no one who left to sail out into the Caleden Sea has ever returned. All are believed to be dead."

"What if they found someplace new and decided to stay?" I questioned as I came to stand next to her. "It seems rather small-minded to think we are the only kingdoms that exist."

Turning her eyes to look at me, I could see the excitement shining in them. "I'd like to think you're right and that more people are out there living their lives, wondering the same thing about us. What if we went? Think of the things we could discover being able to fly dragonback instead of on a ship."

"If you really want to go, I would go with you in a heartbeat, but we need to settle things here first. Leaving would be the same as handing everything over to the Lost King and giving up. You, little mouse, are no quitter. I've seen your determination with my own eyes more than once."

Her eyes fell as she stepped away from me, walking toward the cave. "Of course, it would be after I've dealt with the Lost King. I might need a moment of peace, but I would never turn my back on these people or my own kingdom. What kind of person would I be if I just disappeared without a word? Becoming queen and leading a kingdom into battle might never have been my first choice, but I will see this through."

"Mouse, are you trying to pick a fight with me?" I asked, surprised by her overreaction to my words. "What I said wasn't an attack on you but me simply stating facts about our situation. It's perfectly normal for you to have doubts or want to run away from this fight. You got tossed into the middle of it and were told to fix it, with no say in the matter. I'm trying to show you that having a moment of weakness isn't bad, as long as you understand that's all it is... a moment."

Whirling to face me, she took a step forward and shoved me back with both hands. "Damn right, I was tossed into this. It was your grandfather who showed up in my life and dragged me smack dab in the middle of this shit. Yes, I'm now the Dragon Queen and rule over all the mercenaries, uniting the clans after hundreds of years apart. What little girl wouldn't want to grow up and have that happen to them?"

She paused, hands shaking as her anger and voice grew louder. "You know what they forget to tell you? Once you wear that crown, you're in charge of every life you rule over. Will my people still want me to rule over them when I do whatever it takes to ensure their survival? The Lost King isn't going to hold back, and I can't either, or we'll lose everything we worked to build. That man is willing to bring his dragon back, twisted and broken from the brink of death, as a child. None of us truly know what he's capable of, Cole, but that's where I have to go in my mind to outsmart him. That bastard of a king will die by my hands because I won't allow anyone else to carry that burden for the rest of their lives, just like it should have been me to behead the clan leaders, not their sons."

Finally, my sweet, timid mouse felt cornered by the evil lion who'd been playing with her up until now. Yeah, she'd had her moments of anger at the clan leaders and others around her, including us.

The difference this time was the woman believed to be a mouse was never truly a mouse but a dragon. Cassarah's will and determination were ironclad, like the scales of a dragon, and right before my eyes, the ember of her heart for justice was being stoked. Soon, her flames would be felt across our world, destroying all those who stood in her way while protecting those she'd claimed.

"You know none of them hold that against you and never will. They made that choice on their own, which is one of the reasons they never told you they were planning to do it. While you might be the queen, what power do you have that hasn't been given to you by others? As your guardians, we are placed to protect you but also to ensure your rule is never questioned," I challenged. "A queen and her guardians working together in harmony to protect their people make us a force to be reckoned with. Don't ever doubt that, Cassarah."

Her anger was cooled until it was simmering just under the surface, right where it should stay until we needed it. It would keep her strong and sharp as we worked to end the Lost King. The glow of danger lurking deep within her eyes drew me to her, and I couldn't resist the call. Wrapping my hand in her hair, I pulled her to me until we were chest to chest, noses brushing each other, but I didn't close that last bit of space between us. Right now, I wanted to know if she wanted me as much as I wanted her.

I didn't have to wait long as she surged up, her full lips meeting mine as her arms wrapped around my neck, pulling me down to her. Our tongues danced as we fought for control, refusing to surrender to the other until I pulled back, cupping her face to keep her from chasing after me.

"Cassarah, no matter how deep into the darkness you go, none of us will leave your side. I promise you, I'll make sure you come back from it all, and the girl I met on the balcony is never lost or forgotten. She's the one who stole my heart and refused to give it back, and I will always be grateful to have fallen in love with my best friend," I said, letting my thumbs caress her cheeks as I spoke.

"Is there a reason you're still this close to me?" she asked, using the same words she'd spoken when we first met.

"Does a man need a reason to be this close to a pretty lady?" I responded with a grin.

"Clearly, the man addressing this lady isn't a gentleman."

"I'm no gentleman, only a man who's madly in love with his queen," I said before fusing my lips to hers once more.

We tumbled to the ground, the need to be close driving us into a frenzy. I ripped open her laces, peeling off her bodice, giving me access to her breasts, to which I gave the affection they were owed. It wasn't enough, though. I needed to be inside her. The last time we were together, I took the higher road, but I couldn't find the strength this time. Grabbing her hips, I flipped her over so she was on her stomach and pulled down her pants, exposing her pert ass. If I hadn't already been hard as stone, the sight alone would have done it for me. Tugging at my pants, I got them down far enough to free myself and crawled up her body.

"Little mouse," I whispered along the back of her neck as I situated myself at her opening. "I'm going to show you just how ungentlemanly I can be because no gentleman would have the balls to take his woman the way I want to take you now."

Cassarah moaned under me, wiggling her hips until she managed to get the tip of my cock inside her. "Do your worst. Prove to me how badly you want me."

Nipping at her ear, I thrust in until my balls smacked her clit with the force of my thrust. I wrapped an arm around her chest and pulled her up enough so I could kiss her as I pounded into her. Everything about this moment was primal and desperate. The tension between us had been building until we reached our breaking point here on this beach.

We'd all learned from whatever happened with Abbott last night that Cassarah wasn't a quiet woman when she was being fucked, and this moment was no different. Her moans and cries filled the air as

I rutted into her. I thought I might be too aggressive and eased up a bit for a moment, only to have her look at me over her shoulder.

"Is that all you've got? Is your love and desire for me so short-winded?" she taunted.

I laughed and pulled back only to shift her to her knees to get a better angle on her entrance. "It's dangerous to mock someone, little mouse. You never know what might happen when you antagonize the scoundrel you let into your bed."

"Well, we're not in a bed right now, are we?" she pointed out.

The crack of my slap on her ass echoed off the cliffside as I thrust back into her. "Since when did you become so mouthy? The Cassarah I remember could barely stand up for herself, and now here you are purposefully riling me up. It's almost like you want to see how far you can push me?"

As if to answer me, she thrust back against me as I plunged into her, causing me to bottom out inside her. We both cried out at the feeling catching us both by surprise, but it didn't slow us down. I knew I was on limited time, the tightness of my balls telling me I was close. If my little mouse wanted to play with the big dogs, then I'd give her something to remember.

I spread her ass cheeks and spit right on her back entrance, then swirled it around before pressing my fingertip in.

"What are you doing?" Cassarah demanded.

Ignoring her question, I worked her ass gently with short little thrusts that had her moaning and arching her back. Seeing that she truly enjoyed what I was doing, I added a little more spit and worked my finger deeper, feeling her loosening up for me. As I worked both her holes and picked up my speed, the walls of her core started to clamp down on me, and I struggled to keep a steady rhythm as my climax threatened to spill from me.

"Come for me, little mouse. Show me how much you're enjoying me fuck you here on this beach for the world to see," I growled out, making two more thrusts before she came, squeezing tight enough that I exploded with a grunt.

Unwilling to pull out, I let everything I had spill into her, and visions of her belly growing with my child had me thrusting deeper. One day, when the world was safe again, I would put a baby in this woman I loved. Nothing could mean more to me than having a family with her and the others.

Spent, I collapsed on her back and rolled us to the side, our clothes in shambles covered in sand, damp from the spray of the water, and the happiest I'd ever been. We both laid there catching our breath, watching the clouds across the sky, enjoying the afterglow of finally being together.

"We probably need to head back," Cassarah whispered, kissing my arm as she sat up. "Thank you for giving me some space to get my head on right."

"Is that what we're calling it? I've always heard it called an afternoon delight, but things are always changing," I mused as I tucked myself back into my pants and righted my shirt.

Cassarah just glowered at me and turned, giving me her back to help her with her bodice. I'd torn parts of it, but there were enough holes for me to use that we got it on her well enough it would make the trip back. Good thing she was going back to get cleaned up and changed, or the whole clan would know what we'd done out here.

SEVEN

CASSARAH

"Where the hell have you been?" Becka yelled the moment I entered my chambers. "Do you have any idea how worried everyone has been? The last we knew, you were going to see Vasin, then you and Cole just flew off, no one the wiser of what was going on."

May was standing next to her, arms crossed and looking extremely disappointed in me. "Cassarah, I understand you're under a lot of pressure right now, but with the threat of the Lost King's dragon, you can't do things like that. We trusted you to go see Vasin and come right back."

While I understood their concern, I didn't appreciate how they were treating me right now. "Enough," I snapped. "I understand I should have let someone know where we were going, but I need to remind you that I don't answer to you two. In a few hours, I will officially be crowned your Queen of Sheca. If I need to take some time for myself, then I will do so. I didn't go alone or without protection. I had Cole and Jovid with me the whole time, so I feel this attack is unwarranted."

May and Becka looked at me, their eyes wide with shock at my outburst.

"I'm here now, so we should probably get started on this whole production," I suggested, heading to the bathing chamber.

Since I didn't have much holding my bodice together, I ripped it off on my own. Soon, I was in the steaming water scrubbing the sand out of my hair and crevices I never wanted sand to be in again. When I finished my washing, I didn't leave, knowing Becka would have some grooming she would want to do.

"Are you ready for me, Cassarah?" Becka called from the doorway.

"You can come in," I answered, feeling guilty that now she was being more reserved than normal. I watched as she set down the basket of things she would use as she avoided looking at me. "Becka, I'm sorry. I shouldn't have yelled at you both. Ever since I woke up, I've had someone questioning every move I've made, and I just snapped. It was wrong for me to do that, and it's not the ruler I want to be."

Becka turned her head to meet my gaze. Thankfully, I didn't see anger, but I did see hurt, and that killed me. After all the years we've been friends and protecting her from my mother, ensuring she was safe by taking the beating myself, the last thing I wanted to do was hurt her. She was the sister I never had, always looking out for me and tending to my wounds after mother was done with me. Becka deserved better from me, and I let her down.

"I understand why you snapped at us, but I won't say I deserved it, Cassarah. That was mean and spiteful when all we are doing is trying to look after you," she stated as she slammed down the bottles she pulled out of the basket. "You've spent long enough looking after me when you didn't have to, and now it's my time to look after you, whether you like it or not."

"This seems to be the theme of the day. Everyone who's talked to me today has said almost the same thing." I sighed, sinking into the water.

"Maybe it's a sign you should listen to what we're saying then."

A silence hung in the air as Becka started combing through my long locks, rubbing scented oils into them. I didn't fight the quiet. Instead, I let it stand, knowing there wouldn't be much of it once I left this room, which happened far sooner than I would have liked. Dried and in a dressing gown, I was brought to the sitting room attached to my sleeping chamber.

It was large enough to fit everyone who needed to be present to get me ready. This was the one thing I didn't miss after leaving my childhood home—the poking and prodding of many women bustling around me, chatting amongst themselves. One person did my hair while another did my makeup, and a third and fourth worked on my hands and feet. There wouldn't be a part of my body that someone hadn't touched in preparation.

"All right, everyone… that's it until we're ready to get her dressed," Becka announced, clapping her hands. "Thank you all for your hard work, but I think we should make sure our queen gets something to eat before all the pomp and circumstance."

All the women curtsied as they left, wishing me good fortune, only to giggle as my men started to file in with trays of food. They were a welcome sight, and I couldn't help but smile as they came over to greet me.

"No funny business now. We don't have time to fix the whole look if you mess it up," Becka warned, giving me a wink as she left to give us some time.

Zan held out his hand to me, pulling me to my feet. "We didn't know how hungry you might be, so we brought a little of everything. Paxton even managed to get the kitchen staff to part with some of the cake they made earlier." My stomach grumbled at that, making us both laugh. "Cake it is."

He settled me on the couch and hurried over to get me some cake while Paxton plopped down, put his head in my lap, and smiled at me. "You sure look pretty, but I have to say, I think I like you better without all that stuff on your face."

Running my fingers through his hair, I pressed a kiss to his forehead, leaving behind a red mark from my lip paint. "There, now we match," I teased. "If I have to look like a jester, then so do you."

"Hey now, I didn't say it looked bad!" Pax defended. "It's just I like your natural beauty the best. You don't need all that stuff to get my attention."

I felt my cheeks heat with a blush at his words. For a woman who had eight men, I still wasn't used to getting compliments. "Thank you, Pax."

"Hey, stop being a goddamn brownnoser," Dayson grumbled. "Making us look bad for not saying smooth, romantic things like that to her. Some of us just aren't gifted with our words."

Pax sat up as Zan handed me my cake, freeing me to eat it more easily. "Dayson, I don't need sweet words or gifts. Having you each here beside me means more than anything. The trust I have knowing you'll always have my back is priceless."

"Never doubt that, Cassy-bear. Izel might have been the one to jump after you, but any one of us would have done it in a heartbeat," Dayson shared as he came to sit on the floor, facing me. He picked up one of my feet and rubbed his thumb into my arch, making me moan. "But I'm sure there are less dramatic ways for us to show you how much we love and care about you."

"Feel free to share like this any time." I sighed, leaning my head back on the couch.

I felt someone take the plate out of my hand and replace it with another. Sitting back up, I found the cake was gone, and the new plate was full of meat and cheese with some fruit.

"While I know Zan was trying to be sweet, you really need to eat something that will stick with you for the rest of the afternoon,"

Jade explained, crossing his arms like he knew I wanted to argue with him.

While the cake had been tasty, I agreed with his choice to feed me real food. I sat and munched while the guys talked about their parts in the upcoming coronation, giving me time to just be. Sooner than I would have liked, a knock came at the door before Becka and May joined us, along with Talia, the dressmaker. Two more ladies followed shortly after with the pieces of my outfit, signaling that our break was ending.

"Thank you guys for making this happen," I said, kissing each of them before they left. "I'll find you out there. If you can't find me, I'll be the one getting crowned."

"Look who's got jokes," Pax teased, blowing me a kiss as he left.

Slipping out of my dressing gown, I stepped up onto the platform to be dressed. With all the leather and layers, it took us a few moments to get everything into place, but once we did, I just stared. Everything about my outfit exuded power and authority while showing off that I was very much a woman under it all. The pewter and black contrasted the warmth of my skin and hair, making me stand out from the garment itself. Talia had outdone herself, and I couldn't be more pleased with the outcome.

"They have the crown ready and will place that on you during the proceedings. With how detailed the gown is, I don't know that we need to add much more jewelry unless there is something you want to wear?" Talia asked as she gave me a final look over.

"No, there's nothing. I was never big on collecting accessories," I answered, running my hands over the leather scales that had been carefully sewn onto the sleeves.

May came to stand before me, wearing her uniform, noting her as one of my guardians—black leather pants, black floor-length shirt with slits up the sides, and a fitted leather breastplate with the royal mark on the front. It made her look even more fierce than she did naturally, and that was saying something.

"Are you ready, My Queen?" May asked, holding out a hand to me.

Taking one last glance at myself in the mirror, I took a deep breath and shoved all my scattered emotions into a box to deal with later. "Yes, I think I'm ready."

Taking her hand, she helped me off the platform, and I placed my hand on her forearm as she escorted me from the room. Becka, dressed the same as May, followed close behind, watching my back. Once we reached the second floor, two palace guards led the rest of the way into the throne room.

The space was full of flowers and other decorations the villagers had pulled together, making it beautiful. The giant room was full of people watching as I was escorted to the steps leading up to the throne. What unsettled me slightly was how silent the room was with so many people in it—almost as if everyone was holding their breath.

The four viceroys of Sheca gathered at the top of the stairs, each in their colored robes matching the clans and associated dragons we'd joined together. The guards left to stand at their posts on either side of the steps while May and Becka walked up to join my other guardians standing in a row behind the dragon throne.

"Who stands before us?" Lawrence called out, his voice filling the room's space.

While I'd memorized the normal response to these words days ago, I felt I needed to answer them in my own words. "The woman standing before you is but a humble servant to her people, who has been called by the fates to lead them in this time of great need."

The viceroys looked a little thrown by my answer, but Sal just grinned and stepped up to ask his question. "What gives you the right to claim this throne?"

"I, Cassarah, ancestor of a man who walked away from the clans for the promise of a title, was picked by the black dragon, Vasin. But the truth is, I have no right to this throne other than that given to me by the people standing here with me."

Eleazar stepped forward, presenting his question. "Do you so swear to forsake all other ties in the service of your people, to hold no allegiance to other kingdoms or nations?"

"I willingly forsake all other ties and connections I once held in Norden to their king and queen. I cut ties with my parents, who have forsaken the ways of our people and claimed lineage to the kings of old who ruled before me. In this, I so swear."

Mathew came forward to ask the last question. "Do you swear to honor the cohabitation with dragons, respecting all past, present, and future agreements?"

"As long as the agreements are honorable and agreed upon with the dragons, I so swear. But know that if there comes a time when it is detrimental for dragons and humans to coexist, I will do whatever it takes to end the agreement. I give my honor to humans and dragons alike and will stand by my word defining it to my dying breath."

"Your answers have pleased the fates. Approach and be anointed," all four men called out together.

Lifting my skirt, I climbed the stairs and kneeled on the pillow they placed for me, then tipped my head back for each man to mark me with oil.

"May the fates grant you wisdom to rule justly and without prejudice," Sal said, running his thumb across my forehead.

"May the words of your people never fall on deaf ears," Mathew said, marking both my ears.

"May your eyes see clearly in times of doubt and confusion," Lawrence said, smoothing oil under my eyes.

"May you always speak truth and guidance to your people," Eleazar said, rubbing oil over my lips.

Finished with that part of the proceedings, Gavin stepped forward with the crown resting on a pillow.

In solidifying details for the coronation, I learned I would have to pick one of my consorts who would rule if something happened to me. Everyone agreed it should be Gavin since he had been raised as the crown prince. So, with that honor, he was picked to participate in the coronation, declaring him my heir until I had a child.

Lawrence picked up the crown and held it high in the air. "In the eyes of the people of Sheca, the dragons who share our world, and the fates who have blessed our nation, I crown you the Dragon Queen, ruler of the dragon throne and pair-bond to the black dragon, Vasin!"

The roar of people clapping, whistling, and shouting their excitement was almost deafening in the throne room. Gavin held out his hand to help me to my feet and kick away the pillow before we turned to face the people. Gavin grinned as he kissed my hand and winked before thrusting our joined hands in the air. "Long live the Dragon Queen!"

"Long live the queen!" the people bellowed in response.

The sounds of dragons roaring echoed outside the castle, and bursts of flame could be seen from the skylights as they rejoiced. My heart swelled with emotions as I watched the people before me cheering, their faces full of hope and excitement. To them, this moment had been a long time coming, a promised reward for them being left behind to guard this castle. Now, it was my turn to honor them and ensure this place remained protected from those who wished to take it from us.

EIGHT

CASSARAH

Now that I officially wore the crown and was queen, the hard work began. I'd already dealt with the dragon riders, having them swear their loyalty to me, but I decided to pass on having the village people do the same. There would always be those who opposed my rule, and making them bend a knee in public like this wouldn't change what was in their heart.

Instead, I had King Thomas, Crown Prince Phillip, and Queen Catharine join me in my office. While I had verbal agreements with these men, I wanted it in writing and sealed with blood. I was going to learn from the Raven Queen herself and ensure that none of them could stab me in the back without consequence, and I had the power to do just that.

"This should be a time of celebration, not dealing with this sort of thing," King Thomas argued. "We can just as easily do this tomorrow."

"No," I stated as I sat at my desk. "This will happen now or not at all. There is no telling when the Lost King will make his next move, and I, for one, am unwilling to take a chance. What if he attacks you first, and for some reason, I decided it's too risky to help you? We have no agreement other than our words that we ever had an alliance. Be smart, Your Majesty. This benefits both of us."

With a harumph, King Thomas sat across from me, next to Phillip. It took us a few rounds, but we all settled on agreements for our alliances, creating a bond between the three kingdoms. Each of us is willing to come to the other's aid in the form of military support, food, or supplies if the need should arise. We added in a few other clauses that would cut out loopholes or prevent forced marriages of our children whenever Phillip or I had any. With the wording finalized, I took out a small knife, poked it into the pad of my thumb, and pressed it over my signature.

"Know that this agreement is binding by honor and magic. If any of us, or our children, fail to follow the alliance we've created, then it will result in punishment or death to the offender," I explained as I handed the knife to Phillip.

Without hesitation, Phillip signed his name and placed his blood as I had. However, King Thomas hesitated a moment as he looked between us. "What happens if future generations wish to dissolve this alliance?"

"Then they create another contract and sign that one," I informed him. "Only when all parties agree and come together can this contract be altered or dissolved. It's to ensure that no one party can break the agreement without the others knowing."

King Thomas nodded, reading over the words once more before singing his name and adding his blood, sealing the document for all. A zing of power raced up my arm from the thumb I'd cut, letting me know that the magic I'd infused it with was active.

"Queen Catharine, I would like to be clear that if you in any way try to break or twist the alliance we've just formed, you will suffer the punishment as well. Any interference from the families who formed the alliance will have repercussions. The same goes for any of my consorts or future wife that Phillip will have. This extends to the children in this generation or the next. The magic I've bound to this holds us to this alliance until it is dissolved, no matter how long that might take," I warned, as I held her gaze, ensuring she understood what I was saying.

Her only response was to nod serenely as if there was no reason for me to have been worried. "I will bear that in mind, Your Majesty."

While I didn't trust the woman farther than I could throw her, I didn't think she would be stupid enough to do anything right away. No, if she were going to make a play to get rid of me, it would be after the Lost King was gone and her kingdom was no longer being threatened.

"Come, the feast should be starting soon, and I hear they have some wonderful entertainment set up for the night," Phillip suggested, rising from his seat and offering me his arm. "Come, dear sister, let us celebrate your coronation now that matters have been settled."

He was right. I'd done all I could to prepare for our battle ahead. This feast was going to be the last bit of normalcy we'd have because, in the morning, we would be gearing up for war.

"Your Majesty, might I have the honor of this dance?" Alsten, the captain of the military, asked with a bow.

Surprised by the request, I turned from where I'd been speaking to Dayson to face Alsten. "A dance?"

Dayson's hand landed on my hip, where he gripped it tightly, showing his claim to me.

"Yes, I haven't seen you get the chance to dance once this evening," he explained, meeting my gaze. "I'm not looking for anything more than a friendly dance with my new queen. There is no need for the death glare from your guardian. I don't think you have any need to add another man to your company."

I offered Alsten a small smile and accepted his hand. "I haven't danced in a while, so you'll have to forgive me if I stumble a bit at first."

"Formal dancing isn't something that happens here often, so you're in good company," he whispered conspiratorially as he led me to the dance floor. "Are you sure he won't come and kill me in my sleep later?"

"Dayson, like the others, is over protective, but as long as you behave yourself, I don't see there being any issues," I assured him.

Once we reached the middle of the dance floor, we took up positions and joined the others in the waltz. While dancing had never been my favorite thing to do while under my mother's tutelage, it was actually enjoyable in a much more comfortable setting. A real smile grew as he twirled me effortlessly, showing me he wasn't as unskilled as he made me believe.

"You are a wonderful dancer," I commented as we moved across the dance floor.

Alsten bobbed his head. "Thank you, Your Majesty. I could also say the same about you. I would never have guessed you were rusty on your skills."

We danced another song before King Thomas approached and asked to cut in. "Might I have this dance?"

I agreed, feeling it was a smart move to show how our alliance was already progressing well. "Of course, I'd be glad to share this dance with you."

Alsten bowed, stepped back, allowed the king to take his place, and headed off into the crowd.

"You are a hard woman to get a moment with," King Thomas shared as we began our dance.

His words put me on edge, but I tried not to show it. "I apologize. I didn't realize you needed to speak to me."

"Oh, it wasn't anything vital. I just wanted to get to know you better now that we share an alliance. I feel as though when we first came to Sheca, my wife and I didn't represent ourselves to you very well. My wife is headstrong, and in many ways, I think she believes she is more king than I am. I won't lie to you and say she agrees with this alliance, but I can see the bigger picture," King Thomas explained. "This war isn't something we can run from or hide behind our army like we normally would. I've heard rumblings from our spies about this matter, and she keeps brushing them off. What I want most is to grow old, see my son take over the throne and our kingdom prosper, and that is why I'm fighting for this alliance."

"Your Highness, are you saying your wife plans to hinder that from happening?" I asked in a hushed voice.

"All I will tell you is to watch your back where she is concerned. I will do all I can to honor and uphold this alliance, but I can't say the same for her. She is also trying to poison our children to the idea, so they might one day dissolve the agreement," King Thomas answered with a heavy sigh. "I might have also heard mention breaking her sister out of house arrest and bringing her back with us."

Stumbling at his words, I tried to keep my expression even, knowing how many eyes were watching us. "Was this spoken about before or after the agreement was signed?"

"Before... she was talking about it last night after the attack," King Thomas paused, licking his lips as he looked around a moment before speaking, his voice barely above a whisper. "I have no proof of this other than knowing that woman for the past thirty years, but I think something happened to her. Three years ago, she went on a trip to visit a friend in Utros, and when she came back, things started to change. She's always been opinionated and bossy, telling me how I should rule. Slowly, I almost didn't notice that she started to do things behind my back, like sending supplies to Utros and Errit.

It was small amounts I wouldn't have taken notice of, but one of my stewards came to me asking what it was for. I never agreed to send support to those kingdoms. That's when I sent my spies out to investigate."

"What did they find?" I questioned as my mind started to race, connecting dots of information.

"It was the first time I heard about the Lost King, how he married the crown princess of Errit, and months later, she ended up dead. This made him the crown prince since they didn't have any other children to take the role."

I had to admit I was impressed with Henry's plan to get to this point. He'd systematically taken over two kingdoms in preparation and then conquered Norden, adding to his power base. Now, the only thing standing in his way was Creisal and Sheca. If what King Thomas told me was true, then Queen Catharine might have already been swayed by the Lost King. His power of manipulation was unlike anything we've ever seen. What if he'd managed to implant a thought into the queen's brain that had the kingdom crumbling from the inside out?

"Your Majesty, are you willing to put your trust in me to see if your wife is under the Lost King's control? It might explain so many things about how she is acting and why she is resisting this alliance when it makes perfect sense," I asked, searching his face as he took his time to answer me.

The song ended, but King Thomas had managed to place us in the far back corner out of the way and out of sight. "Is there any hope if he has done something to her?"

"I don't know, but I'm willing to try," I answered honestly. "Here, in this castle, I have access to power I've never experienced before. If there were ever a time I felt hopeful of being able to help, it would be now. If I can't, then at least we know she must be under someone's watch at all times or detained somewhere safe. The Lost King doesn't care about loss of life or ruining someone's mind. I've seen it firsthand."

King Thomas nodded, his shoulders slumping as he answered. "Tomorrow... we will settle things tomorrow. Let tonight be about a happy one, and we will discover just how strong a hold the Lost King has in our world in the light of a new day."

I reached out and placed my hand on his arm, seeing the truth of this man with his royal façade dropped. He loved his wife and children and truly wanted the best for his people. He came here unsure of what to expect, and I'm not sure what he saw in me to convince him that I was worthy of his trust, but I was glad. If the Lost King had a foothold in Creisal, we needed to remove it quickly, or this battle would be worse odds than it already was.

"Come, let us get some cake. I had a sample of it earlier, and it's rather wonderful," I suggested, hooking my arm through his and heading back toward the tables covered with food for people to enjoy.

The second Jade spotted me, he made a beeline to my side. "There you are, Your Majesty... need a break from all the dancing?"

"I was just telling the King he needed to try some cake, but I would like a refreshment." Turning to the king, I smiled. "Would you mind greatly if I left you on your own while you enjoy your dessert?"

"No, my dear, enjoy the night. I've stolen enough of your time. I'm sure your men are getting anxious. You have quite a devoted group of consorts. I hope one day my children will find such loyal partners."

With a quick bob of a curtsy, out of respect, I left with Jade. Soon, I had a glass in my hand that Cole brought over before I was whisked out of the ballroom into the back servants' hall. There were the rest of my consorts along with May and Becka.

"What did the king want?" Jade demanded the moment it was safe to ask.

I held up a hand for them to give me a moment as I took a few gulps from the glass of water. "That's better," I said with a sigh, not realizing how thirsty dancing had made me. "The king and I had a rather interesting conversation. It seems that Queen Catharine and I will be having a chat tomorrow about a trip she took to Utros three years ago."

Even though we were out of the way, staff still hurried back and forth, maintaining things in the ballroom. I knew my people well enough that I figured they could read between the lines.

"I'm sorry... did you say that happened three years ago?" Pax questioned.

I nodded, taking another sip. "Yes, she apparently is good friends with the royalty there. Such good friends that when they requested some help in the way of supplies, she sent them over."

The guys swore under their breaths while the girls did better at controlling their feelings.

"I was also informed about a tragic story about how the Crown Princess of Errit died shortly after being married to a nobleman's son from Utros. Since she was their only child, her husband was named Crown Prince. With how tragic their story is, I'm amazed none of us ever heard anything about it," I mused, knowing full well why the story was kept secret.

Henry wouldn't want people knowing how much influence he had or that he'd left his supposed prison in Utros. Paxton's father had owned up to the fact he didn't kill the boy, and now we are all paying for that man's choice.

"Might I suggest this is a conversation that should be continued in our rooms?" Gavin interjected, giving us all a warning look. "The night is still young, and we have many guests who would like to spend time greeting their new queen."

"Quite right," Izel agreed, nodded, and slipped his arm around my waist. "But not before I get my chance for a dance."

The rest of the night was spent chatting with my subjects and dancing with all my consorts. I managed to put the fears of the future to rest and focus on the here and now. When the clock struck midnight, I made my excuses and curled up into bed with Paxton and Gavin, where we promptly passed out.

NINE

CASSARAH

My dreams were filled with flashes of memories from Miranda on her coronation day, finally claiming her consorts and the beginning of their happiness together. In all the nights I'd dreamed of her, this was a moment I hadn't experienced. It was interesting to see the differences from what I went through yesterday. It was much simpler and reminiscent of a traditional marriage when it came to her men. Magic hadn't been involved at all. When I felt myself starting to wake up, everything shifted, and I was pulled into the void of Vasin's mind.

Panic filled me as I remembered what happened the last time I was here alone, but I'd come a long way since then and understood my powers better. A figure glowed, and I assumed it was Miranda coming to talk with me, as we'd done on occasion. Only this time, it was someone else dressed in armor with her curly brown hair wild around her face.

"Hello, Cassarah. My mother has told me so much about you. I'm Emery, Miranda's daughter," Emery greeted, giving me a soft smile.

Confusion whirled in my mind at this change. "How are you here? I thought it was just Miranda who could communicate with me like this?"

"Oh no, any of the past kings and queens of the mercenaries who shared a bond with a black dragon can reveal themselves to you. We know when we are needed, and my mother was who you needed most.

Now you're on the verge of war, the biggest since the Battle of the King-doms, so I've come to offer what guidance I can," Emery explained, reaching out a hand to me.

I took the offered hand and was immediately swept up in her memory of swords clashing, arrows flying through the air, and people screaming in pain. The smell of smoke burned in my nose as sweat dripped down my back and into my eyes, which I brushed away hur-riedly. Chaos ruled, and it was nearly impossible to see beyond what was right in front of me. A sword descended upon me, and I rose mine to meet it, feeling the hit echo down my arm. Then as fast as the memory started, it ended, and I was back holding Emery's hand in the white void of my dragon's brain.

"War is chaos, bloody, and changes you forever in ways you never see coming. I know the Lost King has left you no choice but to meet him head-on, but I didn't want you to go unprepared," she murmured using her other hand to brush the tears from my cheek. "Your heart is so strong, and yet in that strength, it's weak when it comes to moments where you have to choose your life over theirs."

"How do I make it through this without turning into him?" I asked, feeling that fear wrapping itself around my heart.

Emery smiled and lifted a finger under my chin so I would meet her gaze. "The fact you are worried tells me that it won't happen. War is a test of wills and all about who can outsmart the other, but those who don't have value in the lives that fight for them won't get their best. When people fight for their freedom, homes, and loved ones, they become far more powerful than those who've been ordered to fight." Emery paused, searching my face for understanding. "Last night, your people wanted nothing more than to spend time with you. Trust me when I say they will fight alongside you without a second thought."

"I don't want to have to ask them. There must be some way I can stop this war before it truly begins," I argued.

Emery shook her head. "The time for that has passed, and now you must stand and fight. There is more to the Lost King than meets the eye. When he lost his dragon and brought him back, it twisted something inside him too. Think of him like a rabid dog. It's better to put him out of his misery than to let him live. Sadly, you're the only one who can defeat him with the magic you hold. The dragons have blessed you with what you need to do the deed."

"Is that why you've really come... to tell me it's my duty as the Dragon Queen to slay the monster?" I asked bitterly.

"My dear girl, I was once where you are. I was raised in a loving home with parents who adored me, and then, in the blink of an eye, they were gone, never getting to say goodbye or see their faces again. My last memory was watching them ride off to meet with the king and queen, laughing with each other. Then the darkest time of my life began when a rider informed me that my family was killed. A burning anger rose in me and refused to be put out until I got vengeance for them, but it didn't heal the wounds. Our people still had to go into hiding and were scattered across the nation to keep our people existing. So don't whine to me about getting an unfair hand dealt to you. That was most of my life," Emery stated, her voice cold and her eyes hard. "The fates know what we are capable of, and they push us to the limit, bending until we think we're about to break... but we don't. Keep your men close... you won't make it through this without them."

Feeling thoroughly chastised, I hung my head and nodded, knowing she had every right to scold me like a spoiled child. I wasn't the only one this war would steal from—it was each and every person in this village if I didn't stand up and fight back.

"I will," I whispered.

Emery pulled me into a hug, squeezing me tightly. "You will do amazing things, sweet girl. I have no doubt. Know we are all here for you if you should need us."

Slowly, the dream dissipated, and I was staring at my bedroom ceiling. I could feel Gavin's even breath on my neck where his face was nestled. Paxton tightened his arms around my waist as he nuzzled into my stomach, where he'd managed to push my nightgown up so he was laying directly on my skin.

I could feel they were both still asleep, so I stayed still and decided to enjoy the moment. How soon would we be marching out to battle and sleeping in tents on bedrolls? The weather in Sheca was mild, but when we headed back to Norden, it would be far cooler. Winter was building, making this even more of a disadvantage for us. Thankfully, Norden didn't get much snowfall, but the temperature could be brutal, creating its own risk.

Where would we meet the Lost King in battle? How much of a hold did he have in Creisal, if any? The smartest thing to do would be to lure him there so we didn't need to move that many people on foot to another location. It was easy enough to travel by dragon—transporting our soldiers there would be a far less hassle.

"What are you thinking about so intently, love?" Gavin whispered into my ear, letting his lips brush against my skin. "The wheels of your beautiful mind are working so hard that steam should be coming out of your ears."

A smile tugged at my lips as I turned my head to face him. He rewarded my effort with languid kisses, neither of us feeling the need for urgency. "Good morning," I murmured.

"It certainly is, waking up with you in my arms," Gavin replied, pressing his lips to mine in a deeper kiss. "How long do you think we can pretend nothing important needs to happen today?"

"You tell me. You're far more experienced in this life of a royal than I am," I teased.

The arms around my waist shifted, alerting me to Paxton being awake as they skimmed up my side under the nightgown until they reached just under my breasts. "If the prince is serious, I can think of a few ways to forget all about the real world for a bit. Unless he doesn't want to share, then he's out of luck because I'm not leaving this bed for him to get lucky."

Gavin's eyes shimmered with heat as he traced a finger along my jawline and over my lips. "What did you have in mind? I feel I could be persuaded if all parties were in agreement."

Paxton lifted his head, brows arched in surprise. "Who knew the straight-laced prince could be so open-minded? All right, Your Highness, what do you think about splitting her between us? One gets the cave of wonders, and the other keeps her mouth busy. I'm willing to split fifty-fifty and switch in the middle, or if we're happy where we are, then so be it."

I couldn't help but chuckle at Paxton's description of his plan. Part of me wondered if he'd done this before or was just thinking practically. May had taken it upon herself to share with me about the twins she'd been with at the same time, and they did something similar. Only one was in her core and the other in her ass. Remembering Cole and how he'd introduced that feeling to me made me shiver.

"Would you look at that... our queen seems to like the idea of being shared," Paxton purred, kissing down my stomach until he reached the tuft of hair above my core. "I say we get her squirming and dripping for us before we decide who's going where."

Gavin reached down to grab the bunched-up fabric of my clothes and pulled it over my head, leaving me bare to them. "So perfect," he sighed, letting his fingers glide over the swell of my breasts.

At his touch, my nipples started to peak, and my breathing became faster. When he gently pinched my nipple between his fingers, rolling it ever so slightly, I moaned, arching my back.

"Seems like I need to get to work," Paxton commented before shifting between my legs, which I opened to accommodate him.

Paxton didn't go right for my clit like I expected him to. Instead, he kissed, licked, and caressed every part of my body between my legs but where I wanted, making me pant with anticipation. With Gavin attending to my upper half and Paxton driving the lower half wild, I couldn't help but whimper in desperation.

"Please, someone, please touch me," I begged. "I need to feel you. My body is aching, and it's driving me wild. Someone better fill me with their cock *now!*"

Paxton let out a huff of laughter that hit my clit, making me keen with need. "You know, I think she might be ready for us?" I bucked my hips, trying to close my legs on his head, shoving his face into my core. "Easy there, spitfire. I want to taste you first. Then I promise we will give you what you want."

"Whatever you're going to do, I suggest you do it quickly before I take matters into my own hands," I growled out.

"I kind of like this bossy side of you... it's incredibly sexy," Paxton shared as he ran his finger over where I'd been aching to feel him.

Crying out at the touch, I closed my eyes, and when I opened them, I was presented with a cock ready for me to take into my mouth. Gavin looked down at me, a little unsure of how I would react, but I grabbed ahold of him with one hand, tugging him closer. Licking the crown of his cock, I could taste the pre-cum leaking from it—salty and bitter.

Paxton, feeling that my attention might be wandering from what he was doing to me, shoved two fingers inside me as he descended on my clit. With all the teasing they'd put me through, I wasn't shocked when I was sent into a shattering orgasm. I moaned as I took Gavin's cock between my lips, trying to keep myself grounded as Paxton continued to work me over.

Gavin's hand found its way into my hair, gripping it tightly as I bobbed up and down on his cock. My tongue swirled, feeling the ridges of his veins pulsing as he grunted in appreciation. Paxton got me on the edge of another orgasm but slowed or stopped just before I was about to reach my climax, making me ache in a whole different way. Then he pulled his finger out and crawled up my body.

"Can I take you, Cassarah? Will you let me fuck you, filling you with my seed until we are both sated?" Paxton whispered into my ear.

Pulling off Gavin, I turned to meet his icy blue eyes. "Yes, I want you to come in me as Gavin comes down my throat."

Paxton groaned, hearing my words before surging forward and kissing me senseless as he entered me. "As my queen commands, I will provide."

Ten

Gavin

Never did I expect watching the woman I love getting fucked by one of her other men would be as erotic as it was. Paxton surged up into her, thrusting deep and hard, making her cry out in pleasure. Cassarah reached out and took me in her hand, running it from base to tip and back down again, squeezing just on the verge of too tight.

When Paxton released her mouth, he sat back and swirled his hips, the action making her back arch. While I enjoyed her touch on me, now that I knew what her mouth felt like, I craved it like an addicted man questing after his next fix.

Grabbing her jaw, I turned her back to face me. "Open up for me, love."

Heat simmered in her amber eyes as she did just that, sucking me down until her lips touched the base. Her tongue flicked, teasing me as she slowly pulled back. Reaching the tip, she grabbed the root of my cock and worked it in conjunction with her mouth. My breathing became irregular as my balls tightened, warning me that I was dangerously close to finishing.

Glancing over at Paxton, I could see the sweat on his brow as he pumped into her. He met my gaze, and I could tell he was also closer than he would like to be so quickly. While our woman might not have had much practice in the act of sex, she was clearly a fast study, just as she was with everything else.

"Look what you do to us, love. We've barely even started, and both of us are struggling to hold out," I said, caressing her face as I thrust deeper into her throat. "If you ever doubt whether or not you have bewitched our mind, body, or spirit, remember this moment. A moment where you bring two men to their knees with the simplest touch."

This seemed to spur her on even more, wrapping her legs around Paxton's waist and pulling him in closer as she gulped me down, humming. That did it for me, and with a growl, I came, spurting into her mouth without warning, and she took it all. Soon to follow was Paxton roaring his release as he bucked inside her, doing just as he promised and filling her with his seed. Seconds later, she was moaning out her release, reassuring me she got just as much enjoyment as we did.

Drained and unable to hold myself up any longer, I crumbled beside her as Paxton was recovering, laying on her chest. The only sound in the room was heavy breathing and pounding hearts as we all returned to our senses.

Part of me wondered if we should ask if she was doing anything to prevent a child, yet on the other hand, I would love nothing more than to have a child with her, to see her belly growing with a life we created together. These men I've come to consider brothers would all be excellent fathers, and I hoped one day we each had our own with her. Of course, seeing that we were on the eve of battle, it might not be the best option, but it would be a reality one day.

A knock came at the door, and Paxton swore, rolling off Cassarah, grabbing the sheet and pulling it over her body.

"Enter," I called, not caring to hide. My bet was it was one of the other guys who'd waited for us to finish.

Zan entered the room, his cheeks slightly pink with embarrassment. "Ah, I was sent to check in and remind you that you're set to have breakfast with King Thomas and Queen Catharine."

"Did you draw the short straw, or was it because you're blind and Ezzu isn't with you, so you wouldn't see anything embarrassing?" Paxton asked, lounging on the bed, hands tucked behind his head.

Zan frowned, confused by this question. "Why would any of us be worried about seeing anything indecent? At some point, all of us will be right where you are now. I just didn't want to rush for fear of cutting things short before Cassarah could finish."

"Huh, welp, you can't be right all the time. Glad to hear you're not a prude or anything. I'd thought for sure one of us would be. To be honest, my money was on Gavin, but clearly that's not the case," Paxton mused aloud as he hopped out of bed and started to get dressed.

While I wanted to be offended that he thought I would be a prude, I could see why. Being raised as the crown prince meant I had to keep a certain persona going. The people expected their future ruler to act a certain way, and I gave it to them. The freedom I felt now that I'm working alongside Cassarah was the best gift I could have ever been given. This woman came out of nowhere, and it was only by chance that I met her for the first time at the castle since mother was busy.

I'd assumed it was my Birthright that made her so easy to talk to, but I don't think that was the only reason. She had an openness to those around her and wanted people to get to know her, unlike so many rulers. Everything she was fighting for was so her people could be free to live their lives how they always have. As queen, she wanted to walk alongside them instead of walking on top of them, bending them to her will.

Zan cleared his throat, bringing me back to the present. "Cassarah, do you want me to tell them you're running a little late? I don't want to assume things have ended for you if you need to ah... continue where you left off."

Cassarah smiled and took the robe from Paxton, wrapping it around her before getting out of bed. Walking over to Zan, she placed a hand on his arm so he knew she was there, then kissed his cheek. "No, I believe those two couldn't handle continuing."

I gaped at her, shocked to hear such language coming from her. "Is that so, love?" I asked, hopping out of bed and coming up behind her, snaking my hand under her robe and slipping my fingers into her. "Are you telling us that you aren't satisfied? Zan is here, and I'm sure if you asked him, he would help us tend to your needs," I taunted, letting my fingers slide in and out of her as my thumb flicked over her clit.

She let out a gasp of surprise followed by a moan as she leaned her head back onto my shoulder. With my free hand, I pulled open the robe, exposing her breasts. Then I grabbed Zan's wrist and placed his hand on one. "By the sounds of it, I don't think she's been fully taken care of. What do you say, Zan, up for a little tag team effort?"

"We don't have time," she commented, but I could tell there wasn't much urgency in her voice as Zan now had both hands on her.

"You're the queen, my star," Zan whispered, stepping closer to kiss up her neck. "You're never late, always arriving when you choose to."

I nipped at her ear, catching her attention. "Tell me what you want. Do you want me to keep using my fingers, or do you need something more?"

"More," she groaned, reaching out to fist Zan's shirt. I swept off her robe and lifted her left leg, revealing her opening to me.

Trusting that Zan had her steadied, I guided myself into her and wrapped my hand on her hip for leverage. I pumped into her, gliding in and out with ease since Paxton's seed was still dripping from her.

It reminded me of my previous thoughts. "Do you want me to fill you like Pax did? Claim you as mine in the hopes you bear my child?"

"I won't," she panted. "I'm drinking a tonic to prevent it."

"That works for now, but when this battle is over, that ends, Cassarah. Each of us will fulfill your need and ravage your body as you scream out your pleasure until one of us makes you round with child. Just know that I want my own with you, and I believe the others will be of the same mindset," I warned, rocking my hips to thrust my cock even deeper. "Until then, we will just keep reminding you each time we fuck you that you are ours as much as we are yours."

My words seemed to be turning her on as much as what Zan and I were doing to her. I picked up speed, knowing that as much as we wanted to spend all day with her in bed, we had important matters to deal with. Surprising me, Zan dropped to his knees, and Cassarah dug her fingers into his hair, pulling him so his face was up in her core. As I moved, I could feel him working her with his tongue, and I faltered for a moment.

While I knew some men sought each other's company, I had no desire for anyone other than Cassarah. Sensing my hesitation, Zan pulled back and tipped his head in my general direction. "I'm only interested in her pleasure, nothing more."

Set at ease with that statement, I went back to work, and whatever Zan was doing was speeding her to the finish line fast. Her walls clamped around me like a vice, making me grunt and work harder to keep up my pace. When she exploded around my cock, I lost it, biting into her shoulder as I came to completion within her. With short thrusts and grunts to accompany it, I let her drain me, knowing one day I would have her bear our child.

Her body shook as I slipped out of her, the seed I'd filled her with starting to dribble down her leg. Thankfully, Zan stood and took her from me since I wasn't much better off than she was. My legs felt like I was on a boat, and I managed to stumble back a few steps and flop onto the bed. If I'd thought her mouth did magical things to me, I'd been severely wrong about that. While I'd never turn down an offer for her to take me in her mouth again, fucking her would easily become an addiction.

"Playtime is over," Becka's voice rang out just before a cold, wet rag plopped on my chest. "Time to get cleaned up and get real work done. I thought I was safe sending Zan in, but the pheromones in this room must have been too much for him."

Sitting up on my elbows, I looked at her moving about the room, picking out a dress and other items for Cassarah to wear. "I didn't realize we were on such friendly terms, Becka, for you to freely move about the room while I'm naked."

Becka rolled her eyes. "Seriously, it's not like I haven't seen a cock before, and at the rate you guys are going at it, I'm sure to see more. Chop, chop... no rest for the royalty. You should know this. We have lots to do starting out with... is your aunt under the Lost King's control."

"Trust me, that is one matter I wouldn't forget about," I muttered as I left Cassarah's room and headed to mine.

ELEVEN

CASSARAH

Clean, dressed, and ready for the day, I showed no signs of how eventful my morning had been so far. The only thing I couldn't hide was my smile as I replayed the words my consorts whispered in my ear. I'll admit I didn't know how I felt about having children—after my childhood, I never wanted that to happen to my babies. It was safer to abstain from having any than to risk the chance they could be used like my mother had planned.

However, with how much my life has changed, most of the issues I had in becoming a mother no longer applied. I had eight amazing men who would protect our children and me with their lives. Never would they allow them to be used as a bartering tool in political issues, and they would love them unconditionally as they do me. Any child I had would be so blessed to be brought into this family.

Seeing the doors to the sitting room on the third floor where we were meeting for breakfast, I set those thoughts aside. Even if I decided to change my mind and work toward having a family, it wouldn't be until this whole matter with the Lost King was finished. If there were one thing I'd refuse to do, it's have a child in the middle of a war.

The guards stationed outside the door opened them as they saw us approaching, allowing us to easily enter. There were some things about being queen that would take some getting used to. While I understood their role, and it showed me the respect I deserved, there might be some things we'd have to adjust later when we didn't have guests.

King Thomas and Queen Catharine were seated on one of the loveseats while Princess Ameila and Prince Charles sat on the other. While I wasn't sure I wanted the children here for part of this, I hadn't wanted to cause the queen to have any suspicions. Seeing us enter the room, they rose to their feet, and we all greeted each other.

"I hope you enjoyed yourselves last night," I commented as we wandered over to the table set up for breakfast. "The village worked incredibly hard to make it a night to remember."

"Yes, I'm sure they did, but one can only expect so much from such a humble village. We will have to invite you to our winter ball, then you can see what a real party experience is like," Queen Catharine quipped, taking her seat.

Pursing my lips to hold back my defense of my people, I took a sip of my kavat, swallowing the remark. "That would be lovely. I hear Creisal's palace is quite a sight to see. My consort, Paxton, as you might know, spent quite some time in your fine kingdom."

"Did he now?" King Thomas answered, cutting off his wife. "May I ask what called to you from our kingdom that you left your own for a time?"

Pax looked at me with a questioning eyebrow as if he was unsure if he should be honest. I nodded, having already decided to be transparent when I brought the subject up. Pax just shrugged and turned to face the king. "Well, your Majesty, I was one of your spies. In fact, I was one of the few who had a dragon to work with, gathering information in other kingdoms for you."

King Thomas' eyes grew wide as he turned to look at me. "You knew this and still made him one of your consorts?"

"Of course, he proves himself in many ways to me. Not only can he supply me with information about other kingdoms, but if I should need to build my own network of spies, he understands how other kingdoms use theirs," I answered, waving off his concern.

"My consort, Jade, is an assassin. He used to be hired out often with his specialized skills. Truthfully, all of my consorts are each a master in one area or another that lends aid to me. It's almost as if the fates knew I would be fighting this war."

While I'm sure Cole and Izel were about to strangle me for sharing this much information, I wanted to see how the queen would react. If she were under the influence of the Lost King, she would want to pull whatever information like this out of me she could. I'd given her a taste, not sharing anything that would put us at a disadvantage but enough to draw her out.

"Do you think it's wise to have such dangerous men so close to you?" King Thomas asked, still reeling from the shock.

Queen Catharine sniffed. "Darling, don't be such a dolt... that woman is brilliant to keep them close. Somehow, she's managed to manipulate these men with her body into believing they mean something to her. I applaud you, Your Highness. Truly, your foresight to trap these men to your will as you have is the stuff of legends. Pray tell, what is the skill the blind one provides for you? Obviously, you wouldn't keep around dead weight, so it must be something truly extraordinary. Or is he the one who you picked for the sole purpose of being in your bed?"

Zan shot out of his chair, Ezzu hissing at the queen from his shoulder. I raised my hand, stopping him from moving from his spot. This is exactly what kind of reaction I wanted from her. Now, I just needed to see how much pull the Lost King had on her to fulfill his wishes.

"Now, Your Majesty, you know that a lady never reveals the secrets of her bedchamber. All I will say in the matter is my men can perform well in all areas I have need of them," I shared before turning to Zan. "Please be seated, my love. This is nothing more than two queens comparing notes."

Zan frowned, clearly unhappy with my request, but he trusted me enough to do as I asked. When I took a moment to glance at all my men, I could tell none of them understood where I was going with this. If they could hold on and trust me a little longer, they would catch on.

"What about you? I'm sure you also have your chosen favorites in the castle who provide more than one service?" I challenged, meeting her gaze. "We queens always have to be a few steps ahead of the men around us, don't you agree? Sometimes, they just don't see what truly needs to be done or handled a certain way. One might even say they're too soft or rigid in their thinking."

"My, my. I'm not sure we're good enough friends for me to admit something like that in such company," Queen Catharine answered, glancing at her children.

I flashed her a smile and turned to the children. "Charles, Amelia, would you like to explore the castle? I'm sure sitting here with us is rather boring, don't you think?"

Their faces lit up at the suggestion. "Could we, Mother?" Charles asked.

"Charles, we can't have you wandering around the castle on your own. What if you get lost?" she argued.

"Not a problem." Turning, I signaled Becka, who approached. "Would you please send for Helena? She'll make sure to look after them as they explore, and if anything were to happen, she is quite skilled in defense," I informed the queen.

"All right then, I expect you both to behave as is fitting for your station," Catharine warned, giving them a stern look.

If she were under the influence of the Lost King, I was pleased to see it didn't seem to be affecting how she was with her children. As they left, the table fell silent as we enjoyed the food placed before us, but I could feel an energy simmering in the air. Almost as if by the queen not pressing me for information, the influence on her was growing stronger. Could it be that she was resisting it in her own way? I had no doubt that even if I freed her from his hold, she would not suddenly become my biggest fan. After being told about what happened to her sister, it was clear her prejudice was from her own heart.

"Seems your plan worked," Queen Catharine commented, breaking the silence. "The children are gone so we are free to speak plainly with each other. After all, we are allies and should be open and honest with each other about the resources we have to share between our kingdoms."

I looked at her over the rim of my mug, contemplating how I wanted to approach this. "Yes, that does sound logical, doesn't it? But I have a question I'd like you to answer before I divulge my secrets," I commented, setting down my drink.

This seemed to catch her off guard. "What could you possibly have to ask me?"

Leaning forward, I held her gaze, reaching out with my magic and letting it grip her. "How long has the Lost King been using you?"

Anger flashed across her face before it turned into outrage. "You dare to accuse me of being a traitor and working for the Lost King?"

"I'm not accusing because I *know* you are. What was the purpose in sending all those supplies to Utros? There was no cry for help to any other kingdom, but why would they when there is a steady stream of goods being supplied by *you*? While I'd planned to lure the Lost King's dragon here, the way we were attacked and its central focus on me didn't make sense. Then, when the accusation came that you might be under his influence, all the dots started to connect." I rose from my seat and began to walk the long way around the table, keeping my eyes on her. "His dragon needed a lure to tell him where to strike. He didn't destroy the village because the mastermind needed his informant to gather as much information as they could while they visited. Oh, and let's not forget the fact you wanted to smuggle Queen Mary out of here. If the Lost King had her, he'd also control the queen dragon who can give birth to more dragons for him to use. I'm sure I've missed things, but that's what I can think of off the top of my head."

By the time I was done speaking, I was standing behind her chair. With my magic holding her in place, I reached out and settled my hand on her head. Closing my eyes, I forced my magic into her, causing her to thrash about. I felt something tug on my power, and I let it pull me under. I found myself in something similar to being in Vasin's shared-mind space. Only, instead of bright light and warmth, it was cold and gray with shadows lurking about, reaching out, trying to wrap me up in them. My Birthright began to glow in a shield around me, blocking the tendrils from latching onto me.

"Well, if it isn't the little Dragon Queen herself," Henry drawled as he appeared out of the shadows. "I have to admit, I'm impressed you figured out about my little spy here. It was the king, wasn't it? I figured he might catch on one day. If it weren't more work to kill him than to let him live, I would've dealt with it long ago."

"What did you hope to gain from this?" I asked, still feeling like I didn't see the bigger picture. "If you had her under your hold, why not just take Creisal for yourself already?"

"That's the question, isn't it?" he mused as he circled me. "What makes you think I'm going to tell you just because you asked?"

Shrugging my shoulders, I turned, keeping him in my sight at all times. "It's always worth asking. If you tell me, then I've gained knowledge, but if not, then I really haven't lost anything either."

"You think you're so clever, don't you? Most of my plans you haven't figured out until it's too late to do something. Then you dare to lure me right to you? Like I would ever be foolish enough to send my dragon if I thought it would kill me," he scoffed. "Xotha already died once. The connection we have in that way has been broken and can't be used against us. Why do you think I did the spell in the first place? I couldn't risk someone else figuring that out and trying what you did."

"The more I deal with you, the closer I get to figuring you out. This war won't end with you being the victor, I can promise you that," I vowed. "Even if that means sacrificing my life to make it happen, I refuse to live in a world with you in power."

Henry stepped up into my face. "Bold words, little queen. Do you have the courage to back them up? Are you willing to do whatever it takes to bring me down because between me and you, I have nothing to lose?"

"See, this is where you and I differ. I might have the most to lose, but that also means I have the most to fight for. Come at me with all you have, *Lost King*, and I will meet you head-on with the power of everyone I love backing me up," I taunted. "The dragons chose *me*, the fates blessed *me*, and I wear the crown of the dragon throne, not *you*. The kings of old knew this day would come, and here I am, ready to wipe you off the face of the earth."

Henry tossed back his head and laughed. "You believe those wives' tales that the Dragon Queen was foretold centuries before?"

"Yes, and so do you. Otherwise, I never would have been seen as a threat to you," I argued. "Since you found out who I was, you've tried to kill or remove me from becoming who I am now. While you might be used to dealing with stubborn, pig-headed nobles who can't see past their noses, I always look at the bigger picture. I warned you the more I know, the more I see. Richard told you who I was, the lost who's been found, pair-bonded to a black dragon in the time when evil is rising. If I'd had any doubt, you, Henry, have confirmed it every step of the way."

"Stop calling me that!" he snarled. "I am a *king*! Do not speak to me as if we are equals because we most certainly are not. I might not be able to capture your mind in this place, but remember how close I was once before, and I'll do it again. Distance is your greatest ally right now, but when we meet on the battlefield, I will turn all those people you love against you!"

"The fates saw to that as well," I murmured as I reached out, calling to Paxton. I could feel the mark on my chest warm, making me believe he could feel me. "I will be taking the queen's mind back from you as I leave this place. Creisal is now officially an ally, and even if she might not like me, I will stand by our agreement and save her all the same. Until we meet on the battlefield..."

"No! No, you can't do that!" Henry's scream echoed as I was yanked out of his magical hold and back into my body.

When I opened my eyes, I found myself wrapped up on Paxton's lap. His arms held me tightly as he slightly shuddered, his breath coming in quick, panicked bursts. Queen Catharine wasn't in her chair, and as I looked around, I found her on the couch with King Thomas kneeling beside her, placing a cool cloth on her head.

Sitting up, I looked into Paxton's worried eyes, confused. "What happened?"

"I should be the one asking you that, Cassarah. What the fuck were you thinking?" he snapped. "I almost couldn't get you out. He'd hidden you so deeply I almost couldn't find you."

"What are you talking about? I was with him for only a few minutes?" I countered.

Pax shook his head. "No, Cassarah, you were under for almost an hour."

Twelve

Cassarah

"An hour? How can that be?" I demanded, confusion and panic settled into my veins.

Izel came and sat in the chair next to Paxton, facing me. "Why didn't you tell us what you were going to do? It was obvious you had a plan, so why not fill us in on it so we were better prepared?"

"I wasn't sure it was going to work, and I knew Pax could get me out," I answered and turned to look at the others who stood around our chairs. "Tell me what happened?"

Reaching out, Izel took my hand, pulling my attention to him. "You touched the queen, and suddenly, you started glowing blue as your Birthright created a shield around you. The king tried to catch you as you fell, but it shocked him, preventing him from making contact. The queen passed out as well. When I reached out, your shield let me pass, so the king moved to take care of his wife. With my Birthright, I was able to take a peek at what was going on, and I saw dark magic pulling you under until you vanished." Frowning, I started to speak, but Izel shook his head. "Wait, please. Let me tell you everything, then ask your questions."

I motioned for him to continue, sitting back in Paxton's hold, feeling he wasn't ready to let me go.

"Once I lost sight of you, your breathing became so shallow I was worried he was killing you. Paxton came over and broke your shield, and that allowed me to start searching for you in your own mind. It was almost like you'd left... your body was still alive, but you were gone. All we could do was watch over you," Izel explained, then lifted his gaze to Paxton.

Pax shifted under me as he cleared his throat. "I don't know how much time passed until I felt you call out to me. Both my marks glowed, and it was almost as if I could hear you calling to me, begging me to find you. Cassarah, you weren't in your own body. The Lost King pulled you out and placed you somewhere else. If we didn't have this link to each other, I never would have been able to locate you and break his magic trapping you there. Once I pulled you back into your own body, I felt something like a cord snap between the magic and the queen. She woke up first, babbling about a man who'd trapped her in her own mind, forcing her to do things she never wanted to do." Pax hugged me tightly, burying his face into my shoulder. "He almost took you from us again, spitfire. I'm going to go bald by the time I turn twenty-five at this rate. You can't keep risking yourself like that."

While I wanted to reassure him I wouldn't risk everything to bring down the Lost King, I couldn't. When I'd told Henry that to his face, I'd meant it with every fiber of my being. A world with him as the ruler would never happen while I was alive.

I pulled Paxton to me, letting our lips meet, reassuring him I was very much alive. He'd done exactly what I needed him to do, trusting that he would save me in time. Paxton pressed me against him as tightly as he could, almost to the point I couldn't breathe. When he released me from our kiss with a harsh nip on my lower lip, I knew he was really upset with me.

"Tell me your plan next time. I'll always back you up, Cassarah, but you just need to be honest with me... with all of us. How can we be a team if you charge off ahead, and we don't know how to help you? Even if you don't think it's going to work, it's better to be safe than sorry," Pax chastised.

Nodding, I rested my forehead against his. "You're right, I should have told you. I should have told all of you what I was thinking." Sliding out of Paxton's arms, I stood and looked at my men. "The Lost King pulled me out of my consciousness into that of his dragon. I didn't know he could do that until it was already done. While this was not handled well, I did learn a few things. Killing his dragon will not kill him... the dark magic he did severed that connection, rendering it useless. He's been planning this for longer than any of us realized. Losing the queen was also a blow. I'm not exactly sure why, but he was furious when he figured out what Pax and I had done."

"Maybe she will be able to tell us why when she comes to her senses," Abbott offered. "At the moment, it doesn't seem like she remembers a whole lot."

"I suppose that doesn't surprise me. For the past three years, she'd had someone else pulling the strings in her brain. I feel it might be best for us to travel back to Creisal and investigate. Henry started with Utros, Errit, then Norden when he had someone in place already in Creisal. Although, I suppose we could count Lord Everett as their inside person, along with Payson for Norden," I mused out loud. "If it were me, though, I would have moved on Creisal sooner, knowing how large their army is and they back up to the sea. It was a stronger counter maneuver, so why didn't he? There is something in that choice we need to figure out."

They all nodded in agreement, but I could tell this event so soon after the dragon attack was not going to be let go any time soon. In some ways, I understood them feeling lied to. I'd known this was the tactic I was going to try, and I did so without preparing them.

"You have every right to be upset with me, and in the spirit of being honest, I will state this now," I said, meeting their gaze for a moment. "I vowed that I wouldn't live in a world where he is the ruler. No matter what it takes or the sacrifice I have to make, I will see that promise to the end."

My men froze, gaping at me a moment before they exploded, all speaking at once in a volume so loud I couldn't begin to tell who was saying what. A shrill whistle cut through the room as May stormed over, smacking each of them upside the head.

"Enough!" May barked. "This is your queen you are speaking to in front of guests, I might add. I don't care if you are sleeping with her or not, you will act right."

The guys shut their mouths, but I could tell by the looks on their faces that it wouldn't last for long. "I believe now might be a good time to retire," I commented, removing myself from them and walking over to King Thomas. "How is she?"

The queen lay there on the couch, sweating as she tossed and turned.

"I don't know, Your Majesty," King Thomas answered, shaking his head as he dabbed his wife's face with a rag. "She just keeps speaking nonsense. What if it would have been better for us to leave her as she was?"

I rested a hand on his shoulder. "Have her taken back to your rooms and let her rest as long as you need. The children will be perfectly fine with Helena, and I'll make sure she keeps them busy. The magic the Lost King uses is known to have some side effects. I just pray to the fates that it won't harm her permanently. I will send for my healers to look after her and ensure she is comfortable."

As I started to pull away, he grabbed my hand. "Thank you. I know I just said we should have left her, but no matter what happens, at least I know I have my wife back. You risked so much, and she's been so cruel to you. It was right for me to make this alliance."

Bowing my head in thanks, I gave him what I hoped to be a reassuring smile as I left. Becka fell in alongside me, not saying anything, just lending her presence. When we reached our chambers, I headed straight to my room with Becka, who shut the doors behind us and locked them. Entering the sitting room, I walked to the balcony and stood at the railing, looking out at the village below.

As is always the case with Becka and me, she came to stand beside me and placed her hand over mine. Part of me wondered if I ever should have said a word to my men about what I'd said to the Lost King. *I* was queen of these lands and people. It was *my* responsibility to ensure I did all I could to keep them safe. My mind went back to that moment when I thought I was the woman falling off the cliff to her death, willing to do whatever it took to protect the ones I loved. Miranda might have lost her lovers and dragon, but she saved everyone with that final act. How could I do less?

"Did you really mean what you said?" Becka asked, finally breaking the silence.

I glanced at her, but she refused to look at me as she waited for my answer.

"Yes." There was nothing more to say. I couldn't give her a justification that would make any sense or make it better.

Becka nodded and turned so her back was to the railing and looked at me. "Cassarah, you are like a sister to me, and we've been through hell and back with your mother. If we can survive through that, I'm sure we can handle this."

"Those two aren't even in the same category, Becka. My mother wanted to control and use me for her gai, but didn't want to harm others. Henry doesn't give a rat's ass who lives or dies. How do you even begin to face off with someone like that without putting as much into it?" I argued. "The Lost King has nothing to lose, or so he claims, but what he wants is power and the recognition he never got from his father. He believes he should have been king of Norden, but instead, he was banished to Utros. That's what he's after... to prove they were wrong for doing that to him."

A frustrated growl burst out of my best friend, shocking me. "So what! That man should be grateful he's still alive. The king was supposed to kill him, not just send him away. He can have Utros and Errit, but why does he need everything else? If there is no one left in the world, what good is ruling it?"

"You're trying to get him to act like a rational person. However, I can assure you he is anything but," I explained. "What is it they teach us? To be able to outsmart a target, you have to learn the target. Know their habits, routines, where they are vulnerable, and then you can strike in the strongest way possible. That's what I'm doing," I offered, knowing she wouldn't believe me. "What everyone is missing is that despite the words I said, I have no intention of ever losing to him."

"Did you hear that, you sneaky thieves!" Becka yelled.

Confused, I looked about trying to figure out who she was talking to when my men suddenly appeared sheepishly in the doorway.

"What! How did you do that?" I gasped.

Cole pointed at Jade as if having him to blame would get him out of trouble. "It seems he can use his Birthright on more than just himself..."

My jaw dropped. I knew locking the door wouldn't keep a bunch of mercenaries out of my room, but I'd hoped the message would be clear. Becka knew I needed a moment before I had to explain myself and to get them to calm down. While I didn't have many lingering issues from my mother's treatment of me, the one thing I struggled with was getting the approval of those I cared about. I knew they would be mad at me, and I couldn't talk to them while they were all so upset.

"How long have you been able to do that? Wait, have you always been able to?" I questioned.

Jade shrugged his shoulders. "I don't really know how long I've been able to do it. There hasn't been a time when I wanted to hide others in my shadows."

That was a valid point. He hadn't been all that welcomed in his previous clan after his parents died. "I'm certainly glad we know about it now. We'll have to test this to see how many people you can keep hidden. It will be an amazing tool for the upcoming battle."

"Don't think you can get out of this conversation by distracting us, little bird," Jade warned, coming over to stand before me. "Now, I think we deserve an explanation."

"No, you don't," Becka countered. "You just heard her reasoning while you were eavesdropping on our conversation. What more do you need to know? She had to get on his level and show him she was willing to do anything, up to death, to make it happen."

"Sorry, but that isn't a good enough answer for me," Gavin announced.

As the only person not trained in the ways of a mercenary, I could understand why he wouldn't understand. The others might not like my choice, but they knew where I was coming from. How did you explain to someone who saw the world in black and white that an action cloaked in gray was the right choice?

Walking over to him, I cupped his cheek and held his gaze as it burned with anger and fear. "Did I tell the Lost King I would sooner die than let him become ruler? Yes. Did I also vow I would take him down with me if it came to that point? Also, yes." I pulled him into a hug, squeezed him tightly, then took a step back. "What I didn't say is that I was going to roll over and let him kill me. I needed him to understand I wasn't going into this battle with my eyes closed. It told him I was willing to go as far as I needed to ensure he never won."

I sighed, my shoulders drooping as I sank under the weight of my responsibilities. "He needed to see me as a threat to take me seriously. I needed to push him to get him to spill information, and it worked."

"It worked?" he questioned. "From what you already told us, you didn't get much."

"No, I didn't get much, but we didn't have much before either. Now we know we need to get to Creisal and see what's happening there. What if there is something hidden in that city he doesn't want anyone to know about? Everything he's done is to draw attention away from there. He's leaving it for last, and that tells me whatever we might find there is a weakness he can't outsmart another way," I explained. "My other hope is that the queen will regain her senses and be able to tell us something."

"It still doesn't mean you should have made a vow like that. You have access to magic like never before. What if it holds you to that? We could lose you, and all of this would have been for nothing," Gavin argued.

Tossing my hands up in frustration, I turned to the others. "What do you want me to say? I am queen first, lover second, and mercenary last. My duty the moment that crown went on my head was to my people... all my people, but that doesn't mean I can play it safe just to satisfy those who love me. Tell me what I should have done, staring at the biggest evil we've faced yet as he taunts me, telling me I'm going to fail?"

Gavin looked hurt, but the others seemed to understand where I was coming from. While I could understand why they weren't happy about it, they were trained to look at a battle from all angles.

Gavin must have realized this too because he didn't press the matter when he saw none of the others were going to.

"The question now is how do we proceed?" Zan offered. "You've now been crowned queen and brokered an alliance with what is left of the Norden royalty as well as Creisal. What are you going to do with all of it?"

Rubbing my hand over my forehead, I tried to think of something, but all I came up with were dead ends and more questions. I wandered over to the seating on the balcony and sank into a chair, resting my elbows on my knees and my head in my hands. Everyone slowly came over to join me. No one spoke—we just sat for some time, praying to the fates that something would come to one of us.

Thirteen

Cassarah

The one benefit of being officially crowned queen is that I had a full schedule of things to deal with. My feelings of being lost in how to move forward were pushed to the side with a knock on the door and a steward calling me to a meeting. The viceroys were coming together in their last act in that title to give me all the reports and information I would need. Of course, I'd already been going over them with the three men and Sal before the coronation, but it would give Lawrance, Mathew, and Eleazar closure after their many years of service. While they were closing the door on one chapter of their lives, I was now starting a new one for them as my advisers.

"Your Majesty, we, the viceroys of Sheca, surrender our knowledge to you. May it help your reign be fruitful as you guide our people," Lawrence said as the men set the leather-bound tombs on the conference table before me.

"I thank you for your many years of service to these people and the protection of the throne. Now that you have ended your terms as viceroys, I would like to extend the offer of becoming advisers to the crown," I requested.

Mathew stepped up and bowed. "It would be my honor to advise you."

Eleazar and Lawrance responded the same way, leaving Sal to answer. He walked up and bowed but surprised me when he took my hand in his. "Your Majesty, it would be my honor to advise you, but

I feel I won't be much use to you. I don't have the same knowledge as these other men do, not having lived in Sheca. If you feel I will still be a benefit, I ask you to consider me as secondary counsel."

"If that is what you wish, then I accept your request," I answered, covering his wizened old hand with mine. "You will always be a man I hold in high regard for his sound wisdom and logic. With the way my reign is starting out, I will need people I can trust to turn to."

Sal kissed the back of my hand and stepped back with the others. I turned to the attendant in the room and signaled for him to let the others in. My men filed in along with Ballard, Alsten, and Crown Prince Phillip. To my surprise, King Thomas also appeared, taking a seat at the table.

"Your Majesty, while I am glad you are here, I hope you didn't feel forced to leave your wife if you need to be with her?" I inquired.

King Thomas waved off my question. "She is sleeping peacefully thanks to your healers, and there was no need for me to be there when her personal maid is there as well. This will be good to keep my mind on matters where I can make a difference."

"I'll trust your judgment on that, and I'm grateful to have you here with us as we strategize," I said, motioning for one of the other room attendants to lay out a map of the land on the table.

Another passed out paper and writing materials as well as refreshments. I didn't see us leaving this room anytime soon and wanted everyone to be comfortable. While we couldn't plan how I wanted to deal with the Lost King, other plans could be set in place to protect the kingdom.

"Alsten, what is our current situation with patrols?" I asked, getting down to business.

"As of right now, we have three dragon riders patrolling by air, each stationed at different points north, south, and east. They fly to patrol their section every hour and note any changes we might deem necessary," Alsten answered. "I've also sent out rotating groups of men in various places along the main pathway to the valley and surrounding mountain range."

While Alsten talked, I took notes, needing to see the information before me as I thought through everything else. "All right, that's a good place to start. Do we still have eyes on the mountain hideout the mercenaries used?"

"We do, but there has been no activity," he answered. "My thoughts on that would be they know everyone is here, so there is no need to infiltrate that location."

"I would have to agree with him on that," Ballard spoke up. "We left nothing there for them to use or gain more information from. With the dragons' help, we could remove all the written information we had in the Raven Rose clan and copies protected there. It would be my suggestion not to waste people watching an area no longer deemed helpful to any of us."

Tapping my fingers on the table, I processed their arguments. "Ballard, how many dragons can comfortably stay in that area? I know it had its own roost, but I never was told how large it was."

"I would say a hundred or so, your Majesty," Ballard answered.

An idea was beginning to form as I wrote down more notes to refer back to. "Prince Phillip, Gavin, do you know how many dragon riders Norden had in their military?"

The brothers seemed to confer with each other for a moment before giving me their answer. "There are roughly a little over a hundred dragon riders, but those who are female are not trained for battle like the men. They are more for correspondence between kingdoms, and in the case of a war, they would transport goods and information back and forth. So, with that being said, I'd guess somewhere around sixty to seventy dragon riders who could fight.

Many of which are on the older side. Previous generations had better luck with dragons picking a pair-bond," Gavin answered.

"So we easily outnumber them, but what we don't know is how many dragon riders there might be from the other kingdoms. King Thomas, was that something you had your spies keep track of?" I inquired.

"That isn't something I asked them to look into, but my spymaster would get various reports and only share with me what he thought was important or the answer to the question I had them out there for in the first place," he admitted.

"Paxton, in your work for Creisal, did you share that type of information with your spymaster? I am just trying to get a feel for if we went to them when we visited, would we even find the answer," I explained.

Pax leaned across the table and rested his chin on his hand, thinking. "Many of us reported things the spymaster didn't always think were important enough to write down. While we disagreed on things, many of us kept our own journals of information because there may be a day when they needed it, and we could sell it to the spymaster for a pretty penny. It helped the spymaster save face and kept us on our toes, looking for information to trade."

King Thomas looked shocked to hear this, but it made perfect sense to me. Having gone through my training with the mercenaries and being a strategist by nature, I understood the value of juicy tidbits of intel. Spies were sent to gather information, whatever that information might be, and something else always landed in your hands along the way.

"So, if we called a gathering of the spies, there might be quite a bit of information we could learn," I mused out loud. "Thank you, Pax, that was extremely helpful to hear."

"Always a pleasure to be of assistance, *My Queen*," Pax purred, winking at me.

I couldn't help but smirk at his childish ways. Even if it drove others mad, it brought a smile to my face. Taking a moment, I looked over my information so far and made a decision.

"As long as Queen Catharine is up to it, I would like to leave for Creisal in the next day or two. There seems to be a wealth of information we can find there. I would also like everyone in this room to come with as well, except for Ballard and Alsten," I announced. "Ballard, I would like you to pick up your role as steward of the crown once more in my absence. Alsten, I would like to move some of our people around and double the dragon patrols, only further out from Sheca. On top of that, I would like a hundred of our dragon riders to move to the hideout in the Restless Mountains. I don't want our military all in one location in case there is an attack."

"Your Majesty, while I understand your thinking, is it wise to move so many while you are away from the throne?" Alsten questioned.

"My choice would have been the same whether I was here or not. We need to send out some of our own spies to get a feel for what the Lost King is doing. We've been avoiding drawing his attention so he didn't find Sheca. Well, that ship has sailed. Now, we need to know what we are truly up against. I would also ask that one dragon rider be sent to Utros and another to Errit, taking stock of what is happening in those kingdoms while the Lost King is staring us down," I ordered. "These might seem like requests, but let me assure you, I'm not really asking for permission here."

Alsten flinched a little, knowing I was directing that at him. "It shall be done as you've requested, Your Majesty."

"I do value your thoughts, Alsten, but when it comes to this battle, we need to be prepared for all the worst moments," I pointed out. "If the village gets attacked or, heaven forbid, destroyed, I need to know our people will live on. Those in the hideout will have the chance to fight if they can, but if it looks as if all is lost, they need to run to the Dragon Lands where they will be safe to hide until they can carry on. We've done it more than once, and I refuse to let this noble group of people be wiped extinct. It might not be the outcome we want to hope for, but I don't have the luxury of thinking things might not turn out so bad."

"Our queen is right," Eleazar interjected. "The one thing our people have always done is prepare to have those who carry on." He paused, letting that sink in at the table before turning to me. "How many are you taking to Creisal?"

Taking a deep breath, I pushed up from my seat and stood looking at the men before me. "You are in this room because you are a trusted member of my inner circle or you have an alliance with me. That being said, I will be clear that nothing said in this room will be spoken of outside those doors to anyone. Not your wife, your children, and each other when you think the coast is clear. The Lost King has already wormed his way into our people before and that of every other kingdom. I refuse to give him any more information to use against us." Everyone nodded and muttered their agreement.

"Queen Catharine was manipulated by the Lost King during a visit to a friend in Utros three years ago. He's been having her send supplies and, I'm sure, information along. What doesn't make sense to me is the fact he didn't take Creisal when he already had a strong inside member. Every time I come back to this one inconsistency of his, it makes me believe there is something hidden in Creisal he doesn't want us to find. This is yet another reason I want to go there. In answer to your question, Eleazar, I want to bring all able-bodied men, women, and dragons with us. I don't think the fight will ever get to Sheca. It doesn't serve him any purpose now that I'm the one connected to the magic that was locked within the castle."

Alsten shot to his feet, slamming his fist on the table. "You would leave us here vulnerable with the weak, young, and elderly?"

"Yes and no," I answered, holding his irate gaze. "You will continue to have the members who are guarding the lands, which is also why I want them doubled. They will be the first to know if the enemy is coming your way. At that point, you can choose to fight or run to the hideout where the hundred dragons will be waiting. I won't abandon you like the previous king, but I will *not* bring the fight to these lands. Sheca is an amazing defense, but to have a battle here would put us at a disadvantage, trapping us in this valley back to the mountains and front to the sea. Our women are just as skilled at fighting as our men. The elderly might not make the journey into battle, but I have no doubt they can defend their homes, or do you have such little faith in our people? I will also be creating a shield to protect this valley the best I can to deter dragons laying waste to it."

Alsten seemed to deflate after hearing my words, sinking back into his seat. "I'm sorry, Your Majesty. I never should have accused you in such a manner. While I've never shared the same sentiment as some of my brothers about us being abandoned, I just couldn't help but believe for a moment it was going to happen all over again."

"You're forgiven, Alsten. Times of war bring out sides of ourselves we never knew were there," I commented. "A year ago, I was sitting in my bedroom as a noble lady, praying I would one day be accepted into Norden's court so I could get away from my mother, who beat me. Then I was given the strength and skills to stand up for myself, giving me the courage never to be a victim again. That is what I want for our people. I don't want them to be victims of this war born out of greed and pain."

Taking my seat, I took a long drink from my glass of wine before moving on. "King Thomas, I don't know why I think this, but is there something your wife brought back from that trip to Utros?"

The king rubbed his chin, thinking about my question, and slowly shook his head. "Nothing other than silly women things like dresses, shoes, and other frivolities."

"What about is there a place in the castle, city, or surrounding area where she goes but never lets anyone else but a select few come with her?" I pressed.

A flash of recognition shone in his eyes as he snapped his fingers. "We have a summer house near the sea, and she goes there from time to time to get away. The children aren't even allowed to go with her most of the time. It's just her and her personal maids."

"Is that something that started to happen after she came back from Utros?" Abbott asked, catching on to where I was going with this.

"Now that you mention it, I suppose it was. Before, it was every other time she would go alone. Otherwise, the children always went since they loved the place. It's been awful for them to be denied enjoying time there. When they were first born, we would go as a family, letting them play in the water. I became too busy and couldn't get away as easily, so she took them herself," King Thomas explained. "Then when she returned from Utros, we fought so much more that she claimed she needed space for herself. Our fights were always blamed on me feeling threatened by her trying to step up and take on more. While I can't argue that the matters we fought over the most were things I didn't agree with and didn't see us needing to do, it was never about me not wanting her help."

I gave him a reassuring smile as I saw how much that seemed to weigh on him. "You'll just have to keep reminding yourself she wasn't her normal self. She was being controlled by the Lost King.

The reason I ask you is because I believe she might have something in her possession that the Lost King doesn't want us to find. I have no idea what it might be, but it's important enough to him that he refuses to let anyone get close to it, even himself."

Everyone seemed stunned by this revelation, but it's the only thing that made sense to me. Why else would he control the queen, use her for supplies to maintain his army, but never move for her to take Creisal from the inside out? Queen Catharine could have easily won over the people and removed her husband from the throne over the past few years. The only reason that he wouldn't do that is because he couldn't risk drawing attention to something.

Fourteen

Paxton

Everything Cassarah was saying made sense. While I was a spy for Creisal, I saw many strange things and reported or kept them safely written down, hidden in various places to use at a later time. The spymaster was an idiot, and no matter how we explained things, it was never shared if the king didn't ask for it. We knew there was an army amassing between Errit and Utros, but it was too far away for the spymaster to see any threat to the kingdom. Yeah, well, look at us now, dealing with the problem we told him about.

The rest of the meeting was dull, going over supplies, crops, and other normal life things a queen had to deal with when ruling a kingdom. This is why I'd been so good at being a spy. Being on the move, searching out the things people missed or just didn't see happening in plain sight, was where I excelled—not sitting in boring meetings.

As for Cassarah, that woman had a brilliant mind that could see everything all at once, connecting the dots to things I don't think I'd even consider. To hear her stories of growing up and how her mother used to treat her made me furious. Why the fuck would they want to cage such a person into a role of doting wife and mother when clearly she was meant for something more?

That's what I didn't get about court life. I've watched it over the years in Creisal, and none of it made sense. The mercenaries have always maintained that women have every right to be as involved as the men. In many cases, they were better in certain areas than we were. Royalty and nobles couldn't see past their pedigree long enough to choose what would be best for the kingdom as a whole.

"Thank you all for your time. I will confer with King Thomas and the healers to see when it might be best for us to leave for Creisal," Cassarah announced, snapping me out of my doodlings on the paper she'd given us.

Dayson peered over at my paper and snorted. "Is that what you think the Lost King looks like?"

Lifting the page, I took in the creepy form I'd drawn of a man with multiple arms, sharp teeth, and crazy eyes. In the background was a dragon looking more like a melting stick of butter, but I thought it fit.

"Well, you knew who it was right away, so I must have done a good job," I quipped, flashing the big man a grin.

I still didn't feel like I truly blended with this group, yet things were getting better. Cole still hated me, and Abbott seemed to think I was an insensitive prick, but the others tolerated me fairly well.

When things had gone down this morning with Cassarah, I was utterly shocked to have Gavin, of all people, willing to play my game. Then he'd turned around and done the same thing to Zan. I had to give that man more credit—he had a savvy mind to drive our woman wild and get others to play along. While watching wasn't a major turn on for me, pushing people out of their comfort zone was. I craved knowing just how far I could push someone to see them discover another side of themselves. That is what I thought I was doing until I quickly learned our queen was veracious in the bedroom.

None of us compared notes about our time with Cassarah, but you hear things in passing, and when I found out she and Cole fucked on the beach... well, let's just say I had some mad respect for Cole.

"Come on, you and I are going with Cassy-bear to check on Vasin. The others have things to do," Dayson informed me as he got up from the table.

Blinking a few times, I got up, folded my paper, and slipped it into my pocket. "Guess I missed that part of the meeting."

"You really didn't miss much," Dayson admitted. "I never knew that royalty was responsible for as much stuff as they are."

"Oh, that's Cassarah being Cassarah. Most kings and queens hand things off to a team of advisers and only deal with the large issues people bring to them. My money is that Cassarah will refuse to ever do that and handle everything on her own. That might change over time, but she's only ever seen what it looks like when kingdoms have been mismanaged," I explained. "Queen Catharine was able to get away with so much because the king wasn't dealing with the issues she was manipulating."

Dayson and I walked down the castle's long hall. It was sometimes hard to wrap my head around the fact that this is where I lived. I wasn't just visiting and sharing my observations of my trip, this was my home. I was consort to one of the most amazing people I'd ever met, who happened to be a queen. On top of that, I was also one of her guardians charged with ensuring she stayed alive to make the world a better place.

Who would have guessed the man whose brother tried to kill him while his father was a traitor to not only his people but that of another kingdom would end up a chosen guardian. My family helped create the demon trying to steal everything away from us. I guess the fates decided it was only fitting that I be part of the group that would bring about his destruction.

We reached the dragon platform on the upper level where our chambers were to find Ninnat waiting for me, wings stretched out, sunning herself. Walking up to her head, I gave her eye ridges a good scratch, and she started to hum. I always wondered what it would be like if I could talk to her like Cassarah could with Vasin. Then, I remembered she was a female, and I thought maybe it was best to only have one woman ruling my life. As if she understood what I was thinking, her golden eye flicked open, and she snorted at me, engulfing me in a puff of smoke.

Spluttering, I waved my hand about, glaring at her. "What's the deal? You only do that when you're upset with me about something?"

"Could it be that she knows you have another woman in your life now, and she's jealous?" Cassarah asked, walking up next to me. She smiled at Ninnat as she reached out a hand to my dragon, who crooned and lifted her snout to meet her touch.

"What the hell," I grumbled. "You smoke me out, but you get all sweet around her. What gives?"

Cassarah chuckled as a real smile bloomed on her face. Those were becoming few and far between these days, which is why I always did something stupid to get her to react. "It's a woman thing, unfortunately. We always seem to team up when we feel slighted. My guess is that she used to be the only woman in your life, and with how much you traveled, you two were all each other had. Now you have me, and she gets less time with you."

When she put it that way, it was easy to see the problem. Ninnat and I had been through so much together, and since I became a guardian, that's all changed.

Wrapping my arms around my dragon's neck, I whispered in her ear, "Ninnat, you will always be my girl. No matter what happens in life or who joins us, you are the first ever to choose me and stick by me no matter what."

Ninnat crooned and let out a little puff of fire to add to her answer, nuzzling into me. Many people wouldn't take me seriously and always assumed that since I left my home, I must have been the one to do something wrong. On top of that, being a spy didn't do me any favors either. People hear you're a spy or you work for the Crown, and automatically you're untrustworthy. Gathering intel for the king isn't the same as infiltrating another kingdom to spill their secrets so we could overthrow them. King Thomas just wanted to be kept informed of the other kingdoms in case there was a cause for concern. It was his spymaster who was the moron and missed the signs.

"You two have a very close relationship, don't you," Cassarah commented as she rubbed Ninnat's snout.

I looked at my golden girl with pride and nodded. "She actually saved me when I ended up too close to the Dragon Lands outside the Utros border. I was trying to cross the border, but the patrols were stronger than they'd ever been, so I trekked further through the mountains and stumbled upon an oasis where a group of dragons were sunning. Trying to get away, I fell and hurt my leg pretty badly so I couldn't escape. Ninnat came to my rescue, and she's been with me ever since."

"That's the beauty of dragons, isn't it? They see into our souls and come to know who we truly are inside. When Vasin called out to me the first time, I couldn't understand why he would ever pick someone like me. My mother stripped away my self-confidence year after year until I almost believed her." She looked up at me, her amber eyes meeting mine, full of so much emotion. "They always seem to know who needs saving, don't they?"

Grinning, I nodded in agreement. "Yeah, I would have been a snack for a dragon if she hadn't decided to save me. Then, another miracle was that she never left. She was the first to stick with me through thick and thin, never once hesitating to do whatever it took to keep us alive. Being a spy makes you a target on and off the job."

Cassarah took a step back and bowed to my dragon. "Thank you, Ninnat, for sharing your pair-bond with me. I will do my best to ensure once this battle is over, you get more quality time with him."

Ninnat bobbed her head and folded up her wings, settling herself into position for us to climb on. Hopping up, I got settled and reached down for Cassarah. "Come on, spitfire, stop trying to steal my dragon from me. You'll make Vasin jealous."

Laughing, she took my hand, and I hoisted her up, putting her right in front of me so I could wrap my arms around her. "You're a one-of-a-kind woman, you know that, Cassarah? What queen would bow to a dragon and ensure they are as happy as the rest of the people she cares for?"

"A smart woman," she teased. "Pissing off a dragon, especially a female, is a terrible idea. I'd like to see us all grow old together one day."

I burst out laughing as Ninnat vaulted off the platform and snapped open her powerful wings, allowing us to glide our way to the roost. Dayson and his brown dragon, Hegg, followed after us, drifting from side to side, ignoring whatever Dayson was yelling at him. Those two had an odd relationship. It was almost as if his dragon purposely did things to enrage the mammoth of a man. It made me smile every time but, of course, I would never share my thoughts, knowing Dayson wouldn't find it as funny as I did.

The flight to the roost was short and sweet, but it was nice to get the chance of a flight in. I hadn't noticed how much I hated being in the same place all the time until I was asked to. Of course, I wouldn't change a thing about being Cassarah's guardian and consort. I love the hell out of that woman. Yet, I couldn't argue that my soul cried out for the chance to wander more, seeking the mission's thrill.

Cassarah scrambled off Ninnat before I could help her, dropped to the ground, and ran. Looking up, I saw Vasin standing at the entrance to the roost, and when he saw her coming for him, he moved forward to greet her. She flung herself at the dragon, and he caught her against his chest with his front legs and large head.

We all knew it was hard for her not to have Vasin the past few days, but we clearly didn't understand the level of loss she'd been feeling. Seeing this had me looking over at Dayson, and the same thought was also written on his face. We needed to do better for our woman. We'd been trying to do our best, but it just wasn't in the way she needed right now. We would need to take this knowledge and learn from it for the future.

FIFTEEN

CASSARAH

The rumble of Vasin's purr vibrating against my skin as I wrapped my arms around his neck seemed to ground me. While I knew he needed to heal, and the best way to do that was to put him in a healing sleep, it just happened at a time when I'd needed him. We had been bonded for such a short time in the scheme of things, but knowing he was always there in the back of my mind when I needed him was beyond comforting.

"My dear, Cass, it seems I have missed much in the past few days. I'm sorry I left you to deal with so much on your own."

"Can I tell you how nice it is to hear you in my head once more? Everyone around me has been doing their best, but no one could ever replace you."

"I should hope not." Vasin huffed, letting me slide down his chest until I stood on my own. *"Give me a moment, and I shall catch up on all I've missed so you don't have to waste time explaining it."*

Opening up my mind to him, I placed my hand on his snout. We were past the point of needing physical contact to do this. I just needed the reassurance that he was still here. The feeling of him gathering the information he needed was no longer odd, even though it would never feel truly normal.

"*Cass,*" Vasin snapped with a warning growl. "*How could you even consider doing something so dangerous without me there to back you up? Xotha is an incredibly strong old dragon that has been twisted with dark magic. Thankfully, your Birthright didn't allow him to manipulate you in any other way than by pulling you into his subconscious.*"

"*I didn't even know that any dragon could do that. You and I are bonded so that makes sense to me, but for him to pull me out of another human's mind into that space is mind-boggling. Paxton told me if it hadn't been his link to me as a guardian, he might not have found me.*"

"*You are proving my point for me. That was reckless and something I would have seen one of your consorts doing, but for you to make such a move surprises me. I can feel your desperation for answers, but it's making you foolish.*"

Flinching at his rebuttal, I hung my head, knowing he was right. "*We needed answers, Vasin. I was at a loss as to how to move forward, and doing that gave me what I wanted... the next clue. The Lost King believes he is this all-powerful being who can't be stopped. The only reason he can believe that with so much conviction is that he's ensured whatever weakness he might have is hidden and hidden well.*"

"*Even if your logic is sound, the way you went about it was anything but. There was no need for that to happen so quickly. You could have waited until later in the day when I was once again awake and could be there to guard you.*"

"*If you did that, though, I'm not sure he would have been able to pull me into Xotha's mind. It was because he believed himself to be in control that he let slip what he did. I knew Paxton could get me out of there.”*

“*But he almost didn’t!*” Vasin roared in my head and aloud, unsettling everyone around us.

“*Do not yell at me!*” I shouted back. “*I know what I did was risky, but I got what I needed, and it’s over and done now.*”

Vasin settled, flicking his wings in agitation before walking off to the side where a sunbeam was still left in the waning light. There, he laid his back to me as he spread out his wings. They were no longer filled with holes and rips from the fight, but instead, waxy areas showed where the skin was still healing. The forced sleep had done wonders to speed along his recovery, but I could feel through our connection that he was still weak.

I’m sure Dayson moved in my direction to check on me, but I held him off and shook my head. Inhaling deeply to calm my irritation and letting it back out again slowly, I moved to join my dragon. I didn’t say anything but sat by his shoulder as I always did when we just spent time together. Neither of us were at our best right now, so I didn’t hold his anger against him.

“*You know, if something happens to you, then I am also lost and vice versa. Here I was doing all I could to ensure I was healing as quickly as possible because I knew it made you vulnerable to have me so weak. Then, I awaken only to find out you’ve been all but throwing your life at the mercy of the one man we can’t afford to take it.*”

“*While I can see it from your perspective, that is not what I was trying to do,*” I murmured as I stroked the scales of his neck. “*The others think I’m being reckless because I vowed I would do whatever it took to ensure the Lost King never ruled, even if I gave up my own life.*”

"Yes, I saw that conversation in your memories as well."

"Then you heard my answer."

Vasin's head shifted so one amber eye was focused on me. *"Cass, you are walking a dangerous road. The fates didn't pick you because you were just like him but because you were the opposite."*

That chastisement hit right in the gut. Was he right? Did playing by the Lost King's rules make me just like him? I would never risk anyone else's lives, just my own.

"That isn't true. By risking your life, you risk mine, not to mention the men who love you and would never be able to carry on without you."

Shifting, I looked behind me at Dayson and Paxton talking to each other, giving me the space I needed with Vasin. Could they really be so devastated after only knowing me for a few short months that they would follow me into the afterlife?

"Stupid question, Cass. One of them leaped out of a window after you, hoping his dragon would catch him in time. Their bond as dragon and rider is so new it might not have gone the way it turned out. Would you have been able to catch him if his dragon hadn't?"

Vasin wasn't holding back on his thoughts in the slightest. He smacked down every argument I came up with and showed me just how blinded I'd been in my quest to destroy the Lost King. Each moment I thought I was acting for the betterment of my people or my men, Vasin tore off the blinders and showed me how selfish I'd been.

"How did I not see it? This need to destroy him at all costs has been growing until now, and I've twisted the truth in my mind."

"CASS, THIS IS THE PRICE OF POWER. EVERY PERSON GIVEN A ROLE OF POWER OVER PEOPLE WRESTLES WITH THIS ISSUE. THOSE WHO OVERCOME THE TEMPTATION TO FALL INTO THE POWER'S LUST AND KEEP IT FROM TWISTING THEIR MIND DO SO BY SURROUNDING THEMSELVES WITH PEOPLE WHO HOLD THEM ACCOUNTABLE," VASIN POINTED OUT, FLASHING IMAGES AND MEMORIES OF THIS HAPPENING IN MY OWN LIFE. *"WHERE YOU STUMBLED, AND UNDERSTANDABLY SO, IS AFTER PAYSON BETRAYED YOU. THEN, THE CLAN LEADERS PLANNED A REVOLT YOU PUT A STOP TO. EVEN THE NORDEN ROYALTY, WHO WAS SUPPOSED TO BE ALLIES, TURNED THEIR BACKS ON YOU. IT IS MY BELIEF THAT'S WHEN YOU STOPPED LISTENING TO THOSE AROUND YOU GIVING YOU ADVICE, INSTEAD FEELING IT WAS BETTER TO TRUST YOURSELF."*

Vasin revealed a flood of moments where I did just what he was saying. Not all of it resulted in a selfish act, or even one others didn't support, but were they done for the right reasons? The more I pushed off what others wanted and started to plan things alone in my head, forgetting to tell the others about it, was where I'd gone wrong. The past few days I'd been especially wrong in keeping things from the people who only had my best interests in mind. I tied their hands behind their backs and forced them not to trust me. It angered me, and I lashed out, even though I knew I'd pushed them into this.

"Look what happens when I don't have you to scold me like the petulant child I've been. I don't have you watching over my shoulder, and I fall apart. What does that say about me?"

"THAT YOU ARE HUMAN."

I couldn't help but snort at that, knowing it wasn't meant to be an insult but more a statement of facts. A dragon would never see the need to be so conniving or manipulative.

"How do I fix this?"

"We shall do it together, dear Cass. Now that you are aware of the problem, I don't foresee you making the same mistake quite so easily. Trust your men when they tell you something is off and don't dismiss their feelings quite so quickly. They know you better than you realize. Now, I suggest you head back to the castle and apologize to all your guardians. They have been doing their best for you despite your actions and words."

Standing, I ran my hand along his neck until I reached his head and scratched his eye ridges. *"We hope to fly to Creisal in the next few days, but I can push it back if you won't be strong enough."*

"Give me two days. I shall be ready to fly in two days. My wings are healing well, and the poison has fully cleared my system, but I need a little time. You won't be leaving me here, I'll tell you that right now. It's only been two days, and look at the mess you made. No, I won't be letting you leave to another kingdom without me."

"I wouldn't dream of it. Get your rest, and I will check in on you later," I murmured, pressing a kiss to his giant scaly head.

The guys saw me approaching and started to clear up the card game they'd been playing. Each watched me with careful observation, probably having gathered that Vasin and I fought. Reaching out, I took a hand from each of them and pulled them in close so I was sandwiched between them.

"Everything's fine. I had some hard truths given to me, but they were all things I needed to hear. I'm sorry that I brushed off your concerns, and if I've made you feel like your opinion doesn't matter, I'm so sorry," I shared, looking from one man to the other. "The truth of the matter is, I don't deserve men like you watching out for me. So, the only thing I can do in return is to try and not make it harder on you all."

"Cassy-bear," Dayson said, his voice rumbled in my ear as he kissed my temple. "This has been hard on each of us, but most of all you. The choices you make affect a whole kingdom... one you are still learning about, I might add. Mistakes will be made by you and us while we adjust to this new life."

Paxton wrapped his free arm around me, pulling me against him as he nuzzled into my hair. "What Day said... fights happen, disagreements in how things are handled are par for the course with any relationship, and you have eight of us plus the girls. That's ten people you have to consider at all times. We have it easy since we only have to worry about you, but if we are being honest, we didn't support you the best way while Vasin was healing. All of us can learn from how things have gone the last few days and do better."

Hearing how easily they forgave me worried me as much as it was a balm to my emotions. Never did I want to take advantage of them and their love for me, so even though they forgave me, I needed to earn that forgiveness a little.

"Let's head back and have dinner... just the ten of us in our chambers. I'll make sure the palace staff knows we are not to be bothered unless it's urgent," I offered, hugging them each in turn before we climbed back on the dragons.

This time, I flew back with Dayson, making sure Paxton took a few extra minutes to take a flight, just him and Ninnat. I might not be the best at relationships, but I knew for him to take the time for her would help. The past few days I've been so self-focused I truly wanted to try to be more mindful of what was happening around me with the people I loved.

"Cassy-bear, will you sleep in my bed tonight?" Dayson asked, running his nose along the shell of my ear. "I'd really love some alone time with you. I feel like you and I haven't done that much."

"That sounds perfect," I answered. "I think it would be a wise idea for us to work out a way so each of us can have time together. Like having a meal one-on-one or spending the night together. While you all understand I'm with all of you, I don't need to be with all of you all the time. I think it will help me to focus on the individual needs of each of my relationships."

"Why don't we bring it up at dinner... see what the others think would be a good idea," Dayson suggested.

Hegg landed abruptly, tossing us both forward. Thankfully, the harness kept us where we should be on his back. Hegg let out a snort accompanied with sparks as he shook his head before looking back at us to make sure we were good. I could feel him sending the emotions of an apology for the rough landing.

"It's all right, Hegg. We appreciate the ride, and you've gotten us back safe and sound," I said, rubbing his shoulder before I slipped off his back.

Walking to the front, Hegg dropped his head, and I saw a bunch of feathers were stuck to his face. Chuckling, I started to pluck them off. "Did you catch a snack on the way back? This is why you shouldn't eat and fly at the same time."

"I swear, this dragon is a bottomless pit. He's skinny as a runt but eats like there's no tomorrow. What I'd like to know is where does the food he eats go?" Dayson questioned, resting his hand on his hips, looking his dragon over. "Some days, I wonder if I'm too heavy for him to handle."

Hegg growled at that, swinging his head over to his pair-bond and snapped his teeth at him.

"All right, you two. Dayson, leave poor Hegg alone. Clearly, he needs large amounts of food to support himself, or maybe he hasn't been able to get a decent meal until he came here. Vasin tells me how the Unclaimed Lands are desolate in many areas," I scolded, getting an approving hum from Hegg.

Dayson just grinned at me. "I know I'm not going to win this argument, so I'm not even going to try. I'll just agree with my lady and queen on this matter."

Punching him in the arm, I gave Hegg one last scratch and headed inside. A palace guard stationed at the entrance saw me and bowed as I walked down the hall toward our personal chambers. While I knew they were there as a precaution during this time of high alert, I would be glad when the number of guards posted on our level was reduced. It was becoming clearer to me I needed space to get away from being queen for just a bit, and our castle floor was that vestige. Another guard was posted just outside the main door to my personal rooms with my consorts. Slightly further down the hall were Becka and May's rooms, ensuring they didn't need to hear the more salacious things that happened.

The guard bowed and opened the door for me. "Do you know if everyone is here?" I asked before entering.

"Yes, Your Majesty, all your guardians and consorts are in the common rooms," he answered.

"Thank you. I am relieving you of your post for the night. Could you inform the staff that my guardians and I will be having dinner here? We also wish to be left in peace unless there is an urgent matter," I informed him.

He hesitated a moment before bowing once more in acknowledgment. Entering, I found the front sitting room was empty, so I moved into the library which also acted as my personal office. Becka was at my desk working on something while the others sat around the table, gambling, by the looks of it.

"What are you gonna do, Zan? Three others have already tossed in their hand. You think you have what it takes to beat me?" Cole taunted, tapping his card on the table.

Ezzu hissed in response before Zan tossed in a few coins. "I'll see your bet. I don't think you have the hand you're making it out to be."

Smiling at seeing them all spending time together, I walked over to Becka so I didn't disturb them. "What are you working on so diligently?"

Becka's head snapped up, her eyes wide with surprise. "Oh, when did you get back?"

"Just now," I answered, sitting in the chair opposite her. "Why aren't you playing with the others? I've seen your skill at taking their money. Did they ban you from the game?"

She set the quill down, watching me with her observant green eyes. This woman knew me better than anyone else alive, so when she smiled and leaned back in my chair, I knew what came next would be something less than glowing.

"So, the dragon gave you a good tongue lashing then. It's about damn time. You needed someone to knock you off your high horse, and the only one you'd listen to is him," Becka stated, a haughty look in her eye.

Instead of giving her pointless words, I nodded and smoothed out my dress skirt. "I thought tonight might be nice for us all to have dinner together here. Also, I informed the staff they were not to bother us unless there was something pressing."

"It's a good start. Lucky for you those men love you to the point of insanity. Not every day a man jumps off a cliff after his woman, and he's not the only one who would have done it either," Becka pointed out. "Are May and I invited to this dinner, or are you planning on apologizing in a more personal way?"

My cheeks heated at her suggestion. While I might find myself fully enjoying the perks of having so many lovers, I wasn't sure I was ready to put myself on quite that large of a display. "I'd planned on you two being there since you both are my guardians as well as sisters to me. I owe you both as much of an apology as I do to them."

"Delightful," Becka cheered, clapping her hands together. "Now tell me, is Vasin healing well?"

"He said he needs a few more days, but yes, he is healing amazingly fast in my opinion," I answered, then gestured toward the paper before her. "Are you going to tell me what you're working on?"

"Promise not to be upset with me?" Becka pleaded, sitting up straighter.

"Do I have the right to be upset with you after the past few days?" I countered.

She cocked her head to the side and thought about that for a moment. "No, but this might fall into a different category."

Frowning, I held my hand out, and she gave over the paper. Glancing over the words, I paused, my breath catching in my chest as my eyes snapped back to hers. "Did you plan on telling me you were contacting my parents? Moreover, you aren't just reaching out to them, you're offering them a place of refuge *here* with me."

"Cassarah—"

"No!" I snapped, cutting her off and slamming the paper on the desk. "They were willing to let me die to save their own pride. Why should they see what I've made of myself despite them?"

"Hear me out," Becka asked, reaching out to cover my hand with hers. "You are right, they don't deserve to be offered this chance, but could you live with yourself if they died in this war when you had the chance to save them? The only reason I even considered sending this is so you don't have to suffer that possibility. Once the war is over, if you want to kick them out and never see them again, so be it. They might not even take the offer. They would have to leave everything behind, hoping it would be there when they returned."

I narrowed my eyes at her, trying to think of some reason to prove she was wrong in her logic. "Fine, send the letter with two dragon riders. Have them drop down out of the sky at their doorstep to give them the letter. Once they read it, I will give them an hour to make their choice, letting them only keep the clothes on their backs. If they are going to be here in my home, they will be at my mercy just like I was my whole life with them."

"You might not see it now, Cassarah, but you will thank me later for letting me do this. In the back of your mind, I know you'll always wonder if you should have offered it. If they turn it down, then you are freed from all obligations to them," Becka reasoned, handing me the quill to sign my name and place my seal.

How can it be that one of the first documents I sign and seal is a letter to my parents—the two people who wronged me most in my life, and I'm offering them shelter? Then Vasin's words echoed through my head. *The fates didn't pick you because you were just like him, they picked you because you were the opposite."* If Henry were in my shoes, he would have killed his parents before ever thinking of saving them. Knowing I was doing something he never would told me I was making the right choice, no matter how much I disliked it.

SIXTEEN

CASSARAH

Becka didn't waste any time sending out two dragon riders to deliver my message, but I chose to put that aside for now as I enjoyed an evening with my true family. Dinner was brought up, and I couldn't help but smile as I noticed they selected some of our favorite foods. Having spent time living with Marta when we first arrived, she quickly learned what each of us enjoyed, although everything she cooked was incredible. It was why I asked for her to work at the castle as our head chef.

The atmosphere was relaxed as everyone dished up their plates, having sent the staff away for the night. All of us were more than capable of fending for ourselves, and it was nice to set aside the castle's rules. The only thing we couldn't avoid is that a taster already tested my plate. Regardless of how I felt about things and wished to be a normal person, I couldn't be reckless with my life anymore. Vasin had made sure to hit that home with me in our conversation, and I planned to take it to heart.

"So, we might actually get to meet your parents?" Paxton asked as we all settled into our meal.

He grunted as Cole glared, and my guess would be he kicked him under the table. "Leave it alone."

"What, I'm not allowed to ask? I get that they were assholes to her and didn't treat her right... we've all heard enough stories to gather that picture. I wanted to know if I could meet them so I could look that man who called himself her father in the eyes and see if he knows how badly he fucked up," Paxton defended, waving his fork at Cole, splattering him with food. "You need to back off and take a deep breath. You overprotective caveman."

Hearing the insult and seeing the mock horror on Cole's face, I couldn't help but laugh.

"While I hate to admit this, Paxton isn't wrong, you know," May added. "Out of all of us, you, Cole, you're the only one who seems to baby her feelings the most."

"I do not!" Cole declared, slamming his hand on the table. "What you might see as coddling, or babying as you so called it, is not allowing people to treat her without respect."

"So, what you're saying is everything that comes out of my mouth you see as disrespectful?" Paxton asked, resting his head on his hand, waiting.

Cole opened and closed his mouth a few times before letting out a frustrated growl. "Look, you treat everyone like they are your sibling or your best friend, not taking into account they might be someone of higher status. You speak, but I don't think you ever actually think about what you're going to say before you say it. Most of the time, Abbott or I get after you because you say rude or thoughtless things."

"Are you not my family?" Paxton asked.

"I... well... ah..." Cole stuttered, looking at all of us as if we were going to save him.

Listening to these two men talk, I realized that while I'd been focused on dealing with the troubles happening around us, I hadn't noticed what was going on right in front of me. On the surface, it seemed like all of them were getting along and learning to enjoy one another. Paxton was the last to join us, and he came with some past history that made things challenging, but I didn't for a moment consider they didn't know we were a family.

"Pax brings up a good point," I voiced, pulling everyone's attention. "Do you consider each other family at all? You are no longer just my guardians but my consorts, men who will be forever in each other's lives, raising children, ruling this kingdom with me, growing old together. If things don't go well between you, there is no walking away from it. You're all connected to each other for the rest of our lives."

Looking around the table at each of them, I saw varying degrees of realization register on their faces. The only one who didn't seem at all bothered by this revelation was Zan. He sat back with his hands in his lap as Ezzu napped on the back of his chair. Leave it to my blind lover to see the truth of things clearer than anyone else in the room.

Becka cleared her throat, taking a sip of her wine before speaking. "I know this is slightly different for May and me since we don't have the added nature of sleeping with the queen, but she's right. Most of you have been like brothers to me for most of my life, so adding a few more of you didn't seem to change much for me. I absolutely see you all as my family."

May nodded her agreement. "Same. I've only had Dayson as my family since his father took me in when my parents died. Most of you I've known for years, and if we are being honest with each other, even though you haven't thought about it, you treat each other like you're brothers."

"Isn't this how family works, though? You don't get to choose who is a part of it and whether you agree with their actions or choices, they are still someone you look after. Pax might drive us all crazy, but if anyone were going to mess with him that wasn't one of us, I would take issue with that," Dayson said, rubbing the back of his neck as he looked at the others. "If any of you landed in trouble, I wouldn't ask questions but would just wade in and figure it out later."

Peeking at Zan out of the corner of my eye, I saw him smirking before he hid it behind his glass. My gaze swung over to Jade, Izel, and Gavin, who were completely silent with closed-off expressions. I knew trusting would be hard for Jade, knowing that his family had turned their backs on him. Izel, on the other hand, I was curious about his silence as well as Gavin. Neither of them seemed to have issues with the others I was aware of.

"I have a question," Gavin announced. "Do any of you have an issue with the fact I was selected to take the crown if anything happened to Cassarah before she had an heir?"

"Why would we? Each of us agreed you were the wise choice," Abbott commented.

"That is true, but did you all choose to go along with the others, or did you feel I'm the best option?" Gavin pressed as he looked at the others. "If that isn't the true feelings of this family, then I have no problem giving up the role to another. I've given up being the crown prince once already because I didn't feel it was the right place for me, so I can understand if you think the same thing."

Izel turned to face Gavin, sitting next to him. "Why did you give up being Norden's crown prince?"

"For years, I was educated by our tutors and advisers about our kingdom and the people we ruled over. Some of the beliefs they had I wasn't sure I agreed with. Then when Cassarah rescued me, and I saw firsthand what life was like outside the castle for many people, I knew what I'd been taught was misguided. I wasn't strong enough to stand up to my parents and the people who had raised me. On the other hand, Phillip has always been more confident in himself and challenged those teachings," Gavin explained, pausing a moment as if to gather his thoughts before he continued.

"A new dream started to grow, and I saw a world where I could work alongside my brother to help our kingdom and the mercenaries grow into something more. Both groups have such rich histories and traditions, but in one selfish move, our past rulers broke trust. More than anything, I want to repair that trust and see our world working together, so another Lost King can't happen again, but if it does, then all of us stand together."

Izel nodded in approval of Gavin's words. "If that is truly how you feel, I believe we chose the right man. God forbid that something happens to Cassarah, but if she can no longer rule, I would want someone with the same dream she has to be in power."

Every person at the table murmured their agreement. As if a weight had been lifted off Gavin, he sat up straighter and seemed to breathe easier hearing their answer.

"Does anyone else have something they would like to clear the air on or share with the others?" I asked in hopes of keeping this honest conversation that clearly needed to happen.

"Cassarah and I were talking earlier about how to ensure each of us gets some personal time. Like I asked that she stay in my room tonight, or one of you might request having a meal just the two of you... anything so that we have one-on-one moments together. As I said, I see you all as family, but that doesn't mean I want to be around you every waking moment," he teased. "Sometimes, you just need time with your woman. You know what I mean?"

Zan slapped a wide smile on his face. "That, my brother, is a brilliant suggestion. Thank you for bringing it up. If someone else hadn't, I was going to, but I'm glad to see there are others of the same mind." Ezzu was wide awake now, taking in the room for Zan until her golden eyes fell on me. "Cassarah, I know when we first met, it wasn't under the best of circumstances, but the fates knew far better than we did. Not only have I been blessed to have you as my partner in life and someone I get to love wholeheartedly, but the fates gave me all of you men as well. This is the first family I've had where I feel accepted for who I am and not judged for being blind. I know it took a bit to gain your trust, rightly so, but once you all gave that to me, you never questioned it."

The guys all seemed to be somewhat embarrassed by Zan's words, muttering and looking away. Gavin even blushed a little at the sentiment. Jade, though, still hadn't seemed to break out of his icy shell he had wrapped around himself.

"Vasin."

"Yes, my dear Cass?"

"Has Tahir mentioned anything going on with Jade? I feel like there might be something I'm missing. We are all here having an open and honest conversation, and he just seems to be pulling away."

"Give me a moment to speak with Tahir."

Part of me wanted to call him out and demand an answer, but my heart told me that would only push him farther away. Jade was a man of deep emotions, and I knew I was one of the only people he would allow himself to be vulnerable with. Sure, he would get upset around the others and shout his orders when it came to my safety, but I think back to that moment we shared alone late at night in the late king's office. He told me the story about his family and how he became known as the Grim Reaper. To demand him to answer me now would only result in him storming out of this room, solving nothing.

"How do you propose we do this individual time?" Abbott asked, drawing me out of my thoughts. "I don't want it to be something scheduled, making it feel like an obligation. Also, what if there is a time when one of us needs her more than another for some reason?"

The table fell silent as they considered his words, but I couldn't get over my concern about Jade. I was almost ready to pull him to the side and have him join me on the balcony. What I felt I could confidently cross off the list of problems was something between us. I knew he and I were fine. If we weren't, he would absolutely come to talk to me or drag me off to deal with it. So, it had to be something with the guys or possibly with the war we were heading into.

"What if we take it as a day-by-day situation?" Izel suggested. "The biggest part of all this is ensuring we are vocal about what we need. I don't mind having others around so long as I can sometimes sit next to Cassarah or hold her in my arms for a while. Yet, there might be a day I really need to have one-on-one time, and it's my responsibility to speak up."

"I can get behind that as long as we also agree that if we feel like someone is taking advantage of personal time, we can talk about that too," Paxton voiced.

"Let's not forget that Cassarah gets a say in this as well," Dayson interjected. "Every woman needs a day to herself, and with her dealing with all of us, I feel that is only going to make the need greater."

Becka snickered at that, giving me a wink. "The poor thing is gonna need at least one day she isn't getting poked by one of you. Plus, May and I want our time with her as well. It's not fair that you all get special time with her and we don't."

"That is a brilliant point," I agreed. "I know you all are happy to listen to me grumble about things, but in every relationship there are irritations. Just so we're clear, I will not ever be discussing things with each of you about the others. That is what Becka and May are for. They will be able to listen to me and not need to fix it right away. The last thing I want is for things to get worse between all of you."

"Very wise," Zan agreed. "We will endeavor to do the same and try to deal with our personal issues with others directly instead of coming to you about them as well."

Looking around the table, it seemed that everyone was in agreement with these choices, making me feel much better about how things stood between everyone. Finished with our meal, we all gathered in the sitting room, and Jade surprised me by pulling me into his lap as he sat in one of the armchairs.

"Little bird, I could feel you watching me through the whole conversation," he murmured in my ear. "Give me time, and I will reveal what's wrong. Just trust in the fact that it has nothing to do with you. We are perfectly fine."

"Are you okay?" I asked, turning to meet his gaze.

His seafoam-colored eyes looked back at me with love and a tinge of sadness. "I hope to be soon... it's hard for me when it comes to family. None of my family was ever that loving toward me, and trying to build a new one has brought up some feelings and other things I have to work on."

Pressing a kiss to his lips, I tried to infuse all the love I had for him into it. He tucked my head under his chin as he held me while the others resumed their card games. Soon, the room was filled with laughter, yelling, and the sense of family. This was what we'd been missing—this time to be together just as people, setting aside our titles and role in the world. Right now, we were just family—my family.

SEVENTEEN

CASSARAH

I was awoken as someone scooped me up and started to carry me. It would seem the men had finally had enough of their card battle and were calling it a night. Dayson picked me up from the couch where it appeared I fell asleep watching them.

"Go back to sleep, Cassy-bear. Out of all of us, you need the sleep," Dayson murmured, kissing my forehead. "You don't mind being in my room tonight, do you?"

"No, as long as you're there with me, I'm fine to sleep wherever," I answered, nuzzling into his chest. "Who won?"

"Paxton, the cheating bastard," Dayson grumbled.

Smiling, I couldn't help but chuckle. "Did he really cheat, or was he just craftier than all of you?"

"What's the difference?"

"Skill, seeing as all of you are mercenaries and can read a lie from across the room," I said as he sat me on his bed.

"Then I would say he is an incredibly skilled man because none of us saw it coming. Now, do you need me to help you out of that dress?" Dayson asked with a raised brow.

Rising, I pulled my loose hair over my shoulder, revealing the back of the dress where the laces were. "If you can get the over dress, I can manage the rest."

I felt his body heat as he stepped up to me, resting his hands on my hips before kissing my neck. "What if I also want to take the rest off of you? Will you let me do that? Unless you're not in the mood, then I'll keep my hands to myself."

Glancing at him over my shoulder, I gave him a sultry smile. "I don't think there will be a moment when I'm not in the *mood* to be with of my men."

"Next question... how much do you like this dress?"

"I've got others—"

The sound of fabric ripping echoed in the quiet room as my body jerked from the force of him snapping the laces along with the fabric. He wasn't finished with me yet, though, and I felt the cool steel of a blade glide up my spine, making me gasp.

"Day..."

A hand rested on my neck where it meets my shoulder. "Trust me, Cassy-bear. I'm not ever going to hurt you."

His fingers caressed up the column of my throat then back down, pushing the fabric off my shoulder. Quickly, the same thing happened with the other side, causing the dress to settle at my feet. Using his knife, he cut through all my undergarments, leaving me completely and utterly bare to him. Calloused fingers traced down my back, and I felt the heat of his breath on my neck.

"You are the most stunning woman I've ever seen, Cassarah."

Trusting he would be there, I pressed my back into his chest, letting my head fall back to look up at him. My giant of a man covered in the fierce markings of his clan, rippling with muscle, gave you the impression he would be a hard man. Instead, I knew he was quite the opposite— Dayson was a hopeless romantic with the world's biggest heart, and he gave it to me.

"Thank you for loving me," I said, looking deep into his rich brown eyes. "Any woman would be so lucky to have you as a partner in life, but you, for some reason, chose me."

Shifting in his arms, I turned to face him, letting my hands run down his broad chest before pulling his shirt out of his pants. He gave me a goofy grin, and his cheeks blushed ever so slightly at my words. That look vanished from his face the moment my hands found his skin, and I started to caress the lines of his hips that led down to his groin.

He growled his satisfaction and yanked his shirt up and off, tossing it behind him. Reaching out to me, he cupped my ass and lifted me so I wrapped my legs around his waist as he stalked to the bed. Twisting as we fell, he landed on his back with me on top, and I couldn't help but let out a small scream as the mattress bounced. I shouldn't have been worried. Dayson's grip on my hips was firm to the point I thought they might leave bruises.

"Look at you sitting there above me, perfect tits on display while you gaze down at me like you plan to eat me," Dayson purred as he massaged my ass. "Tell me, what does the queen ask of her consort?"

"What is her consort willing to offer?" I asked, letting my fingers ghost over the markings tattooed into his skin, over his pec muscle, onto his shoulder, and down his arm. For so long, I've wanted to know what they felt like under my touch, and now that I had the chance, I wasn't going to pass it up.

Dayson took my hand in both of his and placed them over his heart. "Everything, Cassarah. I'll give you all of me if you will have it to do with as you please. I know we already made our vows to you, but I do this not out of obligation for you as my queen but as a man who is madly in love with a woman."

Leaning down, I captured his lips with mine, taking the time to explore him. Our tongues battled playfully as we took this moment to share the feeling of our skin and bodies connecting. Slowly, I pulled away and started to crawl down his body until I got to his pants. Undoing the belt buckle, I made short work of the laces that kept his pants snug on his body. It took work to peel the leather off him, but I wasn't to be deterred. Finally, there he lay stripped for my viewing pleasure, and I took full enjoyment in noticing every detail.

His cock bobbed at the attention, begging me to take it in my hand, so that's exactly what I did. Using the bead of pre-cum, I swirled my hand around the head and stroked it up and down a few times, pulling a moan of pleasure out of Dayson's lips.

"Fuck, that feels so good. Do you know how long I've wanted your hands on me, Cassy-bear?" he asked as he pushed up on his arms to watch me work him. "If you keep making me feel this good, I'm going to be finished before you get any pleasure, and I want to see your face as I make you come with my cock buried deep inside you."

I shivered at his words, my nipples hardening into peaks, betraying how much I enjoyed that idea.

"Oh, you liked that, did you?" Dayson murmured, cocking a finger, signaling for me to come close. "Come here, My Queen, let me worship your body the way it was meant to be, and I will ensure my words become a reality."

Unable to hold myself back any longer, I shifted, but instead of letting him take control, I slid down on him until my ass slapped against his thighs.

"Oh God, I feel so full with you inside me, Day," I whimpered as my core burned from stretching wide enough to take him. He might not be as long as the others but he made up for it in girth.

Dayson's hands traced up my legs to my hips and then continued until his hands were full of my breasts. Arching my back, I thrust them forward for him to do with as he pleased. I took my time as I slowly lifted my hips and settled back down, adjusting to the stretch. Soon, my lubrication helped, allowing me to move faster. Swirling my hips, I smiled as I pulled sounds of pleasure from him.

"Use me, My Queen. Ride me so that I can give you all the pleasure possible," Dayson encouraged, urging me deep as he thrust up to meet me. "Fucking hell, this is so much better than I imagined it would be, and trust me when I say I thought of it often."

His words spurred me to move faster, leaning over so I could kiss him as I rode him. His arms wrapped around my back, crushing me to his chest as he decided to take charge, pounding into me to the point I could only hold on. Quickly, the world shifted, and I was now on my back with Dayson pushing my legs to my chest, giving him a better angle to ruin me in the best way possible.

A scream of delight escaped me as he pinched my clit, sending a shock through my body. My fingers curled into the bedding, needing to hold on to something as Dayson's powerful thrusts threatened to shoot me off the bed. His grip on my legs kept me from going anywhere as he owned my body, the look of pure lust written all over his face as beads of sweat traced down his chest.

His continued work on my clit sent me soaring into an orgasm that he milked for as long as he could, making me thrash under him. "Dayson!" I shouted as I could feel another climax building.

"That's right, scream my name so everyone knows I'm the luckiest bastard here tonight, having you wrapped tight around me. Let the others' dicks get hard and painful, resorting to rubbing themselves raw because you are mine tonight," Dayson said with a growl in his voice.

The mild-mannered man was gone, and the warrior was left in his place, waging a war of mind-blowing pleasure on his woman. The slap of skin, coupled with our moans, sounded like a battle, but one I would happily wage for the rest of my life. His pace began to falter, alerting me that he was getting close to finishing.

"Hold me tight as you come, Day," I begged, letting my legs wrap around his hips and my hands pull him down to me.

He buried his face in the crook of my neck so our bodies were pressed together so tightly I could feel his heartbeat pounding against my own. Now, his thrusts were slow and deep, pushing us to new heights only to crash, each crying out our release. Short, jerky thrusts followed as he tried to ensure that his every last drop was forced into me. Part of me feared that even though I was taking my tonic, it might not be enough with the determination of my men to see me with child.

I pushed that worry out of my mind, not allowing it to steal the contentment I felt after this beautiful moment with a man I loved. Brushing the hair off his sweat-slicked brow, I let my hands wander over his body, enjoying the feeling of him in my arms. Dayson nuzzled into me with a hum as if he were a cat purring from being petted.

"To think I could have been destined for a life where I was married off to a man to help my family gain status," I mused, my brain still cloudy from my releases. "Now that I know what it's like to share this experience with men I love with all my heart, I feel so sad for the women who don't get to find their own love."

Dayson shifted us slightly so we were both on our sides, looking into each other's eyes. "Cassy-bear, no one man would have ever been able to satisfy you. When the fates created you, they did so knowing a single person to love you would be a drop in the bucket of what you give to the world. Never have I met a person with a bigger, more compassionate way of loving people. To recharge what you give, they gave you eight men and two women who cherish you in the way you were meant to be." Pausing, he kissed my lips, nuzzling his nose against mine and making me giggle. "As for those other women, we can only hope they've found a way to love the man they are with in their own way."

"Maybe I can work on a way to change how people view their status," I mused as I tucked myself closer to Dayson. "That will be a dream to chase once the Lost King is dealt with. There are many things I would love to see the world around us change and grow into something better."

"Things like this are one of the many reasons I love you, Cassy-bear. Now, get some sleep. We have lots to do in the next few days before we leave for Creisal," Dayson instructed, running his fingers through my hair and lulling me to sleep.

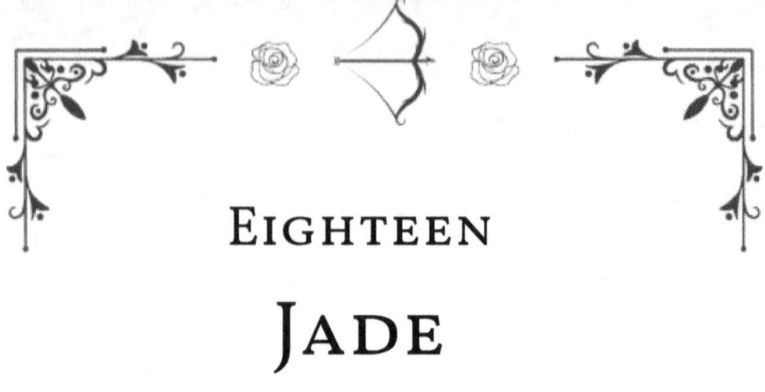

Eighteen

Jade

Everything was set for us to leave for Creisal. Cassarah had us all working tirelessly to ensure things would be settled here in Sheca for Ballard and Alsten to maintain. We had backup plans on backup plans in place for anything that might happen. Our world was at war, and Sheca was a major target since my little bird was the queen.

Since our conversation and the matter of spending one-on-one time with Cassarah was discussed, things have worked out naturally. We all had breakfast together, catching up about what was going to happen throughout the day. May and Becka were constant companions to Cassarah while she had us working on things in and out of the castle. Becka, already having been her personal maid growing up, now turned into her assistant. She ensured that Cassarah got to meetings on time, took time to eat, and checked in with us throughout the day, making sure we knew where she would be.

If there were ever a woman more suited to being queen than Cassarah, I couldn't picture it. She gave every matter her utmost attention, treating each person and their needs equally. The viceroys, now turned advisers, were having a challenging time retraining people to now address matters with the queen instead of them. Cassarah devised the brilliant plan that instead of doing her hearings in the throne room, she would conduct them in the village hall, where they'd been going.

"Guys, it gives me a chance to leave this place and be with the people," she pointed out. "Remember, I'm not the type of queen to view myself as above anybody. I want to be a queen who knows her people. Being in the village also ensures I know what is happening on a daily basis."

Cole and I both knew it was pointless to argue with her once she decided it wasn't worth the fight. While I stood behind the fact that it wasn't the wisest choice for her to make in our current situation, it was true to who she was. The Lost King might be breathing down our necks, moving his people into formation, and gearing up for an attack, but that didn't mean Cassarah would hide away.

Letting out a long, heavy sigh, I leaned against Tahir as I watched my little bird talking with her dragon. Those two had a relationship that would make anyone envious. While I knew in my heart Cassarah loved me as much as I loved her, despite the arguments about her safety, it was sometimes hard to let myself believe that anyone else could care enough about me to watch my back. My own brother tricked me into killing my parents and then hung me out to dry, hoping I would be put to death for their murder.

When Cassarah asked us if we considered each other family—brothers—I just couldn't bring myself to say what I felt. My first interaction with most of these men when I brought Cassarah to the mountain hideout was less than welcoming. Granted, I had been an incredibly closed off person, but something about how Cassarah fought for what was right had me wanting to help, even if the Norden king and queen were owed nothing from us. Of course, I didn't know she'd been raised as a noble, but she didn't risk it all out of alliance—it was the core belief of it being the right thing to do. My darkness craved the light she brought into my life, so I was willing to suffer the other men called to be her guardians.

We've butted heads many times, but even still, we formed a bond of men who all loved the same woman, willing to do whatever it took to keep her safe, even if it was from herself. While I did feel these men were friends, something I've almost never had in my life, the title *brother* or *family* was so tainted for me I didn't know how to get past it. I'd known Cassarah was worried about me, but I wasn't ready to come forward with my thoughts and fears just yet, and now we were getting ready to leave for Creisal, a kingdom we didn't know or trust. The Lost King has had his grip on it for years, so who knows what the queen might have secretly done.

If there was a time that all of us guardians needed to be on the same team, it was now. So, I asked the men to meet with me while Cassarah was dealing with a few last-minute things. While waiting for them to arrive, I paced the library in our quarters, trying to find the right words to articulate what I needed to say. I wasn't the world's best speaker, and my temper was quick to flare, but this needed to be addressed.

"What's up, man? You know we need to leave when Cassarah's done, right?" Cole asked as he entered with Abbott and Izel.

I waved them off, motioning for them to take a seat while the others filed in. There they all were, looking at me expectantly, with a hint of irritation on Cole and Paxton's faces. Stopping my pacing, I turned to them and widened my stance as if I were preparing myself for battle. They might know what happened with my parents, but that wasn't the only mission I'd been sent on over the years. It's just the one that was used to try and get rid of me.

"Look, we all have our pasts and secrets we don't want anyone to know about. I'm the Grim Reaper who killed his parents and was cast out of the clan to be an outlier. While I was left to fend for myself, I used my skills as an assassin to keep myself going. Some of those jobs were pretty high profile, and no one knows that they happened," I explained.

Paxton rolled his eyes. "Come on, Jade, just get to the point. I was a spy for another kingdom. Do you think my hands are clean of shady shit? Say what you need to say so we can all figure out what has you so moody."

While I wanted to punch Pax, he was right. I just needed to spit it out. "Fine, I was the one who killed the Crown Princess of Errit that the Lost King was married to. I didn't know who hired me. They used a third party to make the deal. It was money I couldn't pass up at that time. Now that I look back over the jobs I had, I think the Lost King used me more than once to get people out of his way. No one knew I used to be part of the clans. I kept that to myself, but a man who looks like me with the Birthright I have... word travels fast."

They all sat there in stony silence, staring at me with shocked expressions.

"So, what you're really saying is that the Lost King already knows who you are and what you can do?" Cole concluded. "Did you ever meet him in person? I know you've seen him since you and Cassarah attacked his camp."

"No," I answered, shaking my head. "Never have I met that man... it was always different people. That's why I didn't connect the dots until Cassarah. Now that we are looking at the big picture of all that was done to set up this whole war, I can point out where I helped him remove an obstacle."

Abbott leaned forward, resting his elbows on his knees as he looked up at me. "Why are you telling us this?"

"Cassarah wants us to be a family, and that idea scares the shit out of me. The only family I've ever known betrayed me, and I betrayed them. I killed my fucking parents because my brother set me up to do it. The thought of letting more people in my life who could do the same thing to me is terrifying. Yet, I know when we leave Sheca, that's it... this war has begun. As her guardians and consorts, we all need to be on the same side, trusting each other. I'm coming clean about this to you because I didn't want it to come out some other way, and you see it as me lying to you or holding back information." Sighing, I run my hands over my head and start pacing again. "Telling you this gives you the power to ruin me, but I have to trust Cassarah and the fates that brought us together. It's my proof that I'm in this, fully committed to this family we've created. I'm going to tell Cassarah, of course, but I felt that it would show you how sincere I am to have you hear it from me first."

Gavin stood and walked over to me, pulling me into a hug. Shock echoed through my body at the act, never having expected that kind of reaction. Stepping back, he held my shoulders and looked me in the eye. "Thank you for telling us, Jade. It's clear it was hard for you to do, and I want you to know I appreciate your trust in us."

"Ah... thanks," I answered awkwardly, slightly uncomfortable with the affection.

Gavin sat, looking at the others like they should be doing the same thing. In situations like this, it was clear the prince was raised much differently than we were. Abbott walked up to me, slapped me on the back, and left the room, clearly not feeling the need to dwell on the matter any longer.

"Anyone else have some deep, dark secret they want or need to share?" Zan asked as Ezzu looked around the room for him to see everyone. "No? Great, I suggest we all take this information as the offering it was intended to be and move on. None of you better say a damn thing to Cassarah either until Jade has spoken to her personally. As a family, it's the right thing to do." With that announcement, the others all nodded their agreement.

"It's nice to see what a real family is supposed to be like," I said under my breath as they all left the room, leaving Pax sitting there with his legs crossed, waiting for me to notice him. "What?" I snapped.

His brows shot up at my less-than-caring tone. "Seems that the warm, touching moment is over, and the prick is back, I see. Well, I was just going to say if you ever wanted to talk to someone who knows what it's like to have your family want to see you dead, I'm around. My twin thought he managed to kill me, and my father was an evil bastard who helped to create this monster we're now trying to kill. If you want to keep score, I might be winning."

I realized he was right. We had more in common than I ever would've guessed. Being a spy for another kingdom put him in the same situation as me, helping those who were against the mercenaries. I could imagine he also sees an area where he undermined what we are trying to do now, but at that point, no one knew anything about the Lost King.

"Thank you, Paxton," I said, bowing my head. "You're right. We have far more in common compared to the others."

Paxton made a face and stood up. "Ugg, don't go all soft on me... that's not your thing. Don't even think about trying to hug me. If you do, I'll punch you right in the dick."

"Thanks for clearing that up for me." I laughed and slapped his back as I passed him, heading to grab my bag and load Tahir up for the trip.

Creisal was a coastal kingdom that was flat, lush, and green, scattered with farmlands rich with crops. The flight over had been easy, yet boring as the landscape all blurred together. I missed the mountains and forests that gave Sheca personality. I was thankful that the air stayed warmer, knowing it was entering the winter months further mainland. If the battle were going to be waged closer to Norden, we would need to consider that.

As we flew over the castle perched on the cliffs of the Caleden Sea, I observed the rest of the city sprawling out before it. Red tiled roofs marked the city's wealthy section if the size of the homes were anything to go by. Further away from the castle, the homes became less opulent and simpler until they reached the wall.

Dividing the royal city from the rest of the countryside was a massive stone wall I imagined took years to build and gave protection against attack. It also ensured that those not worthy enough to be in the city limits stayed out. Like so many others, this city loved to make a clear distinction between the haves and the have-nots. I hoped they treated all their people with the same respect if they were in need.

Knowing my little bird the way that I did, she would have no problem encouraging them to change their ways. Many times, she's talked about the future once this war is over and how she hopes her fellow allies will join with her to rebuild our great land. Tonight, I planned on talking to her about what I told the others so we could openly discuss what areas I was involved in. Paxton had already planned to locate his notebooks full of information and gather a few spies he trusted to talk with us. The more we knew about the underbelly of this kingdom, the easier it would be to spot what the Lost King was using the queen for.

She still hasn't completely recovered. There were many moments when she would forget words or events that happened while she was under the influence of the Lost King. It reminded me of elders I've seen when their minds start to fade, and they lose a bit of who they once were. King Thomas hoped that being home in her normal surroundings might settle and help her to remember things.

Since this kingdom wasn't equipped to deal with as many dragons as we had, the landing took a little finagling, but we managed it in stages. I'm sure the city's people were all gawking up at the sky, watching us as we circled above, waiting for our turn to land. Tahir let out a roar, spitting fire and showing off as he saw little kids running down the street pointing at him. The children all clapped and jumped around excitedly at the performance.

Tahir landed in the courtyard, quickly tucking his wings to his side so he didn't crash into Dayson and Hegg next to us. Grabbing my bag, I tossed it over my shoulder and sent my dragon off to play, exploring the new city. Cassarah instructed all our dragons to keep an eye out for anything suspicious. Creisal was a large kingdom, and we needed a clear handle on what was happening within it.

"Trying to create your own fan club?" Dayson teased, shoving me with his shoulder. "I saw Tahir strutting his stuff."

"Believe it or not, that dragon has a penchant for the dramatics. He loves the attention as much as I hate it, but he's spent most of his life keeping us hidden. I don't see the harm in him goofing off now," I answered with a grin.

Dayson and I joined Cassarah where she was standing with Prince Phillip and Gavin, who'd flown together.

"Did you get a chance to say goodbye to your mother?" I heard Cassarah ask.

Phillip shook his head, sadness written all over his face. "She refused to talk to us. Instead, she just screamed about how we were turning her whole family against her, even her sister."

Cassarah placed a hand on his arm, giving it a simple squeeze. "I understand what it feels like to be rejected by the family we love. My parents decided it was more important to them to keep their title and riches than to save their lives. All we can do is accept their choices and know we did all we could."

My anger when I found out that her mother all but spit in the messenger's face at the offer roared in my veins once again. When she first told us, I had to leave the room before I said something I shouldn't. They were still her parents, no matter how badly I wanted to beat some sense into them.

"Excuse me, Queen Cassarah?" an elderly gentleman approached. "I'm Jenkan, the palace steward. Would you allow me to escort you to your chambers?"

Cassarah looked over at us since Gavin, Dayson, and I were the only guardians with her. "Let's have Gavin stay here while Day and I come with you," I offered. "Then, once the others have landed, they can join us, but I don't want you going anywhere without two of us."

Jenkan seemed to take offense at this as he spluttered his indignation. "The queen is an honored guest here and an ally. What danger does she have from us?"

"That..." I said, poking the old man in the chest, "... is for me to worry about. Now, please lead the way so Her Majesty can settle in a little before dinner."

Jenkan scowled as he brushed off his shirt like I'd left something behind with my touch. When he turned to Cassarah, he bowed and gestured for her to follow him. "Right this way. We've made sure to keep all the rooms close since you have so many in your party. There is a room for a lady's maid in your chamber so that she might attend to you more conveniently."

Dayson snorted and glanced at me out of the corner of his eye. "Oh, Becka's gonna love that. Now she can't hide from what might go on at night."

We both grinned and chuckled, but that stopped with the scolding look we got from Cassarah. It seems we would need to tone things down while we were guests in this prudish castle. I guess we couldn't have that wild orgy wanted to suggest now that we'd all been with our queen. It was clear to us that our woman had a veracious side to her that none of us saw coming, but damn, it would be fun to explore.

NINETEEN

CASSARAH

As the palace steward warned, the rooms were close to each other, but none were interconnected or as close as my men would like them to be. Instead, they decided to double bunk to cut down on the rooms needed and keep us all more tightly grouped. Becka and May would switch out who would sleep in the maid's room along with one or two of my men in my bed.

While the castle was in a tizzy about the changes and the clear demonstration of how little we trusted being in our ally's kingdom, they didn't know the whole story. King Thomas agreed it was smart for us to be overly cautious since he couldn't be sure who was with him or who was working for the Lost King. Part of what I hoped to do was root out those moles as I discovered what the Lost King hid in Creisal.

"Mouse," Cole murmured as he wrapped his arms around me, kissing my cheek. "Will you try and rest a little before the feast? You've been up since the crack of dawn working on things. I don't want you to push yourself too hard."

I leaned into his hold, resting my head on his shoulder and letting the warmth of his body slowly recharge me as we stood looking out at the stunning coastline. "I don't think I know how to do anything halfway. When I study, I get lost in the words, memorizing everything I can so that when the time comes and I need to remember it, I will. Look at me, I couldn't even just love one man, so I decided on eight." I giggled, turning so I could wrap my arms around him as I looked into his face. "Being here is so important that I can't seem to turn my brain off long enough to relax."

He gave me a wicked grin as he nuzzled my nose. "Want me to give you something else to think about? I'm sure I could find a way to distract you."

Pushing up on my tiptoes, I sealed my lips to his, letting him draw me into the moment instead of focusing on the future. Lifting one of my hands, I gripped the back of his neck, pulling him down to me as he slipped his tongue between my lips, deepening the kiss. Desire rose in me, causing my breasts to ache and my core to tingle with expectation.

Cole pulled back with a growl, grabbing me by the waist and tossing me over his shoulder. He marched to the bed and tossed me down, letting me plop into the softness of the mattress. There was movement above me, and Izel's face appeared with a knowing smirk.

"Well, hello there, my little warrior. Did Cole finally convince you to take a break from trying to save the world alone?" Izel asked before softly kissing my forehead, nose, and lips. "Now the question is, do we play, or should we behave and let you get some rest?"

The part of me that always leans toward being responsible wants to be good, not knowing what might come in the future, and to rest. Meanwhile, the new urges my consorts had brought out in me had been ignited by Cole's passion, begging for them to free my mind from the seriousness of our situation. Searching Izel's eyes, I saw my answer reflected in them and decided to let my body rule in this moment.

Arching up, I nipped at his lips playfully as they hovered above me. "Who says we can't play then get some rest?"

Izel's face filled with heat and love as his smile grew wider at my words. "Such a brilliant mind you have, My Queen." Wasting no time, Izel slid his hands into my corset to cup my breasts, his fingers finding my nipples far too easily. "Do you feel that, Cassarah? They are begging to be touched, little peaks reaching out for attention. Have we left you needy these past few days?"

While I'd shared the bed with my men the past few nights, things had been so busy I'd been far too exhausted to do much else but sleep. The moment my head hit the pillow, I was out, then all too soon, I was being woken by Becka to start it all over again.

Cole pulled off my boots and started to work on my pants. Knowing we would be flying for a long time today, there was no way I'd wear a dress—it was far too impractical. Lifting my hips, I helped him slip them past my hips then left him to do the rest as Izel managed to free my breasts and wrapped his lips around one of the peaks. I moaned as pleasure flooded my body. Reaching out, I gripped Izel's thighs behind my head.

Opening my eyes, I found that Izel was now crouched over my body, placing his pelvis to hover over my head. Eagerly, I started to undo the ties of his pants, yanking them until his cock was released, hard and ready. Taking it in my hand, I stroked it from tip to root, letting the silky feel glide through my fingers. Pulling it down, I managed to wrap my lips around the crown, licking and sucking as I stroked the rest of him.

"Fuck, little warrior, that feels so good," Izel grunted as he thrust down into my mouth in time with my strokes.

"Stop teasing me with it and give me what I want," I demanded, tugging with my free hand on his hip. "I want you to fuck my mouth as Cole takes my cunt."

"Such dirty words from a queen. What would people think if they heard you," Cole taunted as he stroked his fingers through my wetness. "Look at how her body is begging for us, Izel. She's wet enough that I don't even have to prepare her if I didn't want to, but the chance of tasting her is just too hard to pass up."

"Then feast as you want, brother. I'll keep her busy until you're ready to take her," Izel said, pulling away from me.

"No!" I cried, trying to hold on to him tighter.

Izel removed my hand then leaned down to plunder my mouth with his the moment Cole's tongue started to lap at my core. Thrashing under their hold, my body burned with need at their teasing. Izel pulled my arms up over my head and placed his legs on them to hold me down. Cole wasn't as lucky when my legs clamped around his head, locking him in place right where I wanted him. It didn't seem to deter him as he continued his efforts to drive me wild. When he'd had enough, though, he bit down on my clit, making me gasp. Instead of drawing him closer, I used my heel to shove him back.

"Holy hell, woman, were you trying to suffocate me?" Cole asked, gasping for air as he wiped his mouth with the back of his hand. "I'm all for taking things a little rough, but a man's got to breathe."

"Is our queen too much for you to handle? I'd gladly switch places with you if you need a break," Izel taunted, freeing my arms as he moved to my side.

Cole glared at him and flipped me onto my stomach in a rough, forceful movement. "I think this might help matters... besides, I had something new in mind." As he spoke, he lifted my hips so my ass was up in the air, allowing him to trace a finger between the valley of my cheeks. "If we are going to start having group activities, I think it's time we introduce another place for us to use. The last time I got to play with this spot, she almost blacked out."

"You make a good point. I'm sure you're not the only one who's been looking to expand Cassarah's horizons," Izel commented as he slid off the bed and stripped out of his clothes. When he returned, he laid down, pulled me over his legs so I was draped over them with my face positioned right in front of his cock. "This should be comfortable for you while Cole plays with your ass, but let me know if we need to change it."

Licking up his cock, I flicked the crown, grinning. "I was wondering when you'd remember that I was still a part of this. Seems like the two of you were more than happy to plan things out yourselves."

Cole lowered himself over my back and kissed up my neck to my jaw. "You're right. It's your body, and though we get to worship it, you forever and always have the final say in how things go. The moment you say stop or no is the second we do exactly that. I'm sorry we made you feel like we weren't including you in this choice."

A quick kiss to Cole's lips to soothe him, I answered, "Thank you for acknowledging that, but I'm not the same woman I once was to be pushed around. I will make it extremely clear when I'm not up for something, but I do like to be included in the conversation. As for what you proposed, I'm more than happy to explore your suggestion."

"Let me find something real quick, and I'll be right back," Cole shared, kissing my cheek and rolling off the bed.

Leaning to the side, I slipped off Izel's legs to lay beside them and stroked his thighs' broad muscles, watching his body react to my touch. "You don't mind sharing me like this? The both of you at the same time?"

Izel reached out and stroked a hand through my hair. "Little warrior, to see you in the throes of bliss, no matter who is doing it, is something I never want to miss seeing. Do I want to share you all the time... no, but some things can only be accomplished with a third or even a fourth. Too long have you been denied knowing the pleasure your body can give you when surrendered to those who love you."

"Got it!" Cole called, coming back from the bathing chamber, holding up a clay bottle of oils. "We need a little assistance for this since we don't have the benefit of your natural glide." My face scrunched up in confusion, to which he just smirked and slapped my ass playfully. "Trust me, this is all for your benefit. You'll understand soon enough."

"Have you done this before?" I asked, getting the feeling he learned these things through experience.

Cole paused, cocked his head slightly, and held my gaze. "Do you really want the answer to that?"

"No... no, I don't think I do," I responded, knowing it wouldn't help matters to think of them with other women.

"Do you trust that no matter if we've been with someone else, we are wholly yours now?" Cole asked, coming to kneel on the bed in front of me next to Izel.

"Yes, I believe all of you love me, and I trust you not to stray from my bed," I answered, knowing the ring of truth in my words. "Just so we're clear *if* I ever learn you've been unfaithful, I will chop off your cock myself." Both men looked a little stricken at the idea of me taking their manhood away. "Now, show me what the bottle of oil is for."

Cole shook his head as if to clear out the images of him losing his member and crawled to put himself behind me, settling me back over Izel's legs. This time, I didn't bother to worry about what Cole was going to do and took hold of the cock in front of me that seemed to be drooping a little. As I took it in my mouth, I tried to keep my eyes trained on Izel's as he groaned in pleasure. One of his hands slipped into my hair and fisted it near the root as he tried to control my speed.

Just when I started to get curious about what Cole was up to, I felt the oil being poured on my ass. He swirled it lightly around my back entrance with two fingers, pressing at it but not enough to penetrate. I wiggled back against him, letting him know I was enjoying what was happening since my mouth was otherwise engaged.

"Are you ready to experience something new, mouse?" Cole asked, pressing harder with one finger until it slid in as I pushed back. "So eager. Who would have known there was a woman desperate to be devoured by her men under that queenly exterior?"

His finger glided in deeper, then he pulled it out to add more oil, pressing it back in as he worked his finger, stroking nerves I didn't know I had. My attention was so drawn to what Cole was doing that I stalled my efforts with Izel. Not to be bothered by such things, he took control, clasping my head in both his hands and fucked my mouth. His hips undulated as he tipped my head to the right angle where my teeth wouldn't scrape him as he worked in and out of my mouth. I hummed, oddly delighted he found such pleasure in using me like this. Becka and May told me there was a power in being used by the right person when you trusted them, and they were absolutely right.

Behind me, Cole decided that one finger was no longer enough, and he slipped in two. The stretch was a little uncomfortable, and I shied away from it at first. "Relax, mouse. The more you tense up, the harder it will be. Let your body open for me, and trust I won't take this further than you can handle."

Hearing him guide me through this helped, and I relaxed, giving my body to both my men to use. Immediately, Cole got both fingers in and worked them slowly in and out as his other hand slipped down to my clit. Swirling his finger around my little bud and the new pressure from my ass pushed me over the edge into climaxing. Letting out a scream just as Izel thrust up caused him to end up deep in my throat, making my eyes water.

"Fuck," Izel swore as he pulled out. "I'm so sorry, Cassarah. I didn't mean to give you more than you could handle."

Coughing a few times, I looked up at him through my blurry vision. "It's all right. I was completely caught off guard by that climax. It was so sudden and strong."

"Do you want to keep going?" Cole asked, his voice hesitant.

I looked at him over my shoulder and smirked. "Hell yes, I want to continue. If coming that hard was just from fingers in my ass, what will it be like once your cock is in me?"

"You dirty, dirty little mouse." Cole chuckled, shaking his head. "As my queen commands, I shall do."

"While that happens, I think it's best if we take a break," Izel suggested, sliding me up higher so he could reach my breasts. "I'll help to distract you, little warrior, then we can see if you're up for one more kind of experience."

Now that I was straddling Izel's hips, Cole kneeled between our legs and nudged me with the head of his cock. "Relax and take deep breaths. Once your body stops fighting me, I'll start moving."

Izel cupped my face and peppered it with kisses as Cole started to press in. Izel's hands drifted down to my breasts, where he started to play with my nipples as he caught my lower lip between his teeth, sucking it into his mouth. My brain was so overloaded with sensations it didn't know what to focus on first. Cole sank deeper into me with small, short thrusts, adding more oil each time. The feeling of being overly full was new and different but not unpleasant in the slightest.

The moment Cole fully seated himself in my ass, I arched into him and cried out at the crackling energy it sent through my body. Panting, I leaned my head on Izel's chest as Cole slowly pulled back about halfway then worked himself in again. Each time he did this, it was smoother and easier. The pressure building up in me was to the point I wanted to cry. I needed a release, but I didn't know how to ask for it. "Please, let me come," I begged.

Izel looked up at Cole, and whatever he saw in answer had him lifting me slightly. Then I felt his cock nudging at my core, making me gasp in understanding. "There's no way both of you can fit inside me!"

"Cassarah," Izel said, his tone commanding. "Do you trust us?"

Licking my lips, I nodded, my throat too dry to answer. "We will take care of you, little mouse. This is what you need, and we want to give you the release you're craving."

"Okay," I whispered as Cole pushed down on my hips, impaling me on Izel's shaft.

If I thought I was full before, I'd be lying to myself. With the addition of Izel's cock, I felt like I was going to burst or rip from having so much stuffed into me at once. The climax had faded with my panic but came roaring back the second they both started to move. My hands clawed into Izel's chest, and my eyes rolled back as I screamed. They didn't stop. Instead, they fucked me through my orgasm, filling the room with grunts as they struggled to hold back from release.

I saw movement out of the corner of my eye, and Jade was watching. He leaned against the wall, his eyes full of heat as he undid his pants and pulled out his cock. Holding my gaze, he matched his movements to those of the men plundering my holes, unashamed in his actions. The knowledge that he was watching seemed to kick the whole situation up another level, and I came again, clamping down on both of them so tight they swore. There was no fighting against me that time as I milked them for all they were worth. Jade's hand worked faster, and spurts of cum shot out as his eyes rolled back in his head, letting it fall against the wall as his body shivered with each final stroke.

Utterly spent, I crashed against Izel's chest, my whole body twitching with aftershocks, making me moan as I was still filled with cock. Cole groaned as he pulled out of me and fell on his back, his labored breathing telling me he felt the same way I did. Izel ran his hands up and down my back, making me convulse as little orgasms rocketed through my body. Hugging me tightly, he shifted to his side, tucking me in close.

"Sleep now, my little warrior. We will wake you when it's time for the feast," Izel murmured, kissing my forehead.

The feeling of a blanket being draped over me was the last thing I remembered before letting sleep take me.

TWENTY

CASSARAH

"Cassarah, I let you sleep as long as I could, but now we need to get you up and dressed. A bath might be in order too, since your men just left you after they had their way with you," Becka rambled as she yanked the blanket off me and started to shove me off the bed.

Smacking her away, I climbed out of the bed and glared at her. "Don't I deserve a little respect here instead of getting harassed by you the second I wake up?"

Becka then proceeded to give me a flourishing curtsy and bowed her head. "Your Majesty, your humble servant requests that she be allowed to encourage you to take a bath and wash off all the essence from your lovers as they ravaged your body before putting you to bed. Unless she would like the whole court to know, then, by all means, I'll start dressing you."

"Ugg, this is the problem with having your best friend as one of your guardians," I groaned as I headed into the bathing chamber. "Speaking of my lovers, where did everyone go?"

"I banished them from your room for the time being. You need to get ready, and I couldn't risk them distracting you while you didn't have any clothes on," she replied and followed me.

Sliding into the tub filled with steaming water, I took the rag and started to scrub my body. Muscles I'd never used before ached in a way that reminded me of what happened earlier. Images of them both taking me at the same time with Jade watching made my body start to heat up. Then Becka dumped a bucket of cold water over my head and started to wash my hair.

"Becka!" I shrieked in shock.

"Oops, I'm so sorry. You looked like you were getting a little hot and needed to be cooled down," she teased. "Goodness gracious, woman, you're like a bitch in heat, calling all the boys to her neediness. Do you think you can manage through the dinner without sneaking off with one of your men?"

Glaring at her, I snatched away the bar of soap. "When have I ever not conducted myself in a way that was inappropriate in front of others?"

Becka tapped her chin, thinking for a moment. "Okay, fine. You make a good point, but I'm just telling you there is something in the air with you and those men of yours. Repressing your urges for so long seems to be creating a veracious sex monster out of you. This isn't our kingdom, and we have no idea who we can trust besides ourselves. I worry."

"I appreciate that you worry. It shows how much you love me. What I need now isn't to be scolded but to have those I trust at my back, believing I'll do the right thing. I haven't been living up to my role recently, but I've got my head on right, so please just trust me," I implored, reaching out to take her hand and squeezing it. "Besides, I think you're just jealous and need to find a man or two to play with."

She snorted, pulling her hand free and slapping me on the shoulder. "Right, with what spare time? I'm always making sure you stay on track and out of trouble."

Rolling my eyes, I got down to business cleaning myself while Becka finished washing my hair. Then, it was on to scented oils and hair, followed by getting dressed. Being that this was one of my first events as the queen of Sheca, I was dressed in the royal colors of black and gold. It was stark against my pale skin but set off my honey-brown hair and amber eyes, making it so I stood out against the boldness. The last and final thing was to have my crown placed on my head, ensuring that no one would mistake me for being anything but royalty.

"I swear, the worst part of being queen is going through all this. When I was just in training, I could wear whatever I liked, and it was far less complicated," I grumbled, heading into the main space of my bedroom.

"Have to say I agree with you. Your ass in leather pants is something I'm beginning to miss," Pax shared from where he was lounging on my bed that someone had come in and made.

"You have to admit that seeing her breasts in those corsets might be an even exchange," Gavin countered from the armchair near the fire.

All my men were scattered about waiting for me to be ready. "I'm glad no matter what I wear, you all seem to find something to enjoy about it," I said with a chuckle. "Now, I believe it's high time we made an appearance at this banquet that is in our honor."

Slowly, they all gathered, and I noticed they weren't wearing their guardian uniforms, instead wearing all black with the exception of a gold sash. On the sash was the mark they all bore, claiming them as my consorts, except Gavin's had the addition of a crown. I assumed it was to mark him as the next in line or crown prince, if you will.

"Those are new..." I commented, unsure how I felt about them not being seen as my guardians first.

May came to stand next to me, crossed her arms, and looked them over. "Apparently, it's customary to ensure that all consorts are declared plainly so that no advance might be made on them. People here in this kingdom don't seem to follow the same rules of being committed to one lover. While many have closed marriages, there are many who have open ones that will allow either partner to seek attention outside of the marriage."

Hearing this, my head snapped to look at her. "How common is it for someone to have an open relationship?"

"More common than a closed one," she answered, looking none too pleased. "Queen Catharine called you a whore for having so many committed partners, but here you can just fuck who you like as long as you always return to your husband. Talk about double standards, the bitch."

While I agreed with her, it made me wonder about so many things. It would be so easy for people to use one another to get information. Learning this just made our job that much harder to track down what the Lost King might have hidden in Creisal. What if, in the haze of passion, someone asked about secrets that were better left hidden?

"The queen wasn't herself. I'd like to give her the benefit of the doubt that the Lost King had her acting that way to ensure we didn't get an alliance with them," I pointed out. "As for the other implications, this will be tricky unless they were silenced by magic not to say anything."

"Or they are a spy," Pax cut in. "We know better than to let our lips flap to a pretty piece of ass when it could fuck us over in the long run. I don't think you need to be as worried about this as you are. It's good to keep it in mind, but I believe we'll still find what we're looking for.

"Any other shocking things I need to be aware of before we head to this banquet?" I inquired, looking at the others. Everyone shook their heads, setting me at ease. "All right then, let's go enjoy the feast."

Turning, I went to head out into the hall but paused and glanced at my men over my shoulder. "I assume I don't need to say that this is a closed relationship, and none of us are free to find partners elsewhere."

"No, you have nothing to worry about, Cassy-bear. By putting on these sashes, we are declaring ourselves claimed and off-limits. If someone else tries to make advances on us knowing it isn't welcome, we are allowed to retaliate how we see fit," Dayson explained. "Seeing as we are armed and also your guardians, I think we are safe to assume they will leave us alone."

"Spitfire," Pax said, stepping up to me. "I was a member of this court for years, and there are those who will be unhappy I'm claimed and unavailable to them. Being a spy is something I took seriously, and I would use whatever means necessary to get the information from in and out of our kingdom. I'm saying this to be honest and up front in case something was said to you by those who enjoyed my company."

I cupped Pax's cheek and pressed a kiss to his lips. "Thank you for telling me. I know sharing about your past involvement with other men or women isn't something anyone likes to share with their partner. I love you, Pax. I know I don't say it enough, but I absolutely do."

Pax returned my kiss with more fervor but stopped before it got us hot and bothered. "I love you too, Cassarah. I'm proud to declare that I'm claimed by you and no one else can touch me, so don't let those snakes ever let you doubt my love."

Nodding, I took his hand, intertwined our fingers, and headed out into the hall. An attendant was there to lead us to the room where the feast was being held. We met up with Phillip and his entourage along the way, allowing us to enter together.

"Entering, the Dragon Queen Cassarah of the kingdom of Sheca and her eight consorts. Accompanying her is Crown Prince Phillip of Norden, the nephew to Queen Catharine and King Thomas," a herald called out as we made our way to the head table.

The head table was up on a higher level so we could observe the rest of the feast below us as we ate. I was seated on the left side of the kin, and Prince Phillip was placed next to the queen. My men took their places down the line from me, with Gavin taking his place to my left as my heir. While I'd studied situations like this, it was as a noble lady of the court, not the queen. Instead of having to wait to eat, we were served first, but a taster was presented before me to sample all the items on my plate before handing it over to me once he didn't die.

"Did you find your rooms to your liking?" Queen Catharine asked with a kind smile on her face. "It's been so long since we had guests."

"Yes, Your Highness, the rooms are beautiful, and it's lovely to see right out to the sea," I said, returning her smile.

This was the closest to normal I'd seen her since I freed her from the Lost King. She chatted with Phillip about nonsense things, but I also noticed they were all subjects that were at least three years old.

"The king tells me that you took the role of Crown Prince so that your brother could marry Queen Cassarah. That is a kind thing for you to do. It must be hard to take such a position at such a young age," Queen Catharine tutted, patting Phillip's leg. "I'm sure your father must be proud. Speaking of your parents, why didn't they come with you?"

Phillip glanced at the king then me as if unsure how to best answer her.

"Your Highness, Father passed away suddenly, and Mother is not handling it well, so she has secluded herself in mourning," Gavin cut in.

Queen Catharine covered her mouth in horror. "How am I just hearing about this now? I need to go to my sister. She must be devastated."

"We thank you for your concern, Aunt Catharine, but mother doesn't want to see anyone, not even us. We tried to speak to her before leaving for Creisal, but she denied us," Phillip said in a low voice, not wanting to be overheard. "Do you remember coming to Sheca at all?"

"Sheca? Why no, I haven't left the kingdom for I don't know how long. Although, I'm supposed to be going to Utros to see a friend of mine soon. Her nephew is going to be married to the princess of Errit. Isn't that exciting!" Queen Catharine shared excitedly.

My gaze shifted to King Thomas, who was already looking in my direction, sadness filling his eyes. He shook his head as if to tell me she didn't remember anything of the past three years. While it was wonderful to see the true personality of the queen and to know she wouldn't remember all that she'd done, it meant we were on our own to uncover everything that happened.

The feast was delicious, and everything I ate was amazing. Seafood was new to me, and I enjoyed trying all the different kinds of fish and sea life that had been made in various ways. When it was time for dessert, I wasn't sure I could even manage to take another bite. As bowls of fresh fruit with cream and honey were set before us, I noticed that something changed in the room. People rose from their seats and started to wander, talking with others at different tables.

Some women would sit in the laps of other men as if there wasn't another woman present. Men pulled ladies to their feet and scurried off to the dance floor where a string quartet was playing. This must be what they'd been talking about with people being able to pick partners as they pleased. The room became much more lively and boisterous as wine flowed more freely and pitchers were left on the table to be consumed.

To my utter shock, a handsome younger man climbed the steps to our table and approached the queen. "Your Majesty, I'm happy to see you've returned from your travels. To be without you this past week has been an ache in my soul."

The queen looked at him and blinked a few times before turning to King Thomas. "Darling, who is this man, and how dare he speak to me so informally. We don't have an open arrangement... or have you decided you no longer desire me? Is that what this is? If I'm the one to ask to end our exclusivity, then you get to finally go after something better?"

Before the king could answer, the man spoke. "My love, what are you talking about? We have been seeing each other for almost three years. You approached me, saying your husband was boring you."

"Sir Roulf," King Thomas barked. "I do not care what sort of relationship you have or had with my wife, but you will respect her and me as your rulers. If the queen no longer wishes to share your company, that is her right, and it is your duty to oblige her wishes. Now leave. This is not the time or place to deal with this matter."

Sir Roulf looked as if he was about to burst, the way the vein on his forehead pulsed. Gritting his teeth, he gave a stilted bow and descended the stairs. Most of the room had watched the interaction, and even if they couldn't hear what was being said, the rebuff was clear. I had no doubt gossip would spread like wildfire by the night's end.

I turned to ask Pax a question but found a woman dressed all in blood red, running her hand through his hair, whispering in his ear. Fury like none I've ever experienced before roared through my body. My Birthright started to glow around me as I stood calmly and walked over to the scene.

"Get. Your. Hands. Off. Him," I snarled.

The woman looked up at me with crystal blue eyes and pouty lips painted the same color as her dress. When she registered who had spoken to her, her mouth popped open in surprise. When she still didn't move, I lashed out with my magic, letting it wrap around her throat before it yanked her away, slamming her into the wall. I stalked toward her, closing the distance, my rage burning as hot as dragon fire. I was surprised it didn't slit my skin.

"You dare touch one of my consorts?" I demanded, my voice booming with magic and anger.

The woman clawed at my magic, trying to get it to release its hold on her. I noticed she was trying to answer, but her throat was too constricted, so I let up on my hold just enough to let her speak.

"I didn't know," she croaked.

Reaching out, I slapped her across the face, the sound echoing through the now-silent room. "Do not play me for a fool. He wears a sash that claims him as *mine*. By your own laws, if you disregard that claim, I'm allowed to respond how I see fit. That means no one can save you from me, and I get to make it crystal clear that I am not to be pushed on this."

"He was mine before he was yours," she shot back. "Even if he is claimed, I have the chance to come to an agreement with you."

"Do I look like I'm willing to even consider such a thing?" I pressed, letting my magic press down on her.

"Spitfire," Pax murmured as he came to stand behind me, wrapping his arms around my waist. "You need to let her go."

"Give me one good reason why," I demanded, not taking my eyes off my prey.

Pax kissed along my neck, trying to distract me as he nibbled on my ear, whispering, "She is the spymaster's daughter. If you spare her life, which you have every right to take for what she's done, it will put you in a position where they owe you."

While my anger wanted retribution, I'd calmed enough to know he was right. Forcefully, I pulled my magic back, dropping her in a heap on the floor, where I kneeled in front of her. "This is the only warning you will get. Next time, I will end your life without a second thought. Paxton is my consort and mine alone. You will not approach him again."

The woman looked at me then back at Pax, her face draining of any color that wasn't painted on, and nodded. Standing, I shook out my skirt and walked up to Pax, wrapped my arm around his waist, and cupped his face with my other hand. "Thank you for stopping me. She isn't worth the blood on my hands."

"You are the only woman I'm worried about, spitfire," he murmured, brushing the back of his fingers along my cheek before leaning and showing everyone in this room how he felt about me.

When he released me, I had to gasp for the air he'd stolen from me, making me grin. "You certainly know how to play a crowd, that's for sure."

"Or I really wanted a reason to kiss you and stake my claim on you," he teased with a quick peck on my nose. "Can I steal you for a dance before I have to share you with the masses?"

"I would be delighted," I answered, looping my arm through his so he could escort me down the steps to the dance floor.

Twenty-One

Cassarah

Before I got much further, something had me looking back at the head table. It was then I noticed all my men standing, putting their weapons away as they ensured the spymaster's daughter retreated. It seems I had a little help in making our position clear that they were off-limits to anyone but me.

"Percilla has been trying to tie me to her for a long time, even going so far as to use her father to pressure the union. What she didn't realize was I had so much dirt on her father, there was no way he could ever force me to do something I didn't want to do. His daughter was the source of most of that blackmail and loved to share secrets during pillow talk," Paxton explained as we whirled around the dance floor. "I'm not a perfect man, and I've used every dirty trick in the book to get what I needed from people to survive. I had no reason to be good, honest, or loyal to anyone. Then my entire world turned on its head the moment your mark appeared on my arm."

When I'd first met Paxton, I didn't think there was a chance in hell we would end up where we are today. Even though he was brash with his thoughts, always poking at me, forcing us to talk about the things we'd prefer to leave alone, I could no longer imagine my life without him.

By the time Pax and I had finished our dance, the room settled back into the normal swing of things, aside from everyone giving me a wide berth. I couldn't blame them. I'd made quite the scene and knew it would establish the clear understanding that I was not to be trifled with.

"Your Majesty," Sir Roulf addressed with a bow. "Might I have the next dance?"

I looked the man up and down, trying to discern if he was being sincere or not. "You wish to dance with me?"

"Yes, only a dance. I have no intention of even thinking about asking for more than that. You've made it quite clear that you and your harem are a closed unit," he answered, keeping his eyes lowered.

While I'd planned to speak to this man, I hadn't intended to do so publicly. "You may have one dance. Use it wisely."

Pax gave me a confused look, but when I smiled in reassurance, kissing his cheek, he stepped aside. "I will meet you back at the table, My Queen."

"You have a very loving and loyal group of men, Your Majesty," Sir Roulf commented as he took my hand, leading me onto the dance floor.

I let him spin me into place as the music started up the next dance. We went a few minutes without either of us saying anything, but I'd finally had enough.

"Sir, it's incredibly clear to me that you didn't ask me to dance with you out of the goodness of your heart. It would be wise to say what you need to say, or I'll leave you standing here alone," I warned, holding his gaze so he knew I was serious.

He swung me away from him then I twirled, returning to him, my back against his chest for a few steps. "You're right. I didn't come to dance with you but to warn you. I know you're the one who freed the queen's mind. The Lost King knew it was possible with how light his hold on her was, but the failsafe of her losing her memory was also there to prevent someone like you learning our secrets."

The dance had me slipping under his arm in a complex move that had me facing him again. He gripped my waist and pulled me tight, even though I tried to keep as much space between us as I could.

"Just accept that the Lost King has already won... he holds Creisal in his hands. Many of his men have infiltrated the castle and the kingdom, so you'll never be able to tell who you can trust. I applaud your guardians being so overly cautious, but will they be able to protect you against everyone?" Sir Roulf whispered in my ear. "The Lost King is willing to meet with you and receive your surrender, putting an end to this whole affair. There's no need for any more life to be lost. All you have to do is admit he's outsmarted you, and he might see fit to let you and your men live."

When we reached the point where the dance brought us to the edge of the dance floor, I stomped on his foot as hard as I could. He stumbled, almost falling on his ass, but I caught him and pulled him in close by the front of his shirt. "You tell the Lost King he hasn't seen anything yet. I'm just getting started, and I will find what he's hiding. It's the whole purpose of my visit here. He better get here quickly if he wants a fight he won't lose because as soon as I discover what he's so desperately trying to hide, he's finished."

Done with the wretched man before me, I cast him aside roughly so he crashed into another couple, drawing the attention away from me. May appeared at my side, lightly grabbing my elbow as she escorted me away from the scene.

"Do I need to kill him?" May asked in a low voice. "From what I've gathered from the palace staff, he isn't well-liked. The only thing that's kept him out of trouble is the queen, but now that she's publicly cut him off, he's going to see just how much people haven't liked tolerating his attitude."

"He's connected to the Lost King," I shared as we climbed the steps to the head table.

May's face twitched as she tried to keep her expression neutral. "Seems Henry wasn't convinced his mind control would be enough, so he placed backup to ensure she did what he wanted."

I took my seat at the table and smiled over at King Thomas as I spoke, "It would be wise for you to place a trusted guard with your wife at all times. After a lovely conversation with Sir Roulf, it would seem that the Lost King has more men here than we were led to believe. Even if he were lying, it would be foolish to think it couldn't be possible."

"That is wise advice, Your Majesty. I will certainly take it under advisement. There are a few I would trust with my life as well as hers. Did the gentleman have anything else to share with us?" King Thomas asked.

Reaching over, I placed my hand on his arm. "While this feast has been lovely, I think it's best to retire for the night. Could we possibly have breakfast together tomorrow somewhere private?"

"Yes, I believe that can be arranged. One of my personal staff will come to escort you to the meal. There is a lovely balcony in our private chambers with a stunning view of the sea I would love to show you," he offered, understanding the game I was playing.

"Tomorrow then." Turning to the queen, I caught her eye. "Thank you for your hospitality, Your Majesty. This feast has been a wonderful evening, and I look forward to seeing more of your kingdom in the following days."

Queen Catharine seemed to be pleased with the flattery as she waved me off. "Goodness, child, you put me to shame when you speak like that. A queen for such a short time yet as eloquent as the woman of days past. Gavin is blessed to have such a wife. I can see why he gave it all up for you. Now, off with you. I'm sure you must be exhausted with all the drama that's gone on tonight. Feasts... you never know what to expect from them, do you?"

Seeing this version of the queen added just one more mark of cruelty the Lost King has had on this world. Queen Catharine seemed like a woman who loved her family and did what was best for her kingdom. The changes since her mind was altered must have come on gradually because that woman I met in my kingdom was nothing like the woman before me now.

I bid goodnight to Phillip and the people he was spending time with before I left the hall. Thankfully, another palace worker showed us back to our rooms. Otherwise, we would have been lost and wandering for who knows how long.

As I went to enter my room, Zan grabbed my arm and pulled me back, shaking his head and holding a finger to his lips. He signaled to Jade who vanished into smoke before my eyes, then used the door's keyhole to enter the room. Moments later, a scuffle and a crash had Dayson and Abbott charging into the room.

"Unhand me!" a voice I knew bellowed.

There's no way it could possibly be who I thought it was. Shoving Zan aside, I ran into the room where I found my father on his stomach with Dayson holding him down while Abbott tied his hands. Jade was wiping a split lip and dusting wooden shards off his clothes.

"Wait," I cried out. "That's my father."

The three men froze, looking at me in horror as they released him and stepped back.

"Who the hell are you to attack me like that? Do you know who I am?" Father barked, picking himself up off the floor, his nose bleeding and what looked like a black eye forming.

"No, sir. We had no clue who you were, only that someone who shouldn't be was in the queen's chambers. How did you get into this room?" Jade demanded, not at all deterred by the fact he'd clearly attacked my father.

Father spluttered, looking at me as if I was going to help him. "I told the palace steward who I was and wanted to surprise my daughter with my visit. Is a man not allowed to do so?"

"Father," I said, cutting off whatever Jade was going to say. "How did you know I was here? When we sent the letter days ago, you rejected my offer. I assumed that was the end of it."

The outrage my father seemed to have been feeling drained out of him, and he took a few stumbling steps back to sit on the edge of my bed. "Your mother left me... well, I suppose it would be more correct to say she kicked me out. She didn't even give us a moment to discuss the offer you were giving us. Instead, she spat on the man, sending him on his way. That night, we argued for hours, and the next morning, I had my bags packed and a horse waiting for me. She told me if I wanted to abandon everything, I might as well abandon her too."

Slowly, I approached the man who'd been the one person I looked up to all my life. The hero of my stories, the man who taught me everything I know, gave me the thirst for knowledge that's saved my life more than once. Sitting before me now was a husk of that person. He'd lost weight, his hair was far more gray, and where wrinkles hadn't been, now appeared.

"Father," I started, only to pause, unsure if I truly wanted to know the answer. "How did you find me *here?* The messenger told you I was in Sheca."

"Yes, that's the odd thing of it all. I didn't rightly know where Sheca was. It's not on many maps that I know of. Then, that first night when I was staying at an inn, a man joined me at the table telling me he was tasked with looking after me if I changed my mind about your offer. He shared with me that you were preparing to leave for Creisal in the next few days, and it would be better to meet you there, so here I am," he explained, gesturing with his hands as he told the story.

Something in the pit of my stomach warned me that this whole situation was incredibly wrong. Not to mention, this man wasn't even behaving close to my father's normal disposition. The first thing that tipped me off was he claimed to have fought with my mother. They hadn't even done that when I could have died when the mercenaries first came to take me with them. Father was willing to let me perish to keep our standing in the eyes of those in higher positions.

"That is quite the long journey. You seemed to have made good time," I commented. "Did you get something to eat? There is a feast going on if you wish to join the festivities. I know how you love a good party."

The man claiming to be my father patted me on the leg. "Now, why would I want to do that when I came to see you? Look at you. I can't believe how much has changed in a year."

Letting this man touch me made my skin crawl, but I had to get him to slip up somehow to confirm my suspicion. "Speaking of how much has changed, allow me to introduce you to my consorts and guardians. You remember the once Crown Prince of Norden, now my heir, Gavin. Then there is Jade, Abbott, and Dayson, whom you've already interacted with. You'll have to forgive them, but no one was supposed to be permitted in my rooms, and we are in a foreign kingdom. Izel, Paxton, Cole, and Zan complete my consorts. May is my loyal shadow, and, of course, you know Becka well."

The man pretending to be my father watched with unmasked disdain as I introduced each person in my chosen family. When his gaze landed on Becka, though, she received a brisk nod since I'd made it clear he should know who she was. My gaze flicked over to her, and I prayed she could see what I noticed. Even though Becka was a maid in our home, Father loved her like a second daughter and had always been kind to her above what her station would have called for.

"It's lovely to see you again, Lord Charles," Becka greeted with a curtsy. "I'm so sorry to hear that things with Lady Adeline have turned so sour. You two have always been so in love with each other."

He grunted and adjusted his frock as if he was uncomfortable. "These are not matters I wish to discuss with the maid. If you could please leave the room, I would like to speak to my daughter alone."

While Becka might have been a maid, Father never once held that against her. He would find other kind ways to tell her that she was being impertinent or butting in where she shouldn't. Father knew I loved Becka like a sister and that Mother tried to use her against me, so he never did.

"I'm sorry, my Lord, but that isn't going to happen," Cole stated, crossing his arms. "If you wish to speak to her, there will need to be one of us in the room. That's non-negotiable."

"You dare to tell *me* what can and cannot happen?" Father roared.

At that outburst, I stood, turning on the man. "Enough." With a flick of my hand, a glowing blue dagger appeared in my grasp, which I held against the man's throat. "I don't know who the hell you think you are, but you're not my father. Did the Lost King send you, or is there a new enemy lurking in the shadows I'm unaware of?"

"Seems I over played my hand there. I only had a few hours with the fool, not nearly enough time to make this act believable," the person huffed as the illusion of my father melted away to reveal a woman dressed in all black leather with bright golden hair and glowing green eyes. "Richard warned me you weren't stupid, but I thought I would have managed to get something out of you before you caught on. What gave it away?"

TWENTY-TWO
CASSARAH

My guardians burst into action. Izel grabbed me and yanked me away from the woman, putting himself in front of me as a shield. Zan and Jade held her at knife point while Abbott had his sword drawn. May and Paxton searched the room, ensuring another person wasn't lurking in the shadows. I felt a burst of magic pulse through the room, and the woman changed yet again to be one of the palace attendants who had escorted us down to the feast.

The man snarled, looking around the room. "Who has nullification magic?"

"Why would we tell you that?" Jade asked, pressing the blade against his neck to make him bleed. "You're not in the position to be asking us anything."

I slipped out from Izel's hold and marched right up to the man. "Do you have my father?" I demanded.

"That's the question, isn't it? Is the man still alive, or is he dead? Was what I did an illusion, or did I steal the man's face? One means he could be alive, and the other he is most certainly dead," he said before he started to cackle, his eyes betraying just how crazy he was. "The true king of this world has his army full of people with special talents. In fact, he had your Grim Reaper doing his dirty work before he found you, *little bird*."

Jade roared as he slammed the butt of his dagger into the man's head, knocking him unconscious, making him crumple to the floor.

I stood there stunned, unsure what, if any of that to believe. What did he mean about Jade? Was my father alive? Could he be here?

"Becka, send one of our dragon riders to my home *now*. I need to know if they are still alive from a source I trust," I ordered without taking my eyes off the man at my feet. "Someone needs to alert King Thomas that he needs to be vigilant in every word that comes out of his mouth of those of his family. Nothing is as it seems here in Creisal. The Lost King has had more of a stronghold here than we assumed."

Jade stepped up to me, reaching out to grasp my arm, but I shifted back, not meeting his gaze. "Please, just give me a moment." I lifted my head to see his pale green eyes filled with worry and fear at my rejection. "We will discuss this. I just need a moment to gather my thoughts. Tonight has been one surprise after another."

Turning on my heel, I walked to the balcony and flung open the door. "*Vasin, I need you.*"

"*I WILL BE RIGHT THERE.*" Vasin's voice echoed through my mind. "*ARE YOU IN DANGER?*"

"*No... I don't know. One of the palace attendants just tried to pose as my father hiding in my room. He was spewing all this nonsense that I can't even begin to wrap my head around. I just need to be in the one place I know I'm safe from it all.*"

The whoosh of wind hitting me in the face alerted me to Vasin's arrival. He hovered just under the balcony the best he could, allowing me to drop down onto his back. The moment I was settled, he dropped down the cliffside but thrust his wings down before we reached the beach, shooting up into the dark, starlit sky.

"*TELL ME, UNLESS YOU WANT ME TO SEE IT FOR MYSELF SO YOU DON'T HAVE TO REPEAT IT?*"

"There is so much to tell it might be faster for you to see it," I explained as I started to funnel my memories from the feast to the moment I looked into Jade's eyes.

"It seems the Lost King wasn't ignoring Creisal like we once thought. Instead, he's been working in the shadows much like he did in Errit. I've heard of each of the skills that man was referring to. One can take the likeness of another and create almost an illusion in your mind of what he or she looks like. The latter, though, is dark, evil magic that they literally steal the face of their victim, using it as a foundation for him to create a likeness."

"Do you think my family is dead?"

"Should we go look for ourselves?"

"How long would it take us to get there from here?"

"I can get you there before the sun starts to rise."

"I can't leave without telling the others. That would be wrong."

"Agreed, it would be best if two of them came with you and the others covered for you. We don't want anyone to know you've left. It might be wise for one of them in the morning to go to the king and let him know you still need more rest after traveling since you planned to have breakfast. I will make sure to have you back for lunch instead."

"All right, take me back, and I'll grab Zan and Paxton to come with."

"No, not Paxton. You need Jade for this. He can keep us hidden from sight as we fly."

"Are you sure you're not just trying to fix things between us?"

"Would I do such a thing?"

"Yes."

"Either way, it fixes both problems. I've called Tahir and Ifra to gather their riders."

"Bossy dragon," I muttered.

"Benefit of being your pair-bond. We are of equal status, and you know I'm right."

Vasin dropped me off at the balcony, and I was greeted by Zan and Jade waiting for me. "We're going to check on my family. Vasin said we can be there before dawn and back by lunch," I said hurriedly as I strode into the room to speak with the others.

Gathering by the looks of the others, they'd obviously caught part of what I'd said, and many were not at all pleased.

"You can't be serious, Cassarah," Cole snapped. "There's no way you can just take off right now. What are we going to do with him?"

I looked at the man now tied up and still unconscious on the floor. "I'm sure you will find a way to get information out of him once he's awake. I believe Izel will be quite helpful, and with Paxton here, he won't be able to use whatever magic he has. Zan and Jade are going with me, so I won't be on my own. I *need* to know if they are dead or not. I won't be able to move on without the truth."

"What if the truth is they are dead? That they were skinned like he alluded to? What good will that do you except give you nightmares?" Gavin demanded, anger clear on his face.

"Is there anything I can say that would help any of you accept this choice I'm making?" I asked, to which all of them just grumbled and looked away from me. "I didn't think so. Now, I'm doing my best to respect your wishes that I don't go off and do things on my own. I'm informing all of you what my plan is and bringing backup. Becka, I will need you to contact King Thomas and let him know I'm in need of my rest, but lunch would be lovely to share together."

Becka begrudgingly agreed with a nod. "Fine, but you better make it back, or I'll tell him what really happened."

"That would probably be wise because if I'm not back in time, it means I need help or something went terribly wrong. Gavin, you're in charge as my heir. If anything happens with Sheca or here that I would have needed to respond to, I trust you to make the right judgment." Pausing, I gave them all a sad smile. "I love you all, and I'll be back as fast as I can. I promise."

Having settled things, I removed my crown and placed it in the velvet box it traveled in. For this, I was going as Lady Cassarah, first born of Baron Charles and Baroness Adeline, not as the Dragon Queen. May helped me get out of my dress so I could put on more appropriate clothes for the journey. Dressed all in black, I wanted to ensure I wouldn't be easily recognized as I twisted my hair into a tight bun.

Jade and Zan were already on their dragons, circling the air above while I dropped once more onto Vasin's back. We took off, Vasin leading the way, flying faster than we'd ever flown before. I had to lean down as close as I could to his body so the wind didn't pull me off as it buffeted against me. I prayed to the fates that we would make it there in time, and I would find my family alive. If they were, I would force them to come with me, no longer giving them the option. This no longer just affected them. If the Lost King was going to use them against me, I needed to put a stop to that.

With the world dark and quiet around us, the journey seemed to drag on. It was hard to see anything except for the lanterns in villages as we passed over. When we neared any of the more populated areas, Jade would cloak us in shadow. When it happened, everything turned black and white, his powers removing all sources of color from the world. It was nice to know that if he ever did that to me without me asking, I would know what was happening.

Then I saw it, the home I grew up in. The mansion looked as if nothing was wrong, but I got a sense of foreboding when the grounds looked ill-maintained. I knew having the Lost King ruling Norden would change things, but I hadn't expected Henry to be all that interested in the lives of his new subjects. Could it be that he demanded more taxes, stripping people of what wealth they had? There was only one way to find out what was going on, and that was to land.

It had only been three days since my dragon riders had been here. Granted, they didn't get a chance to do anything other than get yelled at by my mother or at least someone claiming to be my mother. Now that I know people can change their appearance, who's to say this hasn't happened before? They wouldn't have noticed if the grounds were looking rundown because they wouldn't have known what they should look like.

As Vasin landed, I couldn't hear anything coming from the stables—the horses normally reacted to dragons if they hadn't been raised around them. Sliding off his back, I stood for a moment, taking in the sights and sounds but heard nothing other than the chirping of crickets and the cold breeze rustling the trees.

"I don't like this, Cassarah," Zan murmured as he stood beside me. "This place feels… evil." Ezzu launched off his shoulder and started to scout out the place.

I shifted toward Vasin. *"Can you smell or hear anything we might have missed?"*

"It's not good, Cass. What I smell is death. What kind or who I can't say, but blood has been spilled in this place."

Jade joined us, placing his hand on my lower back. "Tahir and I circled the property to ensure there wasn't a trap waiting for you, and the closest living person is miles away."

I nodded, acknowledging I heard him as I stepped forward. I got to the base of the steps and steeled myself for what I might find, already assuming my parents were dead. It was easier to expect the worst and find I was wrong instead of having hope only for it to be crushed. With dread growing at each step I took closer to the front door and my stomach in knots, I turned the handle. It wasn't locked—the first sign something was wrong. Mother never allowed the front door to be left open.

Moving to the side, I shoved as hard as I could when I met resistance trying to get it open. Zan joined my efforts, adding his strength and getting the door to budge. A swath of blood arched, telling me a dead body blocked the entrance. Carefully, I stepped past the blood to enter my childhood home.

The sight before me was graphic, making my already upset stomach heave, but I clamped a hand over my mouth and closed my eyes. Now was not the time to lose myself to this atrocity. I had to see past the blood sprayed all over the floor and walls to understand what really happened. Hands settled on my shoulder, making me gasp, eyes snapping open until my brain caught up to realize it was Zan.

"Sorry, I didn't mean to scare you. It just looked like you needed a reminder you're not in this alone," Zan whispered.

Placing a hand over one of Zan's, I prepared to face the scene before me. Bodies littered the floor and blood pooled around them as flies buzzed around the area, giving me the sense this hadn't been recent. Faces of people who served my family since I was little were there, along with some that were new to me. What I couldn't find was the body of either of my parents.

"They're not here. We should search the rest of the house to see if they might be elsewhere," I said, my voice hollow even to my ears. "I'll take the second floor with Jade if you want to check this level and the barn, Zan."

"Of course," Zan murmured, letting his hands slip off my shoulders as he headed toward the dining room.

Jade was on my heels as I climbed the staircase like I had so many times before. Only now, the heels of my boots echoed in this lifeless space as if the heart of the home was no longer alive. When we reached the top, I looked left toward my room then to the right where my parents' rooms were. They each preferred to have their own since Mother retired early and woke before anyone else. Father and I had always been more of the mind to stay up late.

"This way," I directed, heading down the hall to the right. "This is the wing my parents resided in. Mine is on the other side."

Jade didn't say anything, but his presence was comforting, knowing I didn't have to be alone like I had been so often in this place. The first door led to Mother's sitting room, and it was slightly ajar, making it easier for me to stay in the hall and push it the rest of the way open. The space looked like it always had, everything in perfect order, just the way my mother liked it. Moving on down the hall on the opposite side was my father's study. This door was shut tight, and when I reached out to open it, Jade stopped me.

"Let me... just because we don't think there's anyone here doesn't mean you should be going first. They could have set a trap, hoping you would come back here," he reasoned.

Nodding, I stepped back and let him enter first. His body blocked my vision, but I could tell by the way he froze that something was in there I didn't want to see.

"It's okay," I whispered. "Something in me already knows they're dead."

"You don't need to see this, little bird. They tortured him. By the looks of it, whatever they wanted to know, he didn't give up easily. He went through hell," Jade said, respect for my father clear in his tone. "He wouldn't want you to think of him like this but to remember him alive."

Placing my hands on Jade's back, I rested my forehead between his shoulder blades. "We can't leave him here. He needs to be buried. I may not have always agreed with how my parents acted or treated me, but he is still my father. Knowing he's dead, I'm sure my mother is as well, and they deserve to be laid to rest."

Jade turned and wrapped an arm around me, holding me close as we faced the room. There sat the man who taught me to read, write, instilled in me the love for strategy, and created my ravenous curiosity of the world. His face was so beaten you could hardly tell it was him. Some of his fingers were missing, and his right leg looked to be broken at an odd angle. They had brutalized him for what purpose, I have no clue. Father and I didn't keep in contact other than I had members of the clan check in on them from a distance.

Silent tears rolled down my cheeks as I came to the reality that I no longer had a father in this world. My body began to shake as sobs wracked my body. The feeling of my heart breaking was one I never wanted to wish on another person. Jade turned me into his chest as I wept, my cries echoing down the hall so it sounded as if the house itself was crying over the death of its owners.

"Father?" Zan's voice asked.

I could feel Jade nod in answer. "Can you check the last two rooms? My feeling is you'll find her mother too."

Zan didn't respond, but I heard his footsteps fade down the hall. "What do I do now?" I croaked out. "I wasn't even in contact with them, and he took them from me," I said between hiccups. "Why? Why would he do this to them? They didn't want anything to do with me."

"Cassarah, if I could answer that for you, I would," Jade murmured, kissing my head. "No matter how cruel your family has been to you, to know you are left alone in the world is a heavy thing. While we might not be your blood family, we are the family you chose.

Don't let the lie that you're alone ring true in your heart. That is a darkness that will eat you up inside. I should know. If I hadn't met you when I did, I can only imagine what kind of evil I would have turned into."

"Jade," Zan called.

I peeked out from where I'd been hiding in Jade's chest and saw the look on Zan's face telling me everything—Mother was dead too.

Twenty-Three

Zan

After seeing the shape her father was in, I prayed her mother wouldn't be the same. Cassarah was brave and strong, but everyone hit their limit of things they could handle. Seeing your family beaten and brutalized in such a way was not something anyone should have to deal with.

I paused in the hall and gestured with my head to the door behind me. "She's here, in her bed." Ezzu showed me Cassarah's face, wet with tears. I was glad I'd been the one to investigate, giving her time to break down. "Looks like they dealt with her while she was asleep. It was quick and peaceful."

The bastards had stabbed her in the back, and her mother didn't even see it coming. I'm sure they took her out first then went after her father since he seemed to be the one they wanted. What could he have known that would make them desperate enough to use that kind of torture?

"I want to see her," Cassarah croaked out as she pulled away from Jade.

When she reached me, I held out an arm to block her. "Do you, though? What good will come of seeing her like this?" I challenged, needing to protect the one person in my life who loved me despite my disability.

She gave me a watery smile as she tried to fight back more tears and placed both hands on my arm, pressing it down. "I need to see if only because the memory will be seared into my brain, and if I doubt for a second I shouldn't kill that bastard, I'll remember what he's done to me and my family."

With my ability to see through Ezzu's eyes, I essentially had the perfect vision of a dragon. It also gave me a wide field of eyesight, so I could easily see the grimace on Jade's face while still keeping my attention on Cassarah. He didn't want her to do this any more than I did, but we both knew when she had that wrinkle between her brows, there was no way for any of us to talk her out of doing something.

"If you insist," I surrendered begrudgingly.

Instead of letting her walk past me, I caught her hand, holding it securely as we entered her mother's room. At first glance, you would think she was just sleeping since the coverlet was a deep burgundy color hiding the blood, but the body's smell hit you soon enough. I don't know if it's because she was still under the covers that she was decaying so much faster, but her body reeked, unlike the others we'd come across.

Cassarah let out a sob, covering her mouth with her free hand. Tears once more rolled down her cheeks in large drops. Turning to me, she placed her forehead on my shoulder as if she needed the support to keep standing.

"You've now seen her, my heart. There is no reason to stay and put yourself through more pain. Come on, let's leave... there's nothing more to be gained from this," I urged, wrapping my arm around her shoulders and guiding her out.

She let me remove her, but she dug her heel in the moment we were outside the door. "We can't leave them like this. They need to be buried. I won't leave until that's been settled."

"Is there a place you have in mind for them to be laid to rest?" Jade asked.

She must have already said something to him since he didn't seem surprised at all. "The garden. Mother loved that place, and Father loved her so much he'd spend time with her out there whenever she requested to take her tea there."

"That sounds like a great idea," Jade agreed as he came to stand before her. "Now, what I want to have happen is for you to go to your room. Check to make sure there isn't anything there you want to take back with you. Once we finish here, there will never be a reason for you to come back here again. This place is no longer your home... that died with your parents."

Sniffling, she nodded and shuffled down the hall, looking as if all the life had been drained from her. When I felt she was far enough away, I kept my voice low as I spoke to Jade. "Let me grab a sheet from his bedroom. It will be easier to manage him wrapped up... who knows what else they might have cut off him."

"Smart plan. Her mother won't be a problem since we can just roll her up in the blankets. The garden is just below her balcony so it will be easy to get both of them there," Jade shared as I opened the door to her father's room.

It had been utterly trashed—everything was pulled out and tossed on the floor. Clearly, they'd been looking for something and couldn't find it on their own. Hence, the torture.

"What could they have possibly needed this badly?" I asked, the question pricking at my subconscious. "This is extreme for anyone, whatever they needed, no matter what."

"Part of me hopes we never need to find out, but if they broke him, I have a bad feeling this is going to bite us in the ass," Jade grumbled as he yanked a sheet off the floor.

There was a massive gash running through it, but seeing as they sliced open the mattress, I wasn't shocked. "Her father was only the second generation from the man who deserted the clans, correct?"

"I'm not the right one to ask that. I didn't keep up with all the gossip going around the clans. I was just trying to keep from being put to death by my brother."

He made a good point, but I remember Cassarah saying something about it when they revealed the legend of the Dragon Queen. "Okay, this could be nothing, but the last king of Sheca knew that Cassarah would be born of a deserter. What if somehow there was information given to that man when he left or found its way into his hands along the way? What if the Lost King is trying to find a way to deal with the fact that Cassarah is so much more powerful than him now that she has the Dragon Throne's magic?"

Back in the office, Jade and I laid out the sheet as close to the chair as we could while keeping it out of the pool of blood. With the flick of a knife, Jade cut the man free, and I had to move quickly before the body fell to the side. The man's head lolled back at an unnatural angle. Whoever slit his throat used so much force they almost cut off the head. Together, we wrestled the deadweight onto the sheet and tied it. Hauling it down the hall into the mother's room, out on the balcony, and down the stairs into the garden was no easy feat. Her mother was much easier to handle, already being surrounded by sheets.

Jade located the gardening shed and picked the lock, earning us a pair of shovels. Not knowing how much time we would have left while Cassarah was preoccupied, we got to digging. It was clear this wasn't the first body dump that either of us had done, with how we didn't question how large or deep of a hole to make. When Cassarah finally joined us, we were putting the last few shovelfuls of dirt back into place. Dangling from her hand was a pillowcase filled with what looked like books.

"Did you want to say a few words or any sort of farewell to them?" I asked, not knowing how they'd raised her and their thoughts on death.

Cassarah dropped to her knees between the two graves and set the pillowcase aside so she could put a hand on each plot. "I forgive you," she whispered. "While everyone will tell me you don't deserve my forgiveness, I choose to live a life free from that burden. I know you both loved me in your own ways, even if you were terrible at showing it, Mother. Father, you were my hero, and knowing you would turn your back on me for the sake of appearances hurt more than you'll ever know, but I still choose to forgive you. May whatever secret you kept hidden prove to be one that will be the Lost King's downfall and not mine."

Her voice started to crack at the end, telling me she was most likely crying again. Everything in me just wanted to steal her away from all this. This woman whose heart was so full of love and forgiveness didn't deserve this. With hit after hit the Lost King sent her way, this woman got back up, dusted herself off, and kept moving forward. How anyone couldn't see the power and strength in that didn't deserve to know her at all.

Now, I was supposed to get her back to Creisal, where we were fighting a war on all fronts. King Thomas might be on our side, along with a few trusted members of his personal entourage, but that left us at such a disadvantage. Dark magic was in play, made evident by her father having been killed, allowing that face changer to use the man's death to fuel his magic. What I'd much rather be doing is convince her to run away, get the others, and fly across the sea to discover what might be out there, and leave all this behind and live a life free from this pain. Yet, I knew she would never allow me to do that. Her sense of duty was so strong she wouldn't be able to look at herself in the mirror until she finished the job assigned to her.

"My heart, we should be heading back," I murmured as I crouched next to her. "I wish there was more we could do here for the others, but we can't bury them all."

Cassarah looked up at me, her eyes red and puffy from crying, but they glinted with anger. "We can send them to the afterlife when we set the house on fire."

"What?" I asked, thinking I'd just misheard what she said.

"Like Jade said, there won't be anything to come back to now that my parents are gone. This house holds no life, and only evil remains, so we are going to burn this place down. Let those whose lives were lost be set free in the fires of rebirth," Cassarah explained as she got to her feet and brushed off her legs. "The dragons will be able to do the job with all three of them hitting different points. When the world sees the blaze, the Lost King will know I've been here and received his message."

Jade looked at me, a little panicked at that thought. "Are you sure that's wise, little bird? We don't want to show our hand. That would mean we know about the face changer in Creisal."

"You don't think he meant for us to see through that person? That man had no idea who my father was. He even said he barely had any time with the man. How could Henry believe I wouldn't see through it? No, his plan was to get me here and witness the atrocities he inflicted on my parents." The rage in Cassarah's voice grew the longer she spoke.

It was clear if she hadn't been pissed off at the Lost King before, she was now. While weighed down by sadness, her body seemed to give off this pulse of fury I could feel brushing along my skin. Not having sight of my own was tough, but it certainly strengthened my other senses.

Jade and I wanted to comfort her, knowing her rage at losing her parents was driving this choice, but I didn't think she'd be open to the gesture. "Is that what you really want to do?"

"Yes," she stated. "While I won't drop to his level, I won't be seen as weak either. He *needs* to know I'm not backing down, no matter what he throws at me. Let the Lost King taunt me by sending a man pretending to be my father to my room and steal my family from me. People who get desperate making rash moves like this betray the fact they think they're losing. Right now, it looks like the Lost King wants this to be anything but a fair fight."

While I couldn't disagree with her thoughts, I didn't like it either way. It's true this might never come down to a battle as we've seen in the days of old. Kingdoms lining up to mow each other down, this battle could instead be heading more in the direction of how the mercenaries fight. The Lost King has been playing by our rules more than he has anyone else's. It makes me wonder if he truly wants a massive war. He came and stole Norden in the middle of the night when they least expected it.

When I think back on it, I feel it was more about the fact he wanted his father to know he stole it from him. In his mind, he'd been tossed away, and here he was creeping in to take what should have been his. The fact that Cassarah was there, along with Payson to help him cause diversions made it all the better. A man who has been kept hidden away all his life was now making a splash across our whole world. Everyone knew the name 'Lost King' and why he was doing this. Did he even know or care that his father was dead and didn't know or care about what was happening?

"If that is what the queen wants to do, then we shall see it done," Jade said, his formal tone betraying he wasn't in support of this but wouldn't say no.

Cassarah turned to look him in the eye. "As your queen, I order you and Zan to help me burn this mansion down."

Jade gave her a brisk nod, turned on his heel, and left out the garden gate. Shaking my head at how stubborn they could be and how, in many ways, Jade and Cassarah were so similar it caused them to butt heads, I wrapped my arm around her shoulders and urged her to follow after him.

"You know he gets pissy when he wants to protect you, and you won't let him," I commented, leaning my head against hers for a moment. "I have to agree with him on burning this place down. Do I get your anger and need to show the Lost King you're not backing down because of this... yes. Do I also believe it's foolish to bring unwanted attention while there are only two of us to keep you safe? Yeah, I do, but if you keep that order as you've given it, then we will do as you command," I explained as we exited the garden.

Cassarah slumped against me. "Is it really a stupid idea?"

"Are you really asking me?" I countered.

Pausing, she looked over at Vasin, who was puffing smoke and looking highly irritated. "Vasin agrees with you. But how can I just stand back and let him do this without consequences?"

"You aren't doing that. Just because you wait to unleash your anger at him another time doesn't mean you're giving him a free pass. You are acting wisely and using that anger to fuel your efforts in taking him down for good," I reasoned. "Sure, an eye for an eye sounds great, but what if you could just end it all at once, instead of acting out against the individual acts?"

She took a deep breath and let it out, her head dropping with the exhale. "If you and Vasin are saying the same thing, then I clearly am not thinking straight. Let's head back to the others. There's more to deal with, and if we leave now, I might be able to get a few moments of sleep."

"I think that's the right call, my heart. It doesn't feed your need for justice, but save that righteous anger for the right time, and it will have all the more power in it," I said, unsure if anything I was saying helped at all.

Cassarah reached out, took my hand, and squeezed it before she headed toward Jade to tell him the change in plans. I had to hand it to the man—he could keep his thoughts off his face—but I knew he was pleased she wasn't going to follow through on her order. Without further ado, we mounted our dragons, allowed Jade to cloak us, and headed off into the night. Vasin didn't set a daunting pace for the dragons like he did on the way here, but they still flew with a sense of urgency. When we made it back to Creisal, the sun was low, creating a bright orange glow behind the mountains. This should give us time to catch a few hours of sleep before we had lunch with the king.

Twenty-Four
Cassarah

The moment I entered my room, Cole snapped awake from where he'd been sleeping in a chair by the balcony door. "Everything all right?" he asked, rubbing the sleep from his eyes.

I didn't have the energy to answer him and just shook my head, walking past him to the bathing chamber. I wanted to wash the stench of death off my skin before crawling into bed. Jade and Zan followed me, needing to wash up as well. The thought of them dealing with my parents' dead bodies made me sick to my stomach, but I was glad they asked me to leave so they could handle the situation without putting more nightmares in my brain.

The three of us cleaned up silently, lost in our thoughts as we scrubbed. I could see bubbles tinged with pink from the blood of those who were killed in my childhood home float by me. Before I lost control over my emotions for the umpteenth time tonight, I steeled myself, closed off my mind, and disconnected from the reality of what I'd witnessed. Right now, all I wanted was to sleep and be surrounded by the family I still had living and breathing all around me.

With my hair still damp and only clothed in my bathing robe, I numbly walked to my bedroom. All my men and the girls stood there, watching me with apprehension. I needed to say something to them, but I didn't have the energy to explain it all, so I settled for simple and to the point.

"Everyone in the house was killed. There were no survivors," I announced, my voice cracking as I spoke. Looking at them standing there, alive and breathing, seemed to crack the shield I'd put up, and my bottom lip started to quiver no matter how I tried to get it to stop. "As of now, I am without any blood relations. What family I have now consists of the ten of you."

The air in the room seemed to have been sucked out at my words. Each of my men had lost one or both of their parents. Many of their father's deaths, having been the result of my guardians protecting me, were killed by their own hands. These people before me had given up so much for the sake of our people and this kingdom I now ruled. It appeared it was now my turn to have lost something valuable in this battle.

Cole walked up to me, wrapped his arms around my shoulders, and held me tightly to his chest. I could hear the steady beating of his heart, reminding me that he was still alive. I hadn't lost everything tonight, as much as the Lost King would like me to believe that. Zan had been right. I needed to take this pain, anger, and revenge, using it to bring him to ruin.

Tears dampened Cole's shirt, but he didn't seem to care. Instead, he scooped me up and walked over to the bed. "Come on, little mouse, let's get you into bed. Sleep will help make things more manageable." Izel was already pulling back the sheets as Cole spoke, laying me down in the middle of the large bed.

"Will you all stay?" I asked, grabbing Cole's wrist since he was closest. "I don't want to be alone right now."

"Little mouse, if that is what we can do for you right now, then, of course, we will stay. Did you want the girls to get in on this snuggle pile as well?" Cole questioned, looking over at May and Becka.

I turned my head seeing at how tired they both looked. "With all of them here, I think I'll be safe enough. Go get some sleep so someone is fit enough to see an attack coming."

Becka walked over, crawled on the bed, wrapped her arms around my neck, and kissed my cheek. "I love you, Cassarah. You and I have been through hell once, so we can survive this. You are and always will be a sister to me. While your parents and I had an odd relationship, I will mourn their passing along with you, especially your father. He always seemed like an uncle to me in an odd way. I pray the fates will grant you peaceful dreams, my dear sweet sister."

After saying her peace, Becka left with May, the stalwart warrior woman, wrapping her friend in a side hug as they left the room.

Cole wrapped himself around my back as Izel pulled me against his chest, letting my ear rest over his heart. "Little warrior, do you want me to help you sleep?"

Izel had once before used his Birthright to block out the pain as they tended to my wounds. He could influence a person's mind but not in the same way Henry could. Izel didn't take over your mind. It was almost like he could pull you into a dream-like state, where he convinced your brain it was somewhere else.

"Please, I don't want it to play in my dreams over and over again like I know it will," I mumbled, my hand fisting the fabric of his shirt. "They brutalized him, Izel. There was something they wanted from my father, and he wasn't willing to give it up without a fight. We still don't know if he gave up his secret, let alone what it could be."

"Shh, little mouse," Cole soothed, running his hand through my hair. "Let Izel help you rest, and you can tell us later if you feel up to it. Jade and Zan can fill us in too. You don't have to be the one to share it all if you don't want to."

Nodding, I buried my face in Izel's chest, pulling the blanket they wrapped me in under my chin.

"Where do you want to go, little warrior?" Izel asked, his soft voice already pulling me under his spell. "Tell me, and you will be off on your adventure, forgetting all about today."

"Somewhere across the sea. I want to explore what else might be out there," I shared. "Being here is only filled with sadness."

"Then off across the sea you will go," Izel whispered, pressing a soft kiss to my forehead.

The second I closed my eyes, I was on Vasin's back flying across the open water. It stretched out as far as I could see, our images reflecting at us off the glassy surface. The others were with me as well. All ten of them spread out, joining me on this journey. There was only the sense of peace as the wind blew, ruffling my hair as Vasin lowered enough to skim the water with his claws, sending up a spray that ignited the sight of a rainbow.

"One day, my dear Cass, this will be the life we get to live. That is a vow I make to you."

I could feel Vasin's consciousness retreating from this dream, but I clung to his words like a lifeline. Once this was over, the world would be different—it would be free, and so would we.

"Cassy-bear," Dayson's voice rumbled along my back. "It's time for you to get up."

With a groan, I turned to curl up against him, hiding in his bulk, refusing to face the world yet.

"Hey now, none of that, spitfire," Paxton said, poking my side playfully. I couldn't fight back the giggle that burst out, and I knew I'd just signed away my own fate. "What was that I heard? Did you just giggle, Your Highness? Are queens even allowed to do that? I think I should check."

Paxton started to tickle me, and no matter how hard I tried to fight against it, I burst into laughter as he dragged me away from Day. Now on my back, Paxton pounced to sit on my legs and started to count my ribs, his finger rough on my skin. "One... two... three... four... If you keep squirming like that, I'll lose count and have to start over again."

"Mercy," I gasped, fighting for breath as he continued to count.

"Seven... eig—" Paxton was cut off as Cole tackled him, knocking them both off the bed.

I lay there for a moment, my robe in shambles, showing off my naked body to the room of men, all of whom I've slept with. None of them seemed bothered by this, and many gave me heated glances, but it was clear no one was going to act.

"Come on, little phoenix," Abbott said, reaching out to me with a hand. "We promised Becka we would have you up and ready for lunch. If we fail, then she's going to kick all of us out tonight, and you're having a girls-only sleepover."

"That woman sure knows how to make a good threat," I shared with a grin as I let him pull me from the bed. "So, who's going to help me with my dress?"

"That would be me," Gavin answered, stepping forward to take me from Abbott. "I'm the only one with a clue as to what would be appropriate for a luncheon with a king."

Smiling, I followed after him into the dressing room and watched as he sorted through the dresses Becka had packed. I knew which one she would pick, but I wasn't going to let them cheat—a deal was a deal.

"What do we think about this one?" Gavin asked, showing me a gown more suited to a ball than lunch. "That's a no. You only crinkle your nose like that when you don't want to tell someone they're wrong. Let's try again... that one was too fancy, I think. Lunch, middle of the day, not formal but still pretty."

I covered my mouth with my hand, trying my best to stifle the laughter fighting to come out, but I didn't want Gavin to doubt himself in the least.

"This one," he announced, revealing it to me.

It was a simple emerald-green dress with a gold filigree pattern to it. "That will work perfectly," I answered, letting my robe slide off my shoulders to land on the floor.

Gavin's eyes went wide as I gathered my undergarments and slipped them on. I could feel his eyes watching every move, but he didn't so much as take a step closer to me. It was clear they all came to some agreement that they weren't going to pursue any intimate interactions while ensuring I was ready.

"I'll just need you to help with the corset," I commented, looking over my shoulder as I pulled my hair out of the way. "It doesn't need to be overly tight, just snug to hold things in place."

Gavin licked his lips as he set the dress aside and came up behind me. "I'll admit, I don't have much practice getting a woman into these. It's usually the opposite."

"Can I tell you a secret?"

"Of course, love. I will listen to anything you want to share with me," Gavin answered.

I caught his chin in my hand and planted a firm kiss on his lips. "It's far more sensual to help a woman get dressed than it is to get her out of her clothes. You know what's under my dress that you got to touch what others can't. To know with each breath I take, my breasts press against the corset you helped to secure. It's also only something that can be done by someone that person knows intimately. You don't just let any man into your dressing room where you are bare and vulnerable to the world."

Knowing I was playing with fire, I let my hand glide down his chest until I cupped his cock in my hand. "One never knows what could happen when you're all alone in just your underthings."

"Jade!" Gavin yelled, his voice husky as it cracked. "Help!"

Seconds later, Jade was marching through the door, took in the situation, and removed Gavin from the room, leaving me alone. Laughter bubbled up as I removed that corset and picked another one I could lace from the front. The dress would hide the lacing just fine, and I didn't think any of the guys could make it through the process. I pulled the dress over my head and exited the dressing room. "Can someone lace up the back of this dress? I managed the corset, but that's where my abilities end."

Cole silently approached, brushed my hair over one shoulder, and got to work lacing up the back. "That was a mean trick, little mouse. I'm guessing you figured out the second part of this bet we made with Becka."

"I wasn't sure if it was a bet or just something you decided so you wouldn't get distracted. It also crossed my mind you might think I'm too emotionally fragile for that sort of activity," I reasoned.

When he was finished, I felt his lips kiss the back of my neck. "It could be a little of both, but if you really wanted one of us, we wouldn't deny you." Cole took a step back and waved at Dayson. "She's all yours. Day's going to do something with your hair."

I walked over to the dressing table, sat on the stool, folded my hands primly, and waited for the big man to get started.

"You don't mind braids, do you? That's all I know how to do besides pulling the hair up into a horse tail," Dayson remarked as he grabbed a brush.

"Whatever you manage to pull off will be fine with me," I assured him. "You guys don't need to do this. I'm going to be fine."

Dayson used the back of the paddle brush to cover my mouth. "Nope, I don't want to hear it. Let us look after you for once, all right? You're always worrying about everything, so just sit back and let us handle this."

As he moved the brush away, I made a show of turning the key, sealing my lips shut, and tossing it away. Dayson grunted his approval and got to work on whatever master plan he had for my hair. The feel of his hands in my hair was so soothing, I shut my eyes and drifted off into a sort of dreaming wakefulness.

"Oh, Dragon Queen, did you really think you could hide the fact you went home from me? That my dragon wouldn't sense yours coming into our lands? How does it feel to be an orphan?"

I gasped, nearly falling off the stool as I jolted awake. My heart pounded in my chest as fear clawed at my throat, making it hard to breathe. *Had Henry just spoken to me?*

"Cassy-bear, what just happened?" Dayson asked, crouching down before me. "You look like you've seen a ghost."

"He spoke to me, the Lost King. He spoke into my mind," I said, stumbling over my words.

Shoving to my feet, I moved to the balcony and threw open the doors, gasping in the fresh air. A hand landed on my shoulder, making me scream and lash out, clipping whoever it was on the cheekbone.

"Shit," Paxton swore. "Look, I'm all for taking hits that I deserve, but that one I did not."

Tears pooled in my eyes as I realized what I'd done. "Pax, I'm so sorry. I didn't mean to hit you. My mind was elsewhere, and I panicked." Reaching out, I ran my fingers lightly over the pink skin where I caught him.

Pax grabbed my hand and pressed a kiss to it. "Please don't cry about it, spitfire. I'm glad that your first reaction is to defend yourself. If I really were a bad guy coming after you, I would know messing with you wasn't going to be that easy. Now that you've calmed down some, do you want to tell me what just happened?"

Hearing those words playing over in my head, I lost the battle against my tears. "The Lost King, he spoke to me. I was almost asleep while Dayson was working on my hair, and *he* spoke to me. Henry knows I went home last night. His dragon sensed Vasin and the others."

"That would freak me the fuck out too," Pax murmured as he pulled me against his chest. "You are safe. He isn't here, and whatever trick he used, I bet it cost him a lot of power to do so. Reach out to Vasin... see what he has to say about it."

I wrapped my arms around Paxton's waist, holding him tightly as I reached out to my dragon. *"Vasin."*

"Yes, my dear Cass... what has you so worried?"

"Henry spoke to me in my mind, like we are right now. How could he do that?"

Vasin didn't answer immediately, but I could feel him in my mind as if he were searching for something. *"When he dragged you into his dragon's consciousness, he somehow managed to leave a piece behind. Almost like a hook to make a connection easier. He shouldn't have been able to use it, though, from so far away."*

"What if he isn't? What if he's closer than we think? This has to be tied to whatever he hid here in Creisal. It adds to his power." That thought fueling me, I shoved off of Pax and strode across the room, yanking open the door.

The palace attendant standing down the hall spotted me and hurried over. "Can I be of assistance, Your Majesty?"

"I need to see the king right away," I ordered.

He quickly bowed and gestured for me to follow. "Right this way."

"Queen Cassarah," Dayson bellowed as he exited the room. "What is going on?"

"I need to see the king right away," I answered, not bothering to stop and explain myself.

The attendant led me into a sitting room. "Wait here, and I will inform the king's aide you are here."

"No, it can't wait," I said under my breath, charging past the man into the inner chambers of King Thomas' rooms.

"Your Highness," the aide gasped as he saw me rush past. "This is highly improper!"

"Where is he?" I demanded. "I need to know right now, or I'm going to search every room until I find him."

"Please, calm yourself. He isn't here," the aide explained. "There was something urgent he needed to deal with before your lunch that isn't for another hour."

Pausing, I looked at the man and something about the way he couldn't hold my gaze told me he was lying. "No, he's here. You just don't want me to see him."

"Your Majesty, there is a simple explanation, but I'm not permitted to share the king's personal life," the aide explained, his tone begging me to understand.

"We are at war, and this man is supposed to be my ally. If I can't count on him when I need him, then what the hell good is any of this?" I demanded, throwing my hand in the air. "I will find the king and speak to him regardless of his secrets. This cannot wait."

"Cassarah!" Cole snapped from behind me as the rest of them caught up to me. "What the hell are you doing?"

The palace staff gasped at the way he was addressing me, but I didn't care. I had bigger issues to deal with. I spotted a set of double doors I would guess would lead to a bedroom. If I had a secret meeting with someone, that would be the type of place where it would happen in my logic. Marching up to the doors, I flung them open and found the king on all fours getting rammed from behind by none other than Sir Roulf.

Twenty-Five

Cassarah

"Seems it wasn't just the queen you were sleeping with, is it, Sir Roulf," I said, announcing my presence as I strode to the bed. "Being a messenger of the Lost King, it would only be fitting that you would keep a close eye on the royals."

King Thomas scrambled away from Sir Roulf, snatching up a robe to cover himself. His partner, on the other hand, seemed to have no shame in me discovering them. Roulf grinned at me proudly, placing his hands on his hips, trying to draw my attention to his cock.

"It seems I wasn't able to finish... care to help me out?" he asked with a purr to his words. "I'm told by the palace staff you are quite skilled in your way around men's bodies... two at once is something."

I grabbed a pillow on the verge of being knocked off the bed and chucked it at him. "Cover yourself, you blithering idiot. With eight highly-skilled men to please me, why would I need a rat like you in my bed?" I turned my attention to the king, who looked as if he was praying for the floor to open up and swallow him whole. "So how does it feel to be fucked by the Lost King's informant? It's a miracle he doesn't already sit on the throne with how you handed it over to him on a silver platter."

Clasping my hands behind my back, I slowly rounded the bed to face him. "It's obvious you didn't know about this man, or your binding contract with me regarding our alliance would have struck you down where you kneeled. Tell me why should I help a fool like you? He was sleeping with your wife, for fuck's sake!"

King Thomas bowed his head as no true king ever should in the presence of rival royalty. "I am weak. Men have always been my preference, but as king, I have a duty to my people to produce an heir. I love my wife, she is incredibly dear to me, but I don't feel about her the way I do with men. It was easy with Roulf. I knew he could keep a secret because he never once told me anything about my wife, even when I asked him. I knew something was changing, but I couldn't figure out what. He told me he would tell me what I wanted to know, but then he would do the same for my wife. She would know that I don't love her that way."

I caught movement out of the corner of my eye and saw Roulf trying to sneak out of the room. Calling on my Birthright, I shot an arrow just ahead of him, bringing him to a screeching halt. "Guardians!" I yelled.

Jade and Izel charged into the room, swords at the ready. When they saw the naked man clutching his clothes and a pillow, they paused.

"Would you please keep an eye on Sir Roulf? He has much to tell us," I instructed.

Izel took a moment to check me over, ensuring I was fine, before grabbing the idiot by the back of the neck and dragging him out of the room. Jade hung back, searching the space for any other dangers that might befall me. Satisfied I would be fine, he caught my eye. "We are right outside the door. We've already removed all the king's staff, so it's just us in here now."

"Thank you, Jade," I answered, giving him a soft smile. "The king and I will just be a moment. I'm sure he would like to put on some clothes before dealing with this traitor situation."

Jade nodded and pulled the door shut but didn't let it latch, making it faster for them to get in.

"So tell me, King Thomas, are there any other secrets I should know about?" I asked, taking a seat in one of the armchairs in the room. "I'm fully aware that what you've done by your law isn't frowned upon, but that's not why this is so incredibly awful. If I'd been aware of your intimate relationship with Sir Roulf, then I would have spared you this whole encounter. He spoke to me last night and all but told me the Lost King was far more in control of this kingdom than anyone even knew. Clearly, he wasn't underselling the situation."

King Thomas sat in the chair across from me, letting his head fall into his hands. "How could I have been such a fool? It was so easy to give in to what I wanted rather than to think about what else could be at stake. You'll learn soon enough this role is about giving up everything to serve your people, and I just wanted something that was mine."

"He wasn't yours. He was with your wife as well," I countered, utterly confused. "Wouldn't it seem odd that one person was in both your beds? It's the easiest place for someone to watch, listen, and control things while blinding you to the truth."

"When you explain it like that, I suppose this all seems idiotic to you. Our kingdom wanted to create freedom for our people in a way that would solve situations like my own. We have a duty to family, to our heritage, and to keep the line going, but we also enjoy what we enjoy," King Thomas reasoned, giving me a look that begged me to understand.

"Do you understand that I don't care who you sleep with, be it male, female, both, neither? What the issue here is that because you let your cock do the thinking, you allowed a man who has an allegiance to the Lost King into your bed and probably has been destroying all your hard work from the inside out," I explained, leveling him with a stern gaze.

At these words, the king seemed to wilt in front of me as he nodded in understanding. There was nothing more I could do about what had already transpired. Now, I had to help fix the problem. Pushing up out of the chair, I brushed out my skirts as I tried to process what needed to happen next. "Get dressed, take the time to pull yourself together, and when you walk out that door, I want to see King Thomas, ruler of Creisal. We have a kingdom to save, a madman to stop, and we just found one of his moles doing his dirty work. I'm going to take that as a gift and see what we can get from him."

Without checking to see how he took my instructions, I left the bedroom. Dayson stood just outside the door and clearly listened to everything that had been said. His face betrayed how he felt about what he'd heard, and if I had the luxury of being that free with my emotions, I would be right there with him, strangling the king for his idiocy.

"Where did they take him?" I asked.

Dayson didn't answer. He just led the way, his hands clenched into fists and his steps heavy with anger. I expected to end up in a sitting room of some kind, but instead, they brought me to the bathing room. It was twice the size as mine, and as I entered, I saw Jade pulling Roulf's head out of the tub and plopping him into a chair.

"You and I both know you have plenty to share with us, Roulfie boy. This is just the beginning. You have no idea what the others might be able to do with their Birthrights," Jade taunted as he circled the half-drowned man. He caught sight of me and paused as if worried how I would react to seeing him torture a person.

Unbothered, I walked up to the lying traitor, crossed my arms, and waited. Roulf looked at me out of his one good eye, the other swollen shut from the bruising. He looked bedraggled but not at all like he was willing to talk. The rage in that one eye told me he never thought he would get caught, which was rather foolish of him.

As if we were in a battle of wills, neither of us looked away from the other. He was waiting for me to speak first, but I wasn't going to give him one spec of information I didn't have to. There was no telling what he knew or didn't at this point. I knew some kind of power source hidden here in Creisal allowed Henry to do what he'd pulled on me. There was no other way to explain how he could speak to me in a dream state.

I could feel my men shifting around me, each wanting to step in and make him talk, but they held back. While the mercenaries were never taught interrogation skills, so to speak, they taught us how to use people's faults to our advantage. Sir Roulf was a man of pomp and circumstance. He'd created a nice life here in the castle, and it was all falling away before his eyes.

"Did you spank the king good and hard for being a bad boy?" he snarled, shaking the water out of his face, splattering me with it.

Cole started to move, but I held up a hand to stop him.

"My, my… it seems you have all your men so well trained. I'm sure you'll have the king whipped into shape in no time."

Before my brain could stop my body, I felt my hand connect with Roulf's face, the sound of the slap echoing in the room. "I would advise you against speaking about my men in such a manner."

Roulf shook his head as if I'd rattled his brain with the blow. "I'm sorry, Your Highness, was that a touchy subject for you? I wouldn't want to offend you, seeing as you are in control of whether I live or die."

"Drop the act. I've already seen who you really are last night. Do us both a favor and just speak to me normally," I shot back, my patience growing thin at his tone.

Upon my request, his whole demeanor changed and out came the scumbag he truly was. "If that's what you wish, but you might not like my true personality all that much."

"Anything would be better than what you're giving me right now," I answered and started to pace in front of him. "Obviously, you were sleeping with the king to keep him under your control. The Lost King said himself he would have killed him if it wasn't too much work. Why in the world would you risk what happened here today unless you were just trying to prove a point to me?"

Roulf tossed back his head and laughed. "Oh God, and you think the Lost King is full of himself. What if I just wanted one last chance to give the old man a good pounding? I couldn't have the queen under my thumb any longer, but I could top a king with a wink and a smile. He was so easy to manipulate, desperate to feed his baser needs. That, and it told me you hadn't had a chance to fill him in on things. Unsurprising, since you flew to Norden last night. Tell me, how are your parents?"

Zan came out of nowhere and socked the man right in the jaw, not once but twice. "You will not speak of such things!" he roared. "Clearly, you know they're dead, and if you would like to die with any dignity, then I suggest you keep those comments to yourself."

Blood dripped from Roulf's split lip and tongue. Rearing his head back, Roulf spat a wad of saliva and blood at Zan. Ezzu screeched from her place on his shoulder and shot out a stream of fire, blocking it. Hissing, she flapped her wings in anger almost as if she wished to attack him, yet knew Zan wouldn't like it.

"You think I'm scared of a flying rat?" Roulf snapped but flinched when Ezzu looked like she might launch off Zan's shoulder.

"My money is always on the pissed-off female," Paxton whispered loudly. "Hell hath no fury like a pissed-off woman or dragon. Trust me, I know."

Izel stepped up behind Roulf and met my gaze as if asking permission. I nodded, knowing that he would be able to put the man in a more susceptible state. Izel placed both hands on either side of Roulf's head over his temples and closed his eyes. Surprising me, Gavin also placed a hand on the traitor's shoulder. I could feel the magic flowing out of them as they used their Birthrights to get him to talk.

Gavin could make people feel comfortable with him, allowing them to share more than they would normally. I'd experienced it myself when he wasn't even trying. It came on you so softly you didn't even notice you were doing it right away. Izel opened his eyes to look at me and nodded.

"Roulf, are you truly a messenger for the Lost King?" I wanted to start with something easy.

"Here, I thought you were supposed to be the smart one out of the bunch, but if you're going to waste their efforts by asking such a dumb question, I'm not so sure," he answered, his tone flippant and cruel.

It was clear he no longer had a shield up against sharing how he really felt about things. "Very well, then let's move on to something harder. What has the Lost King hidden here?"

Roulf struggled against Izel and Gavin's hold, trying to fight them off, but he was at a disadvantage.

"Fuck you. Even if you find it, you won't know what to do with it. The beauty of it all is that what he smuggled into hiding is so powerful it will keep him alive forever, but everyone will overlook it."

"Where did you hide it?" I pressed.

Roulf gritted his teeth, fighting the urge to answer, but my men's power was too strong. With our bond and the bond with their dragons, they were becoming more powerful as they used their Birthright. I didn't know if Roulf had one, but regardless of that, he certainly had a strong mind to fight them off.

Taking a step forward, I shoved some of my own magic into him, bolstering the other two. "Where. Did. You. Hide. It?"

A scream burst from his lips as his body started to smoke like it was being burned from the inside out. "Oh God, don't let me die this way, please! If you promise to kill me the second I tell you, I'll give you the truth. Don't let him do this to me!"

"You have my vow as the Dragon Queen that I will end your life if you are truthful," I agreed.

Izel and Gavin withdrew from the man as he sobbed, his tears scalding his cheeks as they trailed down his face. "At the lake house the queen visits, there is a mausoleum with a secret room. That's where it's hidden."

"What is it?" I asked as I called a dagger into my hand. "Just this last bit of knowledge, and I will plunge this magical dagger into your heart."

Roulf thrashed and screamed until his voice went hoarse, kicking out his legs as his skin started to blister. "Dragon heart... it's his dragon's heart. He removed it and kept it sealed in a metal box no one can touch. If they do, they'll die." He wept as he tried to breathe through the pain of being burned alive from the inside out.

"Thank you," I whispered before doing as I promised.

Roulf sagged, and on his dying breath, I heard him whisper one last thing, "Your father didn't tell..."

I released my hold on the dagger, and it disappeared as I stumbled back. Abbott caught me and held me tightly against him as the reality of what I'd just done hit me. I'd let him suffer just so I could get the answers I needed. How could I have done that? It was clear how much he was suffering, and I let it go on to drag out the answer. How am I any better than the Lost King who was torturing him to keep him from speaking?

My body shook, warning me that my legs were going to give out, but I couldn't say anything. Abbott scooped me up and carried me out of the bathing chamber, only to be confronted by King Thomas.

"What's happened?"

TWENTY-SIX

CASSARAH

"Not here," Abbott instructed as he carried me past the king into the sitting room.

Instead of placing me on the couch, he sat and continued to hold me against his chest. All my guardians but Jade joined us, taking up positions around me, subtly making it so if the king tried anything, they could intercept.

"Look here, I'm the king and when I ask what's happened, I expect to get an answer," King Thomas demanded as he squared off with us.

None of my men spoke, unwilling to share anything with the king unless I divulged the information first. While I still didn't trust myself to stand on my own two feet, I shifted so my back was against Abbott's, using him for support. "I'm glad to see you've pulled yourself together, Your Majesty. While this wasn't the plan or our doing, Sir Roulf is no longer with us. There must have been a trap set on him that he would self-combust if he shared things he shouldn't have or got caught doing."

The king's face went pale, and he stumbled back a step. *Had I misjudged the king's feelings? Did he truly care about Roulf? I'd just assumed it was a means to getting a physical need met.*

"Did he..." the king paused and cleared his throat. "Were you able to get any information out of him?"

I nodded. "It seems that the Lost King has indeed hidden a powerful object here in Creisal, and it's in the mausoleum of your summer home. We will need to head there directly and without anyone knowing our true agenda. It would be best if we also came up with a reason for Sir Roulf to go missing so suddenly."

King Thomas wiped a hand down his face as he paced the room. "Yes, as far as I know, no one knew he was involved with me. Now that the queen has declared our marriage to be closed, it is within my rights to send him away if he continues to persist. He wasn't born of Creisal. He hailed from Utros and returned with the queen when she came back. They didn't become lovers right away... that happened more naturally, or so it seemed. It's been far shorter for us, but he wormed his way into my bed soon enough."

"Very well, that takes care of that issue. What about taking a visit to the summer home? It's becoming winter in most other kingdoms, but here and in Sheca it tends to remain mild," I mused, trying to get my brain to engage with the matter at hand. Instead, it just kept replaying Roulf's screams, begging me to end it.

"That won't be hard at all. The queen went up there all the time, no matter what season it was. She would say that she'd had enough of court life and leave with her personal attendants," King Thomas shared.

"So, it's safe to assume the attendants are also tied to the Lost King," Cole muttered. "He wouldn't risk them going out there being so close to something so powerful if he couldn't trust or control them."

"Is anyone going to tell me what *it* is?" the king asked.

I took a deep breath and stood, meeting the king's gaze head-on. "Please understand that what we learned could end this war. I have no problem telling you, but I won't do so with so many eyes and ears around that we can't trust. In situations like this, it's safe to assume the walls are listening and that information is just too important to let slip out." Clasping my hands together in front of me to keep them from betraying how unsteady I still was, I forced a smile. "I believe it's about time for us to have lunch. We wouldn't want to draw any more suspicion than I already have bursting into your chambers."

"Yes... what exactly are we going to say about that?" he drawled.

"It's simple really. I'm a woman who simply lost control over my emotions, fearful that I was being attacked in my rooms. Overwhelmed with fear, I came in demanding to speak with you to place more guards outside my rooms while I'm not there for protection," I explained. "That is something no one will have a hard time believing. Women are always underestimated and assumed flighty."

"Did you get attacked in your room last night?" King Thomas asked, suddenly concerned.

Before I could answer, Jade strode out of the bathing chamber, wiping his bloody hands on a towel. "Yes, it was one of your own people posing to be her father. They used dark magic to copy his likeness after having killed him in his home back in Norden."

The king gaped at Jade, then looked back at me like I was going to correct the story. "It's true." I glanced over at Cole. "Where is that man, by the way?"

"He had the same spell on him that Roulf did. We locked him away, and when we went to check on him, he was dead and burned to a crisp," Cole answered. "While we didn't know if your parents were still alive or not, I was worried we'd lose out on information with the man ending up dead, but it seems we got it anyway."

"Things have been cleaned up in the bathing chamber, so there shouldn't be any reason for people to connect things that happened here," Jade informed me.

King Thomas spluttered and strode to the bathing area, only to return a moment later. "It doesn't look like anything at all went on in there."

Jade gave the king a patronizing look. "Yes, Your Highness, that would be the whole point. If you sent the man away, you can't leave evidence around the place that he was killed here."

"Is this the type of thing they teach you mercenaries?" King Thomas snapped. "You just kill people and make it so no one ever knows?"

Sensing what might be the real reason for his irritation, I walked up to the king and placed my hand on his arm. "I'm sorry you didn't get to say goodbye to him. You will just have to trust me when I tell you, you wouldn't want to see him that way. The spell was destroying him from the inside out, and I highly doubt he would have wanted that image to be the last thing you think of about him."

The king's shoulders sagged at my words. "I know I shouldn't mourn the loss of a man who was using and manipulating me, but I just can't seem to wrap my head around that yet."

"When this is all over, there will be time to mourn those we've lost along the way. Right now, we need to put on a good show and enjoy a meal together. We can talk to the queen and see about getting out to the summer home," I said, speaking to myself as much as him.

The loss of my parents I couldn't lock away last night, but now it was tucked away behind a door in my mind. Eventually, it would be opened, and I would allow myself to feel that pain once more, but now wasn't the time.

"Yes, you're right," King Thomas agreed, clearing his throat and dabbing at his eyes. "Come, I believe my wife will be waiting for us. She's rather overly punctual to these sorts of things."

I waited a moment for Abbott to come alongside and tuck my arm into the crook of his elbow, leading me out of the room. He'd always been so skilled at knowing when I needed someone to lean on emotionally—my stalwart knight, ready to defend my heart along with my body. It just showed me once more how each of these men provided something for me that another couldn't, but together, covered it all.

The king led us out of his personal chambers, further into the private section of the castle into a dining room. It was stunning with murals painted on the ceiling and a highly polished marble floor of white with gold veins running through it.

"Oh good, you're all here," the queen said as she came to greet us.

She took her husband's hands and kissed both cheeks before moving to Gavin, then offering me the same greeting. "It's so lovely to have family here in the castle. We never get to use this dining hall. Did you know that when the castle was first built, it was so small that *this* very room was the main hall? Now look at us, it's incredible!" She continued to chat, pointing out this or that in the space. "Now, you must be famished. I hear you were too tuckered out even to eat breakfast. You need to take better care of yourself, especially if you're already with child. When I was pregnant with Charles, I was so tired and slept all the time."

I was so shocked by her assumption I didn't know how to respond. *What possessed the queen to believe that I was with child? Could that even happen with how recently I've been engaging in sex?* My stomach was tied in knots at the thought of it.

"I'm sorry, Your Majesty, but I'm not pregnant. I've been making sure to take my tonic since now would not be a good time for that to happen," I corrected.

Queen Catharine paused to look at me with a frown. "No, that can't be." She strode over to me and held out both hands.

"Ah…" I stammered unsure of what was happening.

"Your hands, dear girl. It's my gift to be able to tell these things," she informed me, motioning for me to hurry up.

"Are you saying it's your Birthright to tell if a woman is pregnant, Aunt Catharine?" Gavin inquired.

"Of course, didn't your mother ever tell you that?" she tutted. "Well, I suppose since I'm the elder sister and she didn't get the Birthright, she wouldn't want to share that. Mary hated having me best her in anything in life."

Licking my lips, terrified of what she was going to say, I placed my hands in hers. Queen Catharine closed her eyes and took a deep breath. The room was deathly silent as a smile bloomed on her face. "Yes, there it is, the glow of a little life growing within you. Oh... wait, there are two! That's odd... one seems to be slightly further along than the other." She opened her eyes and looked at the men around me. "I suppose with so many to meet your needs, it shouldn't be strange that you might bear two different men's offspring at the same time."

My hand shot out, grabbing Abbott's arm, my fingers digging into his muscle as the magnitude of what I'd just been told hit me.

I...

I... was...

I... was... pregnant... with not one baby but two.

The world started to tunnel around me, my vision growing darker until I passed out.

"I didn't mean to upset the poor thing," I heard the queen say, her voice seeming miles away. "Here, lay her down. No one will bother us in my personal sitting room."

Someone placed me on something soft, but my mind still refused to return to the world. Hands lifted my head, and when it was set back down, I knew I was resting on someone's lap. Fingers combed through my hair as I felt magic pressing at my mental barrier. Part of me wanted to stay shut in here where it was safe. If I didn't acknowledge that I no longer was the ruler of my own body, then what I've already gone through never happened. Scene after scene of my reckless actions flashed through my brain. I'd been carrying a child, and I didn't even know it.

"Little warrior, let me in."

I knew it would be Izel. He was the only one who would be able to enter my mind at this point besides Vasin. Being my pair-bond, I wouldn't have been able to keep him out, so that left my consort.

"Tell me it was all a dream you fed me, and I'll let you in," I countered.

"You know I wouldn't do that. As much as I want children with you, that isn't the way I'd go about convincing you to consider it. Everyone knows now isn't the right time, but it seems the fates had other plans," Izel reasoned.

"Damn the fates!" I screamed. *"How could they do this to me? I did everything I was supposed to do to ensure this didn't happen. We are at war. How can I possibly do what needs to be done knowing I carry not one but two other lives inside my body?"*

"Cassarah, this is not a conversation to have like this. Come back to us, and we will manage just as we have through everything else... together."

I knew he was right. While I might be upset about this sudden twist in my life, it affected them as much as it did me. Two of them would be fathers far sooner than we had planned. It would make sense to be Jade and Abbott since they were the ones I slept with first. How far along could I possibly even be? It's only been a few weeks. Without the queen's gift, I doubt I would have shown any signs for another few months.

Would that have been better?

Does knowing now change how I would have handled things?

"Cass, stop acting like a child. You are going to be a mother now, and while it might not be what you planned, this is how it is. Yes, this wasn't something you saw coming, but it changes nothing about what needs to happen. If anything, now you have more reason to finish things," Vasin cut in, speaking the hard truth I needed. *"Get up, Cassarah. We are near the end of this, so you better finish what you started."*

I could feel Izel's magic caress over me. *"You're not in this alone, little warrior. Let us walk through this with you. These babies already have eight fathers and two aunties who will do everything in their power to keep them safe."* A ghostly image of him appeared in my mind with a hand reaching out to me. *"Trust us, just take the first step, and we will meet you there."*

Taking a deep breath, I clasped his hand and let him pull me out of the mental bubble I'd put myself in. As I opened my eyes, I found my men standing around the settee I was placed on. Izel helped me to sit up, but he pulled me close so I could lean on him as he wrapped his arms around me.

"I'm sorry. I didn't mean to scare you all. That was just not information I was expecting to receive," I apologized.

A maid approached with a goblet of water, which I took. Paxton swiped it out of my hands and took a sip of it first, paused a moment, and handed it back to me. "Can't be too careful right now."

"So you think drinking the poison yourself would be the right call?" I snapped. "What if there had been something in it, then you'd have died. Trust me when I say that would not have made things better."

Paxton gave me a guilty look as he rubbed the back of his neck. "Sorry, I wasn't thinking and just reacted."

Queen Catharine waved Paxton aside so she could speak to me, sitting on the edge of the settee. "I'm so sorry, dear. I didn't know you didn't want children. Sometimes, my excitement about things gets the better of me, and I don't always take into account how you would feel about the news. The world is changing, and not every woman wants to be a mother."

"That's not it. At some point I do want to be a mother. My hope was this war would be over before that happened, though. Right now, all I can think about is how I'm going to put my children in danger. In war, there is no predicting what could happen, and that is what had me so out of sorts," I assured her.

"You know what would be good for you... a visit to the summer house. It's out of the city, a little quieter, and has beautiful views all around. That's where I went when I was pregnant with both my children. Then you don't have to worry about prying eyes watching you blow up like a balloon and eat everything in sight," Queen Catharine shared, patting my knee.

My jaw dropped at how easily she'd just offered a fantastic reason for us to leave the city. If anyone heard about the trip, word would spread about my condition, which the Lost King might believe, or he might think it's part of the plan to get me there. In no other way has there been the slightest speculation that I could be pregnant.

"Thank you, Your Majesty. That's such a kind offer," I said, giving her an encouraging smile. "Only if it's not too much trouble. I wouldn't want you to feel obligated to offer that to me."

"Nonsense, child," she answered, waving off my worry. "I think a trip out there sounds lovely. We can even take the children, and you can start to see what it's like to be a mother."

Panic at the idea of the kids being there if something went wrong had me turning to her husband. When he noticed my attention on him, I gave a slight shake no, hoping he would step in and make some excuse.

"My love, while I'm sure you have good intentions, it's still early in her pregnancy. Let the poor thing wrap her mind around it for a few days, then we can send the children up," he reasoned.

The queen pouted but nodded. "I suppose you're right. We still have eight months yet before she has to be ready. Keeping her calm and healthy should be the focus of this whole thing after such a spell."

My body sagged in relief, knowing that innocent lives wouldn't be in jeopardy. While I didn't trust Roulf to be honest about much, I didn't think he was lying when he said if anyone touched the box the dragon heart was in, it would kill them. That sounds exactly like something the Lost King would do to ensure he stayed immortal and protected from danger.

"Do you feel well enough to head back into the dining room? It would help settle you to get some food in your stomach. I know you probably feel like eating is the last thing you want to do, but it will help," Queen Catharine urged, rising from the settee.

"Yes, of course, here I am causing everyone else to go hungry with all my drama," I answered, motioning for Dayson, who was close by to help me up.

While I felt perfectly fine, the queen clearly expected me to act a certain way now that I was carrying a child, and I would pretend the best I could. Granted, it looked like my men were just as concerned about my situation as she was. That would be a conversation for later when it was just us. I didn't plan to be the woman who hid herself away while she created life. I'd been instructed my whole life that it was unseemly for a woman large with child to be wandering about where people could see her. There is nothing unseemly about creating life, and as Queen of Sheca, I wouldn't be hiding behind any closed doors.

Dayson wrapped my arm around his as he led me back toward the dining hall, walking extremely slow. "Day," I whispered. "You aren't going to break me by walking at a normal speed."

He glanced down at me as if he didn't believe a word I just said but sped up to a normal pace. "It wasn't just a shock to you."

"I'm fully aware of that," I agreed. "When we finish lunch, I plan for all of us to sit and talk. This isn't just about me or you, there are nine of us directly affected by this surprise."

"Are you happy?" he questioned.

It was a fair question, and I didn't blame him for questioning that. "Now that I've had a moment to wrap my head around the idea, yes, of course, I'm happy. What makes me sad is the moment is overshadowed by the fact I have a madman to kill."

"You mean *we*," Dayson corrected. "We have a madman to kill. That duty isn't resting solely on your shoulders, you know. The rest of us have more than enough reason to end him before this factor was added to the equation."

"Let's get through lunch, then we can all talk. I have a feeling the queen is going to smother me with all her good intentions." I sighed, resting my head on his arm as we returned to the dining hall.

"All right, everyone, take your seats, and I'll try not to share any more earth-shattering insights," Queen Catharine said with a chuckle, sitting next to her husband.

Twenty-Seven
Dayson

The last thing I wanted to do right now was to sit here and play nice with the stupidest, kindest queen I've ever encountered. Was this normal for royals? Did they all have a few marbles missing in their brains? Gavin's father went mad, and his mother now thinks everyone is out to get her since her children want to steal the throne. King Thomas couldn't use the head that actually did the thinking, and Queen Catharine had an entire personality change once Cassarah freed her mind.

I was a simple man who grew up with things being black, white, and gray when it came to the jobs we took. There were rules we followed, but when you knew them, you also understood which ones you could break if need be.

The Bronze Reaper clan I grew up in were warriors. If people needed help in a fight, we were who they came to. Our clan was simple and slightly more barbaric than others, but we lived in the harsh mountains closer to the Unclaimed Dragon Lands. Not much grew, so we fought and scraped for everything we had. The black ink markings I bore on my skin proved my prowess in battle. Being the son of the clan leader meant I had expectations to live up to, and I did.

If you'd told me I'd be a consort to a queen of our people, sitting at a fancy table, eating food I've never heard of before, I would have laughed in your face. Why would I give up everything I worked for to have that kind of life?

The answer to that would be—Cassarah.

My Cassy-bear, the woman who was so strong but allowed me to protect her. For the most part, she let me guard and shield her from dangers, even though she didn't have to. From what Cole and Abbott told me, she was a fighter in her own right. Even Jade had commented he was impressed with how she handled herself in the first encounter with the Lost King when they saved Gavin.

Now the woman I cherished more than life itself was growing life inside her. The urge to snatch her out of her chair and lock her away somewhere safe away from all of this rode me hard. If there was one thing Bronze Reapers treasured more than their reputation, it was children. Not many women chose to have them, knowing the world was only becoming more dangerous. So when it occurred, those women were looked after by the whole clan and banned from taking any jobs that would endanger them.

This world was on the verge of another great war, and my woman was in the dead center of it. How could I let her go after the Lost King now? Of course, if she knew what I was thinking, I'd get my ass chewed out. She was as fierce as any Reaper, and I had no doubt she'd take the same stance as many of them, furious at the coddling.

"Lovely, then we will plan to leave for the summer home in the morning. The trip isn't long... about half a day's ride in a carriage," Queen Catharine shared.

"Oh well, we would be going by dragon, so it might be slightly faster for us," Cassarah said.

The queen paled at this. "You can't ride those beasts while you're *pregnant.*"

The stony anger that appeared on Cassarah's face at the queen calling Vasin a beast made me cringe. I've learned in our time together not many things will flip the switch and make cold Cassarah present herself—that was definitely one of them.

"Vasin is not a beast," Cassarah snapped. "He is my pair-bond who I would trust with my life and my children's lives. There is nowhere safer than with him. Riding in a carriage, we could be attacked, horses spooked and driven off a cliff, or a wheel breaks, and we are stranded with no other option than to wait for help. No, Your Majesty, I would much rather take my chances on the back of my dragon."

Queen Catharine quickly realized her mistake and took Cassarah's scolding with grace. "I apologize. We here in Creisal don't have much experience with dragons. I fear I've let the stories we've been told growing up influence me."

"Your sister ended up with a dragon," Cassarah countered.

The queen nodded. "Yes, that happened after she was set to marry the late king. With her status, this allowed her to be at the next dragon hatching. The golden dragon picked her, and there you have it, a woman who'd never thought she'd have a chance as the second sibling secured a crown and a dragon."

Interesting. The queen seemed bothered by this for some reason. "Were you ever at a dragon hatching?" I asked.

She looked over in my direction, and I could tell by the sour look on her face that she had not been picked. "I attended one before I came to Creisal, and that was more than enough interaction with a dragon for me. While all of your dragons seem to be well-mannered, I've seen what they can do left un-paired. When food gets scarce in the Unclaimed Dragon Lands, they venture out here and go after our farmers' livestock. The devastation they bring is unmanageable."

"While I understand your experience with them has left a bad taste in your mouth, I do request you keep in mind that, like people, there are those that are good and those that are bad. In many ways, dragons have been slaves to us until recently. The reason Birthrights ever came into existence is the bond with dragons. Their connection to a human when cemented with a bite injecting their venom into us, is what gives us the magic we share through the generations," Cassarah informed the queen.

The king and queen looked shocked.

"I won't bore you with the details since things have changed with the dragons, and only those they choose to share their gift with will receive it. Thank you for this lovely lunch, and I look forward to visiting your summer home you've described with such love," Cassarah said, rising to her feet. "I will retire to my rooms if you should need me for anything, King Thomas."

Taking this as a signal, I shoved out of my chair and headed right for Cassarah. She smiled at me as I took her hand, leading her out of the dining hall. Once we were back in the main section of the castle, I took a deep breath and rolled my neck to shake out the tension that had been building.

"Did you enjoy yourself, Day?" Cassarah asked, a teasing lilt to her words.

I glared down at her. "I'm not a man meant for palace niceties. My place is out in the training yards or on a job... a man of action."

She nodded in understanding. "Trust me when I say I want our visit here to be as short as possible. I don't find Creisal to be as agreeable to my senses as I first thought."

"It's certainly made an impression," Pax muttered as he fell into step with us. "I swear, the more time I spend here, the happier I am that I never have to come back if I don't want to. It's part of the reason I would take any and all jobs I could to keep from being trapped here."

"That surprises me," I commented. "This seems just like the kind of people you would hang around. So many secrets for you to learn and use against people."

"Maybe that's who I was, but *someone* seems to have been rubbing off on me, and I couldn't imagine having to deal with all that drama now. Just seeing Percilla the other night made me so uncomfortable, nothing about her appealed to me in the slightest," Pax shared, shivering at the thought. "Speaking of her, I really should take some time to catch up with her father. I feel like he might be useful to us."

Cassarah reached out and grasped his arm, drawing his attention. "I would greatly like to meet this man as well."

Pax's eyebrows rose at this. "What possible reason would you have to do that?"

"He was a great influence on your life and possibly to apologize for my actions toward his daughter. Whichever one you think he'll believe more," she answered with a shrug.

"Oh, spitfire, I do truly love that brain of yours. It comes up with the best situations," Paxton praised, kissing her cheek. "All right, I'll be off to visit my old friend and see what he's up to."

Breaking off from the group, Pax gave us a wave before disappearing down a hall. "That man worries me sometimes," I commented.

"He's just a wild spirit who hasn't had a reason to be tamed," Cassarah shared, leaning into me. "Much like the warrior who's now the noble."

I grunted at that, seeing as she made a fairly valid point.

"Mouse, wait right here. The rest of us are going to check your rooms before you enter," Cole instructed, giving me a look to stay with her. I nodded, to which he returned, slipped past the door, and entered her room.

"Is this going to be a new step in how things go?" Cassarah asked.

"Yes. I'd get used to the fact we are going to be highly overprotective for the rest of your life," I answered.

She chuckled and shoved me gently with her shoulder. "Weren't you already doing that?"

"Not to the degree we are now with you being pregnant," I pointed out. "You might not like it, but we're their fathers, and no self-respecting member of the clans would allow their woman to place themselves in danger unnecessarily."

"Yes, well, we are going to have a conversation about just that once everyone gets back and settled," Cassarah informed me.

I tucked my free hand under her chin, lifting her face to mine. "We know you aren't going to like it, but this is one moment where you are not allowed to be queen and just make an order for us to follow. I know we will find an agreement, but don't think both parties won't have to give a little."

Cassarah didn't answer, but I think she heard what I was trying to say. There was no way we would let her do something drastic if another option was available. This needed to be discussed tonight before we left for the summer home, where danger would be lurking.

Becka helped Cassarah into more relaxed clothes, and she laid down. She was asleep almost instantly, but that didn't surprise me. The few hours she got before lunch wasn't enough for her to be rested. Then, you add on all that happened in such a short period of time, and I don't blame her for shutting the world out and sleeping.

The guys and I gathered in the sitting area, looking at one another in shock.

"How did this happen?" Gavin asked, dropping his head into his hands. "She told us she didn't want kids right now, and we did nothing to prevent it."

"She was taking the tonic," Abbott pointed out. "We should have been told if we couldn't finish inside her or if there were other precautions we should have been taking. Plenty of women use the tonic and stave off pregnancy."

"How many of those women have eight men they're fucking?" Jade asked bluntly. "Cassarah might not have been in danger if it was only one man's passion she was dealing with—"

"Our passion? Now I know you know that isn't the case. That woman is more veracious than any man. She needed to have eight of us to control it," Zan pointed out.

I gave an approving grunt to that as I nodded. "When it was my night with her, she rode me 'til we both passed out. There really shouldn't be any surprise at her being with child. Plus, it sounds like it happened right away, and if I'm not mistaken, that leads me to believe you two are the true fathers to those babies," I said, pointing at Jade and Abbott. "Not that it matters... whatever child Cassarah has is all of ours, just so we're clear."

"Dayson's right. What happened, happened, and now we need to ensure that Cassarah realizes what's at stake here. It's no longer just her life she holds in the balance but those of our children as well," Cole commented, his face scrunched in a scowl.

Izel shot to his feet, surprising us all with this reaction. "Listen to you guys," he whispered harshly, trying not to raise his voice. "Do you honestly think she isn't fully aware of what's at stake? She was going to hide away in her own mind where it was safe instead of returning to reality because she was terrified of what this meant. Who is the one person we can *always* count on to think of everyone else but herself in these moments? Shame on each of you for getting blinded by your own fears and not seeing just how scared she is."

As much as Izel's words hit me in the gut, I knew they did because it was true. Yes, we needed to adjust to this reality as much as she did, but none of us were the ones growing life inside our bodies. Never had I met a more selfless person than my Cassy-bear, which made me doubt her all the worse.

"So what do we do then?" Gavin asked. "How can we still let her fight?"

"As much as I would like to say that was our call to make, it's not," Izel reasoned. "Cassarah is still her own person, even if she's carrying our children. What we need to do is support her, protect her the best we can, and let her know, as always, she's not alone in this."

Jade let out a groan of frustration, sagging into his chair. "I know you're right, Izel, but that doesn't mean I like it."

"None of us are going to like doing it, but it's what must happen if we don't want her to pull away from us," Zan added. "Now, who's going to stand guard while the rest of us get some sleep? No one got much last night."

I raised my hand. "I'll stay. It looks like May and Becka are too, so go. In a few hours, I'll wake one of your asses up to switch with me if Paxton doesn't come back with the spymaster before then."

They nodded in agreement and shuffled out of the room, leaving me to watch over our woman and unborn children.

TWENTY-EIGHT
CASSARAH

A loud knock at my door snapped me out of my sleep and had me sitting up in bed, panic squeezing my chest. Becka walked up to the door and opened it a crack while May came to stand beside me, her blade drawn and ready to act. Abbott came over to the bed, waving for me to go to him, which I did quickly.

He strode across the space and pulled me into the dressing room. He kept the door cracked so he could hear what was going on. I could hear Becka's voice but not what she was saying and the bass tone of another man's voice in response.

"Please wait, My Lord. Her Majesty isn't ready to receive a guest at the moment. If you wait in the sitting room across the hall, I will alert her to your presence, and we will join you there. I know she has been eager to clear the air with you on the situation that occurred during the feast," Becka said, loud enough that we could hear her.

"It's the spymaster," I concluded. "Here, help me get into this dress."

I pulled my nightgown over my head and grabbed what I needed for this meeting. This man needed to know I was queen and to be respected in that position. The fact that he came banging on my door, already told me he didn't think I deserved any reverence for my status. I pulled the gold silk underdress over my head and slipped my arms into the long sleeves.

"Help me with the skirt... this material is rather heavy," I requested, handing the black brocade fabric to Abbott.

He fumbled a bit, but we managed to get it to work. Once he secured the skirt, he pulled on the bodice of matching black brocade, but this had the Shecan royal crest stitched onto the front of it. If that man thought he was going to play ignorant, then he had another thing coming to him.

"Oh, good. You're almost ready," Becka said as she stepped into the room. "I'll help her finish up, Abbott, if you'll get the others. I think it's best if everyone is present for this discussion since he decided to bring *her* along."

"That bastard brought his daughter along with him?" Abbott demanded.

"Yes, now go. I don't want to leave Paxton in there with them longer than I need to," Becka explained as she shooed him out.

Now, it was my turn to get upset. "Why is he in there alone with them?"

"Cassarah, I need you to trust your man right now," Becka scolded as she laced up the back. "That wily idiot has some sort of plan going on that I can't figure out, but the sooner we get you in there, the better. I'm afraid he might kill her himself if she keeps ignoring his brushoffs."

"You'd think me almost killing her would get the point across," I muttered.

Becka grabbed my shoulders and spun me around. "Yes, well, one might just believe you put him under a spell and forced him to become your consort."

"Is that the nonsense she's spouting?" I demanded, ready to charge out of the room.

"Whoa there. You need one more thing before you go all Dragon Queen on her ass," she said as she held me back. Pausing, I took a deep breath and waited for her to set my crown on my head. "There, now you can go kill the bitch, and she won't be able to mistake you for anything but the queen you are."

I couldn't help but snort at that as I let her escort me out of the room and across the hall. All my men were present, standing behind a couch where Paxton sat glaring at the woman across from him. Percilla looked at him as if she wanted to eat him more than she wanted to kiss him. Anger seemed to be making her one eye twitch as she turned her gaze to me. She wore a sickly green color that did no favors to her complexion, but I guess it was the height of fashion right now.

Paxton rose, walked over to me, took my hand, and escorted me to where he'd been sitting to face the spymaster and Percilla. "My love, this is Lord Belin, the king's spymaster. Lord Belin, the Dragon Queen Cassarah of Sheca, ruler of the mercenaries and friend to the dragons."

Lord Belin and Percilla remained seated, looking up at me as if I were beneath them.

I turned to Pax and cocked my head to the side in confusion. "Is it not customary for those of lower stations not to greet a royal properly? Do they not bow or curtsy? I believe I did see that happening for King Thomas and Queen Catharine. One might believe these two mean to slight me when I have done nothing to deserve such treatment."

"That custom is the same here as it is in all other kingdoms," Paxton informed me.

Nodding, I turned to look at the two idiots seated before me. "I see, so they do mean to slight me..."

Abbott and Dayson drew their swords, marched over, and pointed the tips of their blades at their throats. When neither of them moved, the blades got closer, and Dayson even nicked the spymaster, a telltale drop of blood rolling down his neck.

"If you wish to live, I suggest you recall your manners quickly. Otherwise, you leave me no choice but to end your lives here and now," I informed them as I sat on the couch, spreading my skirts as if I didn't have a care in the world.

Percilla let out a sob, and fat tears rolled down her cheeks. "Please forgive me, I was only doing as my father directed me to. He said you were weak-willed and didn't deserve to be bowed to or shown any respect at all."

Glancing at her father, I saw his face pale, and his eyes flick in her direction as she spoke those words. "You lying whore, this was your idea. All I've heard since you got back from the feast last night is how the bitch queen stole Paxton from you and beat you up in front of everyone. You wanted to get back at her by pulling this stunt, and I told you it was an awful idea." He then faced me, his eyes beseeching. "Please, Your Majesty, have your guardian stand down, and I will get on my knees to beg for forgiveness."

Percilla let out a snarl at her father. Seeing that they were no longer concerned about the blades at their throats, I waved them off. No sense in killing them when they were going to spill their guts.

"Spymaster, ha! You are nothing but a pathetic old man who doesn't know a goddamn thing going on in this world. How many times have you brushed off information that was useful, only to have these bastards make you pay *them*," she ranted, pointing at Paxton. "Those spies knew you were useless, so they milked you for all you were worth, leaving us noble only in name and nothing else. You used my dowry to buy back secrets you tossed aside. Then, this bitch shows up taking the only man I ever wanted from me because you didn't see his value. He could have been the next spymaster and been brilliant at it."

Part of me wanted to let this go on, letting her spill all the ammunition I needed to get the spymaster to tell me what I wanted to know, but then again, maybe he knew nothing at all.

"I think that is quite enough," I cut in. "Abbott, would you be so kind as to remove Percilla and have one of the palace guards place her in a jail cell? I believe she needs a night to reflect on her behavior toward others."

Abbott nodded and dragged the screaming woman out of the sitting room, leaving me alone with the supposed spymaster. The second the door was closed, the man dropped to his knees and groveled. "Please spare me, Your Majesty. I never should have let her talk me into something so foolish. I'll do anything to save my life for this heinous way I've behaved."

"Then tell me everything you know about what the queen has been doing behind the king's back. I'm positive someone has brought it to your attention, and the king himself had you looking into things." I raised my hand to stop him from speaking. "Before you speak, I want to know *everything*. The information you thought was useful and the crazy theories you tossed out. Leave nothing unsaid. Do I make myself clear?"

His head bobbed up and down in silent agreement.

"Then you may speak," I ordered.

The spymaster moved to sit on the couch again and settled himself back into a person I believed should be given the position he held. "As you said, the king became suspicious of the queen and situations he discovered after investigating. He asked me to have my men and women look into what she's been up to. At first, it didn't look like anything was going on, but then we started to follow the people around her, like Sir Roulf. That man is one sneaky rat, exchanging notes with people in the dead of night and helping to coordinate supplies to be sent to Utros. Through investigating him, it was revealed a network of people had been brought in from other nations to work in the city."

"You didn't tell the king this?" Paxton demanded, cutting into the story.

"Of course I did, but there was nothing about the interactions that I could say for certain were traitorous. They could be exchanging notes with their families for all I knew," the spymaster countered.

Paxton let out a frustrated growl. "Why didn't you have someone intercept one of the exchanges, allowing you to see what was written in the notes? Then you would have had proof you needed, or better yet, just arrest one of them to question them for information. Clearly, you felt like things weren't as they seemed."

The spymaster's jaw clenched at the attack, his hands balling into fists with anger rolling off him. It was almost as if I was seeing the real man for the first time. This whole thing had been an act. He'd tried to play me into believing he really wanted to help, that his daughter was the problem, not him. The problem with that was he wasn't a good actor himself, and this bumbling idiot act wasn't working for him.

"Something upsetting you?" I questioned. "All of his questions were reasonable. You forget you're talking to a group of mercenaries. I might be queen, but I was trained just like the others to spot deceit and get information out of people. What you've been saying are things I already know, but you know that, don't you? Did the Lost King pay you off? Offer you something you couldn't refuse in exchange for being the worst spymaster in history?"

This had Lord Belin on his feet, his face bright red with anger. "You two-bit dragon whore! The Lost King is who should be ruling our world. He sees what's become of us and how to make it right. We need to be united under one ruler instead of divided, allowing some to become prosperous while others fight and scrape to make a living in desolate lands."

Dayson, who'd stayed close by, held out his sword, blocking the man from advancing on me.

"Tell me, Lord Belin, where were you born? By the sounds of it, it wasn't here in Creisal. My guess would be Errit," I mused. "Could it be that your family sent you to this court to be raised and trained in their military? That's the only thing that makes sense for you to land yourself in this position without being noble born in Creisal. You must have been quite the soldier to impress your superiors... now look what you've become."

"Do not speak of what you do not know! Errit is a dying land, a dry desert wasteland no one can make anything grow in. When the Lost King married our princess, it was the best thing that happened. We got supplies from Utros, the people began to flourish as traders, other merchants started to sell to us, and we could travel to their lands doing the same. While I was lucky to make it into the military here, I still have family back home who have suffered greatly. I did what I could to help them, but the previous king was cheap and felt that food and lodging were enough for his soldiers," Lord Belin roared. "So yes, I'm loyal to the Lost King but out of my own choice and not by being bought."

I watched him for a moment, absorbing all he'd told me, which was far more than he knew. Dearest Henry had started this whole thing by gaining the trust and respect of the people in Utros and Errit, then sent them out into the world to sow the seeds of him unifying the kingdoms together under one rule. Then, he knew he needed to start a war when people started to resist the mind games in other kingdoms that weren't as hard-pressed for that type of change. The Lost King was patient, placing what tools and people he needed in the right positions and watching them eat away at the kingdom from the inside out.

"So, I'm guessing you aren't going to help us destroy him then?" I asked, calmly folding my hands in my lap.

"I'd sooner slit my own throat than help you," Lord Belin spat.

Nodding, I turned my gaze to Dayson. "Would you be so kind as to help our spymaster out with that request?"

Without hesitation, Dayson grabbed the man, dropped him to his knees, grabbed his hair to pull back his head, and slit his throat. There was a gargled gasp as the spymaster's life leaked onto the rug as he dropped, eyes wide in shock, mouth moving as if he was trying to speak.

"It seems I owe the king and queen a new rug." I sighed. Paxton pulled me to my feet as the pool of blood seeped closer. "Jade, I don't know how you got rid of the other body, but will you be able to do it again?"

"Yeah, there is window access, so it should be fine. I dropped the last guy out the window, and Tahir burned him to a crisp. No one will be able to tell who or what it was once dragon fire is done with it," he explained.

Leaving him to it, with Zan's help, I returned to my room and sat on the edge of the bed, holding my stomach. "I feel like I'm going to be sick." Becka quickly grabbed the basin used for washing my face and placed it in my hands. "The smell of his blood brought me back to the house last night. There was so much blood and gore everywhere, bodies rotting, having been left there for a few days," I shared, ducking my head and rubbing my belly.

Becka worked on getting me out of the bodice, and the moment the ties were loosened, it helped to make breathing easier. A cool cloth was placed on my neck, and I looked up to see Gavin next to me with concern etched on his face.

"Are you sure that was a wise move to kill him? What if he was able to tell us more, or we could use him to find other connections?" he asked, taking my chin in his hand while using another cool cloth to wipe my face.

"He would never have told us anything, and what he did tell was by mistake," I shared, closing my eyes as his soothing touch brushed over my skin. "The loyalty he had toward the Lost King was rooted deep in his heart and soul. There was nothing that man wanted more than to have Henry rule over this world, giving the dream of a united front where everyone was taken care of."

"Still, what was the purpose of killing him before you spoke to the king?" he challenged.

I reached up and grabbed his wrist, pulling his hand away from my face so I could look him in the eye. "A man with that much power would have been incredibly dangerous to leave alive. There is no telling what kind of system he actually has running through this kingdom. He might have acted like a fool to throw people off, but, in reality, he was incredibly smart and conniving. We need a miracle for any chance we get to the summer home without an army descending upon us. The battle won't happen in the fields between Creisal and Norden. It's going to happen right here on the shores of the Caleden Sea, hidden from sight just as everything else had been done in the shadows."

"So, us going to the summer house tomorrow will be the beginning of the end?" Gavin questioned, finally realizing what I'd known all along.

"Yes, the final battle will be waged, and whoever gets to the dragon heart first gets to determine how this will end. What I don't know is if the magic also repels Henry from taking the heart. All magic has consequences, some worse than others, but a spell that cheats death will require something great in return," I shared, feeling the truth of my words like a rock in the pit of my stomach.

Everyone looked at me, clearly uneasy. I could tell some of them wanted to argue or keep me from going, but they kept their thoughts to themselves.

"It's all right... say what's on your mind. You have every right to share your feelings, even if we won't see eye to eye," I encouraged them. "We are partners in every aspect of our lives, and you deserve to be heard as much as I do."

No one spoke right away, and the sound of the door opening had everyone burst into action, but they quickly realized it was Jade and Zan returning. They both paused, looking wary, seeing something in the other's expressions.

"What did we miss?" Jade asked.

"I just explained to them that in going to the summer home, we are meeting the Lost King and his wrath head-on," I explained. "They were just about to tell me how they felt about the situation."

"You don't really want us to do that, little bird. What we think you won't like," Jade stated.

"All the same, you have every right to speak your mind and be heard," I countered. "I won't say anything. I'll just listen."

Cole walked up to me and cupped my face in his hands, holding my gaze intently. "Cassarah, you are now carrying our children. I know you understand this, but it worries us to no end since we've seen you pull some crazy stunts. As Izel reminded us, there is no one who has a heart as big as yours for others as you do. We need to know that applies to doing everything possible to keep you three alive and healthy. None of us have said it because, like you, the news was shocking and unexpected, but we are over the moon that we will be fathers someday in the near future. All that we ask is that you protect them with everything you have while we do the same for you."

My heart ached at his words. While in a way they hurt, feeling like they didn't trust me to protect the children growing inside me, I also understood why they would feel that way. The last time we were in a battle, I did things that would certainly put them at risk. Then some events have recently unfolded that could have caused me to lose them. I'd promised I would hear them out, and I would. I needed to understand their fears so I could help them move past them the best way possible.

I covered his hands with my own and smiled. "Thank you for being honest, my love." He pressed a kiss to my lips and stepped back with the others. "Does anyone else have something to say, or did he speak for the group?"

"Little bird," Jade said, crossing his arms. "I need you to look me in the eye and tell me that putting your life on the line is no longer a thing you'll consider."

Holding his seafoam green eyes with my own, I answered. "My life is no longer my own, Jade. There are two other lives who share mine, and I will do everything in my power to protect them so I will get the joy of being their mother." I paused, taking a calming breath before I continued, "But hear me when I say I'm not going to be treated like an invalid just because I'm with child. No one is going to lock me away for the last few months of my pregnancy just because I grow too round. The fact I'm going to be a mother has nothing to do with how I will rule the kingdom I'm in charge of. None of you will be able to keep me from having a normal life before or after these children come into the world. I love each of you more than life itself, and I understand you want me to be safe, but don't put me in a bubble. I will only resent you."

"If you allow us to keep you safe, Cassy-bear, then we will happily let you live the life you want. We want our lives to be filled with joy and happiness. None of us want to strip that from you in this new journey, but for that to work, we need to do this together," Dayson interjected.

"I agree with everything you've said, even if it does sting a little that you're convinced I won't protect myself," I shared, dropping my gaze at the bowl still in my hands.

Someone kneeled in front of me, took the bowl and set it aside, then grasped both my hands.

"My heart," Zan crooned, causing me to lift my gaze. "That is not what we believe, but we also know how strong your conviction is. Ending this battle is all we've been focused on for the past few months, and it's consumed our every thought. All we want is to know this mission you've been set on doesn't overshadow the future we now see growing inside you."

He reached out and placed one hand on my stomach. "I never thought I would have a family of my own... no one would want to risk the chance of their child being born blind. This is the greatest gift I could ever receive, and it scares the hell out of me that it might be ripped from us before it can ever start. The Lost King is not one who believes in the sanctity of life."

"What Zan said, none of this is an attack on you," Gavin assured me. "This is all because we don't trust the Lost King not to play a trick on you or somehow force you into a situation where you put yourself in danger. We wish we could take you out of this fight, but we won't. You need to see this through. It's your purpose in life, and the fates have decided you are the one who will bring this war to an end. We only wish it wasn't the case, but we will be beside you the entire time." The others all nodded in agreement.

"Now that you have got all this off your chests, I suggest we get some dinner and then call it an early night so everyone is well-rested for the world to implode around us," Becka interjected, breaking the tension hanging in the room. "Let's get this bodice on you, and we can join the rest of the court for dinner. It would be best for them to see things happening as if we didn't kill two people today."

That made my stomach lurch again. I quickly grabbed the bowl and emptied my stomach of what was left from lunch. A cloth and a goblet of water were handed to me to wipe my mouth.

"Do we think we could keep the talk of death, killing, and corpses to a minimum?" I groaned. "That seems to be incredibly upsetting at the moment."

"Damn, if I didn't know you were pregnant, I would have thought you'd gotten soft on us," Becka teased as she took the bowl from me. "Seems you were going to start showing signs soon enough."

"You might be my best friend, but I kind of hate you right now," I muttered as she helped me redress.

Becka planted a sloppy kiss on my cheek. "That's how it works with sisters... get used to it. Now pull yourself together, and let's get this show on the road. We need this to be believable."

Twenty-Nine
Cassarah

Thankfully, dinner went off without further incidents, and we enjoyed our meal with the king, queen, and Prince Phillip. It was decided he would remain at the castle with the king and keep an eye on things. We arranged it so my people would follow along with us since we were leading everyone to believe I would be out there for some time. The king would have men ready if they needed to come to our aid, but my feelings were this battle wouldn't be an all-out attack.

Abbott and Cole spent the night with me, and we did little else but hold each other as we slept, needing the reassurance that everything would be all right. I kept waking as nightmares plagued my dreams of all the people who'd died the past few days. Their dead eyes and condemning words made my sleep fitful. Each time I would awaken, sweating and panicked, Abbott would soothe me, humming a song I didn't know. His tone was deep, and sometimes he would whisper the words of hope and love in my ear, chasing away the shadows. Cole buried his face in my chest, wrapping his arms around my middle, holding me tightly so I knew I wasn't alone no matter what.

I was thankful when the sun rose in the sky, and I could get up, ending my losing battle. Washing my face with cold water and shocking my system seemed to help. Becka had packed my things last night, leaving out what I was going to wear or need for the day.

It was refreshing to wear my leather pants and billowy shirt with the leather vest that fit snuggly instead of the heavy fabrics and corsets. The guys were still asleep, so I wandered out to the balcony to take in the view and breathe in some fresh morning air.

My father and I had talked about taking a trip to see the Caleden Sea before I was introduced to the court and married off. Of course, Mother squashed that plan, saying it was improper and much too far to travel with a girl so young. It made me wonder what caused Mother to be so fearful of the world around her that she dared not step out of turn.

The sound of someone walking up behind me made me pause, but I knew it was one of my men the moment they settled their hands on my hips. "Did you end up getting any sleep last night, little mouse?" Cole asked.

I let out a heavy sigh. "I suppose some, but it wasn't a great night for rest, that's for sure."

His lips pressed to my head as he wrapped his arms around me. "I should have gotten Izel to come sleep with us so he could help. Today is going to be an important day, and you being tired is a risk."

Turning in his hold, I slipped my arms around his body. "Everything will be fine, Cole. We don't even know that Henry will come after us right away. News of our journey wasn't announced until late, and it takes time to gather people. I doubt he has as many dragon riders as he would like. Vasin had to push rather hard to get us there and back as fast as he did. It's not possible for that many people all at once."

"Forever the optimist." Cole chuckled. "Come on, let's get some energy in you and see if that helps to perk you up."

"Can we eat in the room? I don't want to join the castle for a meal," I requested.

Cole tucked a hand under my chin, lifting my head to kiss my lips. "That is something I can make happen. Stick close to Abbott while I'm gone, please. It makes me feel better knowing there are two of us with you, but he's formidable enough on his own."

I nodded as I followed him back into the room, where Abbott was pulling on a fresh shirt.

"I'm going to get food sent up... stick close," Cole called as he left the room.

Abbott walked over to me, scooped me up, and settled us in an armchair. "Finally, some time alone. I know things are different right now, needing to keep a closer eye on you, but can I just say I'll be glad when this is over."

I let my head rest in the crook of his neck as he ran a hand along my thigh. "It's crazy. We've been around each other all this time, but in a way, I still miss you."

"That is exactly how I feel," he commented. "Cassarah..."

Lifting my head, I met his gaze, concerned that something was wrong, but all I saw in his gaze was overwhelming amounts of love. "What is it?"

Abbott placed a hand on my stomach reverently. "I'm going to be a father..."

A smile pulled at my lips. "Yes, you are. I'm sure that one of them has to be yours. It's the only thing that makes sense unless the fates have a way of making things happen faster than they should."

"Did you know all I've ever wanted in life is a woman I love with all my heart and a son?" Abbott whispered. "Of course, I'd be happy with a daughter too. It's just when I think about it, I always picture a little boy. Who would have thought I'd get everything I wished for?"

I hugged Abbott around the neck, pressing our cheeks together before kissing him soundly. He was quick to keep the kiss going, angling his head to deepen it with a moan. My fingers curled into his long hair that was brushing his shoulders. The silky feeling just added to the moment as I shifted to straddle him. His hand grabbed my ass, keeping me pressed against him so I could feel his hardening cock in his pants.

He pulled back, breaking our kiss. "Little phoenix, we can't. Cole will be back, and the others will be joining us..."

"They've all seen me naked. It won't be anything new," I countered. Sliding off his lap, I yanked open my pants and shimmied them off as quickly as I could. Before he could argue with me further, I loosened his ties and pulled his cock free. "You wanted time with me, didn't you?"

"God, yes, but this doesn't need to happen," he answered with a grunt as I pumped my hand up and down his shaft.

Crawling back on his lap, I hovered over him, searching his face. "Tell me now if you don't really want this, and I'll stop."

Abbott let out a strangled growl and pushed me down as he thrust up, impaling me on his cock. I gasped as he filled me—the slight burn of being unprepared only added to the moment. Here I was on the eve of a battle for the future of our world as we knew it, and all I wanted was to feel all that was good in the world. My body craved to be fucked, loved, and filled with a reminder that I was growing life inside my womb.

Each time he thrust up, I met the motion, rocking into it, forcing him as deep as he could go. My body burned with delight as our breaths became quicker. There was nothing romantic about this—it was need-driven and reassurance that we didn't die without showing how much we loved each other. Abbott pulled me close, cupping my face in his hands as he devoured my mouth. Our tongues battled and twisted around each other, neither winning, but that wasn't the point.

"Shit," Cole swore.

I lifted my head to see him standing there holding a tray full of food. His gaze was hungry, even if he looked slightly uncomfortable. I reached out to him and curled a finger, beckoning him over.

He hesitated for a moment before setting down the tray and coming over. I paused in my movements to twist so I was now sitting on Abbott's cock, my legs between his. When Cole joined us, I grabbed his pants and tugged him to stand before me. Undoing his ties, I reached in, pulled out his semi-hard cock, and licked my lips. Looking up at him, I held his gaze as I took him in my mouth. With him not fully hard, I could get the whole thing in my mouth and kiss the base of his shaft. It didn't take him long to harden and become just slightly too much for me to handle. His hand slid into my hair and helped keep me at a steady pace as Abbott thrust up into me.

I was quickly becoming a fan of having two of my men sharing me at once. There was just something about being able to control two men while watching them crave my touch as we exchanged pleasure. Cole tossed back his head, moaning as I swirled my tongue around the crown of his cock. He was no longer able to hold himself back from thrusting into my mouth, and I enjoyed every moment of it.

Abbott pushed me forward so I was now standing as he pumped into me. My hands on Cole's hips kept me from crashing into his chest from the force of Abbott's thrusts. The pressure began to build low in my body, alerting me that I was heading for a climax. Needing both men to finish along with me, I clenched on Abbott as I sucked and hummed around Cole.

"Fuck, mouse, I'm gonna come," Cole warned me as he tried to pull out, but I dug my fingers into his skin, holding him still. "Little mouse, you don't need to do this."

My eyes flicked up to his, and I tried to tell him to shut up and let me finish this. I wanted him to come in my mouth, to know that I drained him and found pleasure in what I did to his body. Abbott started to lose his rhythm, which was a good sign he was getting close as well. Then, as if something tipped the scales, Cole shot off down my throat, and Abbott slammed home one last time, throwing me off the edge into a world of ecstasy.

"Oh God, she's clamping around me so tight it's like she's trying to drain me dry. If she wasn't pregnant with my child already, she would be now," Abbott muttered and pulled me off Cole and sat back on the chair.

Still with him inside me, I relaxed into him, curling my arms around his neck so I could comb my fingers through his hair. "That was exactly what I needed," I shared with a sigh. "I need to remember that sex is wonderful for dealing with stress."

A knock on the door had Cole stuff himself back into his pants and jog over to see who it was. He cracked open the door, his shoulders relaxed, and pulled it open enough to let the rest of my men in. When they caught sight of my legs splayed, filled with Abbott who was softening, letting his cum leak out of me, they groaned.

"That's so not fair," Pax muttered, adjusting himself in his pants. "There is no way we have enough time for us all to get a taste."

Cole just grinned. "She's pretty great at taking two at a time. It might happen."

Laughing, I kissed Abbott deeply one last time before I stood up and sauntered my way into the bathing chamber to clean up before putting my pants back on. While sex was amazing, wet leather rubbing up in some sensitive places wasn't.

With my hand over my eyes, taking in the courtyard of the castle where we were staging things, just as we had when we landed in Creisal. This time, I would mount up last, ensuring my guard was ready to protect me as we flew. My additional dragon riders were happy to be on the move, not enjoying city life after the quaint normalcy of Sheca. The summer home was out in the countryside farther south, leaving plenty of open space for the dragons to roam.

King Thomas came to stand beside me. "Are you sure it's safe to allow my wife to go with you?"

"Nothing about this is safe, but we need to keep it believable," I reasoned. "The Lost King can't have reason to suspect we know what's hidden at our destination. He has eyes and ears everywhere, and I'm assuming all the staff there is his. They will be the hardest to work around until we know what we're dealing with. Leaving the children here, keeping you out of the situation, along with Philip, is the best we can do. Your wife doesn't have a clue what she's done, and they know that. It will be interesting to see how they deal with her at this point."

"You make it all sound so simple when it's anything but," King Thomas shot back. "I'm supposed to be your ally, but all I've done is create terrible messes you keep cleaning up."

"Once Henry is out of the picture, you can rebuild your kingdom. I have a few dreams of how I would like to reinvent our world, so maybe I can share them with you later?" I offered.

He looked at me with amazement. "Here you are, walking into what could be a trap or certain death, and you're dreaming of the future?"

"If we don't have the future, what do we have?" I asked with a shrug. "I refuse to believe after everything I've been through and the things I've learned, that Henry will take me down so easily. If we destroy what we need to, then his trump card is gone. He'll be as human as I am... the only difference is I have others I'm protecting." I rested a hand on my stomach, trying to picture what it will be like as it grows bigger to make room for my babies.

King Thomas turned and bowed deeply to me, pressing a hand to his heart. "It is an honor and a privilege to be in your trust, Queen Cassarah. I wish you safe travels, and may the fates bless your mission, for it is one that will save us all." Saying what he needed to say, he returned to the castle without a backward glance.

Since the queen was traveling by carriage, she'd left much earlier in the morning while we had time. A dragon roar filled the air, one I knew well. Vasin landed, spreading his wings wide as he shot a burst of fire into the sky.

"Goodness, did you wake up on the wrong side of the roost?"

"This is war, Cass, and all us dragons know it. This city has been asleep for far too long, distancing themselves from the rest of the world. It's time they return, join the united front, and allow dragons to coexist."

"Have the dragons been avoiding this palace?" I inquired as I walked over to him, double-checking the harness. Taking a moment, I secured the supplies I wanted to keep close at hand, including my sword.

"They were the first to break the treaty and abuse us. We quickly cut them off and chose to shun their people, but with the new agreement with dragons, it might be time for those who are willing to come pay a visit. The countryside is teaming with life, and dragons are a good judge of character, which isn't found here."

"I couldn't agree with you more. This city needs to be purged, and everyone's roles in the world shuffled about. That, however, is a job for later. First, we need to keep the world from being taken over by an evil dictator."

Mounting up, I strapped myself in and gave him a pat on the neck, taking hold as he launched himself up into the sky. The sight of my dragon riders filling the horizon was something I don't think I'd ever find anything but awe-inspiring. These were my people— brave, true, and loyal. They didn't know the whole story but trusted I would guide them wisely.

Thirty

Cassarah

It was an easy flight to the summer house, full of beautiful scenery I wouldn't be able to find anywhere else in our kingdoms. My guardians stuck close while the others hung back in formation like the trained mercenaries they were. When we got to the summer home, it wasn't a home but another castle, just smaller. It was three stories high and spread out more like an estate, but still far larger than anyone really needed.

Surrounding the summer castle were farmlands with cattle roaming the fields, making a rather picturesque visual. It gave me some peace of mind that there weren't too many people close by to the summer castle so innocents wouldn't be slaughtered when the fight inevitably broke out. I could see from my vantage point the queen was already there, her carriage being pushed into the stables for safekeeping.

With the much more open landscape, I landed along with the others of my guard all at once. Servants came running from the castle to assist where needed, but I brushed them off, not needing to be fussed over. I handed off my personal luggage but kept my sword, strapping it to my hip. It had been a few months since I felt the weight of it, but it served as a reminder of our purpose here.

"This is what they call a summer home?" Cole muttered under his breath.

Paxton snorted, trying to keep from laughing as we entered the front gates to the castle courtyard. The gravel crunched under our feet, making it impossible to sneak in, which was helpful.

"Where are they going to put all of our men?" Abbott questioned, looking around the property.

"King Thomas told me there was an old barracks down the way they maintained in case there was ever a need to retreat out here. It isn't much, but they will have meals provided and a place to sleep. They will be taking shifts guarding the castle, so we can keep *some* loyal people around us," I explained.

The guys all nodded, but May didn't look pleased at all. "So, are the guards who are normally stationed here also going to be on watch? How is this going to work, blending the two?"

"I plan to talk to the head guard here and have them split who will be watching when and where. If we can have one group inside and another outside, then it will be flipped when the shift change happens," I shared, pausing to look at them all. "My hope is they won't feel like we are stepping on their toes but afford us the protection we actually need. Our biggest challenge will be not tipping off those who work for Henry. They can't know until it's too late what we're really up to."

"Cassarah, everything about this is a huge risk, and your men might be willing to bend to your requests, but just know I'm not going to be so easily swayed," May challenged. "You and those babies you're carrying are my responsibility, and I will do what is needed to protect you all."

"I would expect nothing less, May, but all I ask is that if you have a problem with my choices, you speak to me directly about it," I countered. "There will be no questioning my authority in front of the enemy. It can wait until we've removed ourselves from the situation."

May gave a sharp nod. "That I can abide by unless it will put you in immediate danger."

"Fair enough," I said, offering my hand to her.

Grinning at me, she shook my hand before pulling me in for a hug. "Ah, we made a mercenary out of you despite your noble upbringing. Never give into the first offer, always negotiate for better terms, but *never* forget to shake on it, or the deal is null and void. You make me proud to be part of your family, Cassarah."

I laughed and hugged her back. It wasn't often she allowed such obvious affection, and I wasn't going to waste the moment. With a slap on the back, she let me go, still grinning, and headed toward the castle, expecting us to follow.

"What in the world was that?" Dayson asked, his expression shocked. "That woman never says anything nice, let alone give hugs."

"Guess you just need to be special," I teased, grabbed his arm, and tugged him to follow after her. "May is unlike anyone you'll meet, and to be considered her family is one of the biggest compliments I think I've ever received."

"Oh, I wouldn't be too sure about that," Day muttered. "Once you're family, she no longer feels the need to protect your self-esteem."

"I love that she speaks her mind. It lets me know exactly where I stand with her, and that is something you don't get often in this world," I stated as we walked up the steps to the castle.

"We'll just see about that a few years down the road," Day warned.

The interior of the castle was far more relaxed than the one we just left. Oddly enough, it felt more like a home—a space to be lived in—not just presented as a show of status. Hundreds of windows let in the afternoon light, making the space warm and inviting.

"Your Majesty," an older woman said as she bowed before me. "I am Lady Blanch, and I run this estate for their majesties when they are not here. If you should need anything while you are staying with us, please don't hesitate to ask. I've been informed of your situation *personally* and *physically* so that I might be able to assist where I can. There is a wing of the castle I've set up that will be for just you, your consorts, and ladies while you sequester here for your pregnancy."

My hands immediately went to my stomach as she spoke, feeling the need to shield them from her judgment. I wasn't sure if it was the fact that I had more than one partner or if she just was this blunt with everyone she interacted with.

"The queen has retired for the afternoon to rest. Carriage travel has always been hard on her," Lady Blanch informed me as she clapped her hands together.

A young woman scurried from somewhere to appear at Lady Blanch's side. "Yes, m'lady?"

"Would you escort Queen Cassarah and her companions to the room in the west wing we prepared?" Lady Blanch requested, even though we all knew she wasn't asking.

The woman bobbed into a curtsy and set off, assuming we would follow. The rooms were on the second floor, and we passed many sitting rooms, game rooms, and I believe what I might guess to be a library. We were moved along so quickly I couldn't be certain. This castle was fully functional and could be used full-time if they ever wished to. Having more than one didn't make sense, but I was fine with the simple life.

We were led to a massive set of double doors the girl struggled to push open, revealing a long hall with various doors on either side. The hall ended in floor-to-ceiling windows, facing out onto the countryside.

"This whole wing is yours. All the rooms have been prepared, so feel free to choose where you'd like to stay. There is a dining room, two sitting rooms, bathing chamber, and a veranda that leads down into the gardens," the woman informed us before she bobbed another curtsy and went on her way.

The guys ventured down the hall, opening all the doors and checking the rooms as I waited with May and Becka. I promised I would let them do this, especially in this place, since we didn't know who to trust. Feeling uneasy, I looked back at the doors, noticing that they could be locked from the outside, and the inside didn't have a way to open it again.

"May, why do I feel like they put us in this wing for more reasons than to give us space?" I asked quietly, knowing that in old castles, the walls had ears.

She looked around calmly as if taking in the space, stepping over to a wall hanging that portrayed a group of hunters out chasing a buck. Pulling back the corner of it revealed a door, but there was no way to open it from this side. It could only be pushed open from the other side.

"Seems they are fine with things entering this wing... just not leaving again. This is not going to be a space where we can relax, I'm sorry to say. I think it would be best if we keep this to ourselves and not mention it to the queen. She will only stir up more trouble with her good intentions," May shared as she stood next to me once more. "That sword better be your new and fervent companion."

I nodded, understanding what she was alluding to. While I was always armed with my Birthright, this would help others to understand I was not to be messed with. The feeling that crawled along my skin, making my hair stand on end, told me this was the Lost King's home, and he ruled here whether he was present or not.

"All clear," Zan called from the end of the hall. "The rooms remind me of our home, much less about show and more about comfort," he shared as he walked up to us, Ezzu flying around him, chattering her excitement.

I smiled and took the hand he offered, seeing how excited he was to show me through the space. The first room was one of the sitting rooms, and across the way was the dining room. Both were simple yet welcoming, not at all austere in their decoration. Then started the bedrooms. Clearly, there were more than we needed, but it was nice to know it would just be us. The bathing chamber was like home, more of a community space for us all to use instead of individual ones.

"There is only one room that would work for you," Zan commented as we approached the last door. "It has the biggest bed *and* sitting area for us to hang out in."

Everyone else agreed since they were all there relaxing and chatting, pouring drinks from the pitchers of wine and snacking off the trays filled with food. At first glance, one might think we were totally unaware of what was going on around us, but I knew them well enough to see the watchful glances. They might have looked relaxed and enjoying themselves, but they were incredibly aware we were in enemy territory.

Gavin walked up with a goblet and handed it to me. "It's not wine since I wasn't sure your stomach would like that right now, so instead, I poured sweet fruit juice. The fruit can only be found here in Creisal. It's a bit tart but incredibly refreshing."

Leaning in, I kissed him on the cheek. "Thank you, my love. It sounds wonderful."

"Come sit. I know you've been flying, but I'm sure the babies will want to remember what it feels like to have their feet on the ground," Dayson ordered, pointing to a soft-looking armchair.

The second part of our plan was to play up the fact I was with child and was fulfilling my role as a noble woman to be at rest, hidden away while I completed the demands of creating an heir.

"Goodness, you act as if I'm made of glass. I move about just fine, but if it will make you feel more at ease, I will rest," I said with a sigh as I took my seat. "I think it would be lovely to take a stroll around the countryside to get some fresh air and sunshine, don't you agree, Becka?"

"Oh, don't get me pulled into this picking-sides nonsense." Becka chuckled. "While I do agree with you, the eight grumpy possessive males you have might not."

"Someone needs to be on my side, fending them off from keeping me in bed all day. I came out here to rest, but also it will be good for me and the babies to exercise," I pointed out. "What do you say, men? Can we take a tour of the countryside?"

They all grumbled and muttered to each other, then Jade spoke up. "Tomorrow. Today you will rest after the stress of journeying here. Maybe take a turn in the gardens for that fresh air to keep it close today as we get settled."

Hmm, he had a good point. Better to know what was going on around us to avoid issues later.

"You make a good point. Today, we will investigate the castle and then explore the lands around it at a later time," I conceded.

So that is what we did. We relaxed, used the bathing chamber to clean up after our travels, and I helped Becka unpack all my things. We requested that the palace staff remain out of our space unless we needed them. More people underfoot was the last thing we needed. We found three more doors in the common rooms, leading in but not out. Part of me believed that, at one point, they were normal servants' entrances that have since been altered. None of us found anything suspicious in the bedrooms, which helped me breathe a little easier.

Lady Blanch found us in one of the sitting rooms, the men playing card games while I read some reports that had been sent to me from Sheca. Things back home seemed to be going well, and Alsten had implemented the changes I requested before I left.

"Your Highness... and consorts," she greeted with a bow of her head. "The queen would like to invite you to dine with her and a few friends from the area."

"That would be lovely. When does she plan to have the meal?" I asked.

Lady Blanch blinked at me in confusion. "Now..."

I rose from my seat and calmly walked over to her. "So am I to understand that the queen has just requested my attendance? Could it be that you've known and neglected to tell me? While I am here to rest and see this pregnancy through, there are still matters of decorum that need to be attended to. When you look at me, do I look ready to join the queen of Creisal and her friends for dinner?"

"I... I assumed this is how you dressed in your kingdom and wouldn't be following the standard of decorum we have in Creisal. I beg your pardon, Your Majesty," she stuttered, bowing low before me. "Let me inform her of the situation, and I'm sure she will understand."

"Becka, would you please run back to my room and bring my crown back for me? It appears that everyone here already assumes I lack propriety, so why deny them that experience," I requested, then turned back to Lady Blanch. "You will not say a word to the queen because I know she isn't the one who led you to believe this was true. I will deal with the twittering court ladies who have nothing better to do than stir up trouble to entertain themselves."

May stepped up and used her dagger to lift Lady Blanch's head. "It would be wise to treat our queen with the respect that she is owed, or you might find yourself without a job… or maybe a head."

I could hear the woman swallow at May's threat, her eyes wide with fear. I reached out and placed a hand on May's arm, urging her to lower it. "Easy, May, it's our first day together, and people do not know much about us who hail from Sheca. I'm sure Lady Blanch has now learned her lesson."

May grunted as she dropped her dagger, sliding it back into the sheath on her thigh. "Don't test me again, *m'lady*."

Becka returned quickly, settled the crown on my head, and fixed my hair to help hold it in place. Then we were off, but Lady Blanch stopped us just before leaving our wing. "I do apologize, but this meal is for women only…"

All of my men started to argue, but I cut them off. "Stop," I barked. "Becka and May will attend with me. Two of you can come and stand guard outside the room while the rest of you remain here. I'm sure there is something you can come up with to entertain yourselves for a few hours."

Begrudgingly, they let us leave with Izel and Paxton in tow, muttering to themselves. I hoped they would take this time to do some exploring since the attention would be on this dinner. We were led to the castle's first floor and into a more lavish dining hall, where the twittering of women could be heard. I groaned internally, having always hated these kinds of events when Mother forced me to go to them. The difference this time was that I outranked these women, but it was clear from Lady Blanch's treatment that might not matter.

THIRTY-ONE

CASSARAH

Six ladies sat at a round table, sipping on glasses of wine and popping sweets in their mouths like we weren't going to eat dinner. I enjoyed sweets, but Mother had made them as undesirable as possible so I didn't ever gain weight. Of course, with the life I led now, that wasn't going to be a problem. I worked too hard for fear of that.

Queen Catharine stood and clapped her hands in excitement when she saw me. "There's my sweet niece-in-law. Come, I would like you to meet my friends."

I headed right up to her, seeing there was a seat on her right-hand side left open for me. I took in the ladies—some were older, closer to the queen's age, while some younger, possibly daughters to these women.

"Ladies, this is Queen Cassarah, gracing us with her presence all the way from Sheca to take a respite with us while she is with child. Poor thing didn't know. I surprised her with the news a few days ago." She turned back toward me, clasping my hands in hers. "I hope you don't mind. I asked them to bring their daughters so you might make some friends while you're here as well."

Looking at the table of hopeful faces, I bowed my head. "It's lovely to meet you all. Thank you for taking the time to join us here tonight."

"Sit, sit," Queen Catharine urged, taking her seat. "We like to do things backward when we have our ladies-only dinners. Dessert first, then work our way to the soup, which none of us enjoy all that much as it is."

Smiling, I reached out for a chocolate-covered strawberry and popped it into my mouth. "That is a brilliant idea."

Then they were off telling me everything I could possibly need to know about what was happening in the small town of Cliffshire. It was the largest town in the southern half of Creisal and where these ladies lived.

"You'll never guess what happened, Cathy," Edith announced. "A young man came to town and took up residence in the old Neely Estate near the church. No one has been there for years, but over the last few months, crews of people have been working on it, fixing the place up. He must be the one to have inherited it."

"The man is so handsome he'd make an angel weep," Tilda, Edith's daughter, gushed, fanning her face. "Those piercing blue eyes, almost like they see right into your soul."

That had my attention.

"I'm sorry, the Neely Estate?" I questioned, trying not to seem too interested. "Why would someone take the effort to restore something that's been empty for so long?"

Lillian cleared her throat as she prepared to tell the story. "The last family to live there went mad, killed his whole family, even the children not yet able to walk. Since no one was left alive, it fell to the church since that was in the man's will, if you believe that. The church didn't need the estate so they've had it up for sale for some time now. It was bought, oh... about three years ago. They've been fixing it up ever since, and the young man must have been the one to buy it. Cathy, aren't some of your husband's relatives buried there?"

Queen Catharine nodded, her cheeks glowing pink with how much wine she'd had. "Yes, that bastard of a grandfather. He had to be one of the worst men I've ever known, staying alive on spite alone. They didn't want him in the normal family plot, so they banished him out here. This castle used to be his full-time residence. Then when he passed, I took it over for a reprieve. We all know what it's like to be married to a man who actually doesn't want you. Rather have the stable boy in his bed, but they can't give you a child now, can they?"

The old women all nodded in understanding, lamenting over their own marriage problems with their husbands. Some preferred not to engage in sex at all, saying they just didn't see the need. Glass after glass, pitcher after pitcher, these ladies drank most men under the table. I abstained, gleaning more from their stories than they realized.

"You know what the crazy thing is?" Queen Catharine asked, followed by a hiccup. "I have these odd dreams that I've lived a life that doesn't make any sense. In these dreams, I'd go to the cemetery to visit that old bastard, but you know what... he wasn't there any longer. Nope, instead there was a box, one that glowed a sickly yellow color like it was oozing filth. What does that say about me? Am I oozing filth? Did you know someone told me I've been seeing another man for the past few years? The same man my husband was boinking."

The women gasped and covered their mouths with their hands in horror.

Queen Catharine waved her goblet around, the wine sloshing over the sides. "Why would I do that? I got my two children out of that man so Harriet and I could be in love without him bothering me." The queen's shoulders sagged. "She left me, you know... after fifteen years together, she left me, believing the lies that I took up with another man."

"I wondered why she didn't come with you. This was your home together," Edith tutted, dabbing a napkin at her eyes. "Poor Harriet, I hope you can get her to see reason. You both were so in love."

Clearing my throat loudly, I drew their attention. "Forgive me for not understanding things here in Creisal, but is it now allowed for you to love someone of the same sex? I know you have the whole open-marriage agreement, but why wouldn't that apply to that type of relationship?"

"While it isn't forbidden, it's also not welcome. The family name, fortune, and property all go to the male child of a union. For the union to count, you have to be married, so they created the law of an open marriage. That still doesn't mean the other person you're with can be your wife or husband. You have to be tied to a loveless marriage while you find your joy with someone else you can never love publicly," Lillian explained. "From what I hear, you people in Sheca have the right idea."

"I am incredibly fortunate to be with every person I love," I agreed. "Speaking of them, this is the longest I've been out of their sight since we've found each other. I bid you ladies a goodnight, and I hope you're all remaining here for the night to sober up before returning to your homes. We wouldn't want the men to know what you really think, now would we?" I teased.

The raucous laughter that burst forth from that comment made me smile as I left the dining hall. May and Becka were grinning when they joined me, nudging me in camaraderie, laughing at my joke.

"I have to admit that was actually a lot of fun and helpful," I shared when Izel and Pax walked up. "It would seem Henry has already arrived."

"What," Pax demanded. "This isn't good. It means he could take what we need and leave."

"I'm not so sure about that," I mused. "The item was brought here and hasn't moved. He bought a home near the item and has been restoring it for the past three years. Now, of course, that could be a cover to conceal that he was keeping an eye on it, but there could be something more."

"Spitfire, you know this changes the game no matter what, right?" Pax questioned. "If he's here, then we are out of time."

Nodding, we fell silent as a servant arrived to lead us back to our wing. A wave of tiredness fell over me, and I wrapped my arm around Izel's and leaned into him. "Are you all right?" he inquired.

"Just tired, seems the day has finally caught up to me. I didn't even have any wine, but it just feels like my body is so heavy," I answered.

Izel paused. Before I could protest, he scooped me up and continued on his way.

"I can walk perfectly fine," I grumbled.

Pressing a kiss to my temple, he chuckled. "I'm fully aware of that, but can you blame a man for wanting to hold his woman? Make the most out of opportunities... isn't that what you once told us?"

I scowled at him but gave him a quick peck on the lips. "Of course, you'd be the one to remember what I say even when I don't."

Relaxing into his arms, I wrapped mine around his neck and soaked in the contact, knowing I was well and truly loved. Of course, when the others saw me being carried, they converged, convinced something was wrong. Jade pulled me from Izel's arms to stand me up and look me over.

"Nothing looks wrong, but she could have eaten or drunk something that might have upset her stomach. Wait, you didn't have wine, did you? Are you drunk?" he asked, shooting question after question at me, not allowing me to answer.

Seeing that he was opening his mouth to speak again, I slapped my hands over it to keep him silent. "May I speak now?"

Rolling his eyes, he nodded.

"Thank you," I said with a smile, removed my hands, and kissed him on the nose. "I'm just tired. The dinner was lovely and surprisingly enough, I learned a lot."

"Tell them the important part first," Pax muttered, arms crossed and looking rather disgruntled.

"And what would that be?" Cole asked, coming to stand in front of me as if he could ever intimidate me.

"I believe he wants me to tell you that Henry is in town." The guys froze. "Seems he got here yesterday and has an estate, which just so happens to be right next to the church where the cemetery is. King Thomas' grandfather is buried there, and from what I hear, he wasn't a nice man," I added, knowing they didn't care, but I felt it was important.

If the tomb of the person was as evil as the magic it holds, it would make sense why it could keep it contained. It might also add to why no one could get to it if an evil spirit guarded it.

Pax growled and tossed his arms into the air. "Look how calm she is like none of this is a big deal. How can she just say that shit and not feel the panic I'm feeling right now? He's here, and he has to know we are too. Someone has been feeding him information faster than we anticipated."

"Or..." I cut in, "... he already was planning on coming here, and we just happened to show up at the same time. Either way, it doesn't matter... we were going to have to face him as it was. Henry isn't one to charge headfirst into a situation. No, he'll take a calculated position then choose what to do next." Not having the energy to argue, I stepped out of the circle of men.

I removed my crown and handed it off to Becka, shaking out my hair as I faced them once more. "This is nothing new, you guys. We were going to have to face off with him at some point. At least now, we have a heads-up. The other part is we know where he is and where we need to go. Right now, we need to act as if he isn't here, that we have no idea what's hidden in that graveyard, and lastly, that we plan to kill him." Sighing, I let my shoulders sag. "Last night wasn't all that restful for me, and I think it's finally hitting me. Who's going to stay with me tonight?"

"Izel," Cole blurted. "She had nightmares all last night, and you're the only one who can help her with those."

He nodded in agreement and turned to Zan. "I think having you here also will help... your soothing energy will be welcome. Also, having Ezzu as a backup pair of eyes if something happens will be invaluable."

Everyone agreed, and those going to their rooms kissed me good-night and left. When it was just the three of us, I plopped onto the bed, my body drained.

"Little warrior, I'm concerned this isn't normal," Izel whispered as he combed his finger through my hair. "I've never seen you this tired before, even after sleeping in a cold tent in the mountains. Are you sure you're feeling all right?"

"It's as if my body is just too spent to do anything like I'm a water flask with a leak. What I can't tell is if it's the babies who are taking it or if it's something else," I answered, rolling onto my side, tucking a hand under my head, and letting my eyes drift shut.

"Cassarah," Zan snapped.

My head snapped up, looking around, but nothing was wrong. "What? What is it?"

"You just fell asleep in seconds," Izel explained. "I tried to shake you awake, but that didn't work."

Tears started to fill my eyes. "Does that mean I can't sleep? I'm so tired I just need to rest. It's so much, and I'm so incredibly tired."

"Let's get you in more comfortable clothes first," Zan suggested, dropping to his knees to remove my boots.

The energy it took for me to do this simple task wasn't right. Fear made me shake as I helped to get my pants off, leaving me in my undergarments and shirt. "What's wrong with me?" I whispered as the feat of keeping my eyes open was becoming too much. "Don't let him take me, get Paxton. If something happens, he's the only one who can break his hold…"

"*Vasin!*" I screamed in my head as the world went black.

"*Little Dragon Queen…*"

"*I know you can hear me. I don't like to be ignored.*" Henry's snarl echoed in my head.

Desperately, I tried to reach out to Vasin, the guys, anyone or anything that might free me from this nightmare.

"*Oh, it won't be so easy this time. I'm far too close to my power source for you to possibly win,*" Henry taunted.

The world around me started to illuminate as Henry stepped into view, a sickly green glow around him.

"*You're too late. Now that I've gained enough power, I will all the kingdoms and even the dragons. I know you did something, changed the agreement somehow, but it won't stop me from draining them of power the way I have with my own dragon. Xotha couldn't be trusted any longer. He stopped following orders after his ordeal with your pet. He died for a good cause, though, and his body was wasting away. That happens, you know. Without a heart, nothing was left to give him life but the power I fed him. Now he's fed me all his power!*" Henry cried, raising his hands, letting the energy around him crackle like lightning.

I tried to push myself up, not wanting to leave myself at a disadvantage lying on the floor. No matter what I tried, there was no strength to do anything but keep my body breathing. *"What did you do to me?"*

"Me? Oh no, it is not I who has sapped you of your power. See, the tainted heart of a dragon needs life to sustain itself. It can take life from people, animals, dragons, humans... unborn children... The purer the life is, the stronger the power. You, little Dragon Queen, have both power and life inside you. The dragons blessed you with more than you should have, more than they ever gave me!" Henry raged, dropping to his knees before me. *"Now, I'm going to take it from you... all of it, every last drop."*

"CASSARAH," Vasin bellowed, breaking through whatever barrier that had been put up. *"GET UP!"*

"No, no you won't get away this time. I can't let you win... everything I wanted is so close. You're already drained past the point of being able to survive. All I need is your soul, then this will be over, and the world is mine!" Henry babbled as his hands clasped my head, trying to keep me from fighting as he pulled the last drop of life from my body.

"DO NOT BELIEVE HIS LIES, DEAR CASS. GET. UP. NOW!"

The faces of everyone I loved and who I would be leaving behind if I didn't do as Vasin demanded flashed before my eyes. The devastation on their faces was something I never wanted to inflict on them. Digging deep, I latched onto my bond with Vasin and pulled, screaming all my rage and agony out as I dragged myself out of whatever version of hell this was.

"Cassarah!" Izel yelled. "Pax, it's not working. Nothing is working."

"Vasin's out in the garden, and he looks fucking pissed," Zan called from somewhere in the room. "He keeps trying to climb up the stairs like he's going to fit in here."

The bed moved under me, and I was lifted. A groan escaped my lips as my body burned with pain. "We need to bring her to him. He has to know what's going on. Their connection is stronger than anything I've seen before," Izel said as he jogged, doing his best not to jostle me too much. "I knew there was something wrong, but I didn't know how to fix it or figure out what was happening."

"It's not your fault. I can't even break through whatever's holding her," Pax stated. "Right now, she feels closer to the surface than before, but it's like she could slip back under any second."

Vasin's roar rattled the windows as they brought me outside, the cool evening breeze brushing along my skin that felt so hot.

"She's burning up," Izel muttered.

"Quick, place her on the ground and let Vasin do whatever he thinks will help," Cole ordered.

It seemed all of them were here now, but no matter what, I still couldn't open my eyes. My hearing was sharp, and I could feel most things if I blocked out the pain. Izel settled me on the soft grass and soon a familiar scaly head was butting at my hand.

"*Cass, you need to fight the spell. We dragons blessed you with life, magic, and wisdom, which this curse seeks to take from you. You are more powerful than you know. Fight, use what we have given you to break free from its clutches. If you don't do it soon, your children will die.*"

I could feel tears streaming down my face. "*How, how do I fight when everything is gone?*"

"WHAT IS GONE? EVERYONE IS HERE... YOUR MEN, YOUR FRIENDS, AND AS ALWAYS, I'M HERE RIGHT BESIDE YOU. EVERYTHING YOU NEED TO KEEP LIVING IS RIGHT IN FRONT OF YOU. ALL YOU NEED TO DO IS LOOK."

I just need to look. How can all my other senses be fine, but I can't see?

"Is there something on my face? Over my eyes? Why can't I see?"

"THERE IS NOTHING BUT THE LIE HOLDING YOU BACK. OPEN YOUR EYES, DEAR CASS. FOLLOW MY VOICE AND SEE THE TRUTH BEFORE YOU."

See the truth...

What is the truth?

The truth is that I'm not alone. I have so many people who love me and have cheered me on since day one. Ballard helped me to believe I was worth it. Helena showed me I could be strong as a woman and still have a soft heart. Sal showed me how knowledge is power but also something that should be held with great respect. Person after person came to mind, helping me in big and small ways to get me where I am today. I'm in this fight for them—this world deserves to be free. Those who have fought for me have given me the chance to fight for them in return.

The truth is, all you need is love and hope.

Two things that I had massive amounts of these days. Turning inward, I dove into the well of magic I discovered when I was plummeting through the air toward almost certain death. Hope and love are what grew those wings for me because I was not alone.

Crashing into the well of blue magic, I coated myself in it and wrapped it tightly around my body like a blanket on a cold night. This power was mine—it had been entrusted to me by those who knew the world needed to see change. What is the first thing to bring about change? To *see* what's wrong with the world and do something about it.

The magic that encased me thrust itself into me, breaking whatever hold the curse had tried to use. It shattered into a million pieces, and I emerged like a butterfly out of the cocoon. This time, when I opened my eyes, I found everyone I loved standing there watching me with awe. Everything was lit up by an ethereal blue cast of light from the dragon wings on my back. The second the shock wore off, everyone surged toward me, but I held up a hand.

"Now is not the time. Now is when we end this," I declared.

Reaching out, I woke all the dragons and had them find their partners. The dragons that belonged to my people were already on their way, feeling Vasin's call. Ezzu darted over to me and perched on my shoulder, rubbing her small, scaled head against my cheek.

"Ezzu," I cooed, stroking her back. "Now, I need you to take the very best care of our man, all right?" She chirped her agreement back to me and flitted off to take up her station on his shoulder, wrapping her tail around his neck.

"Everyone is coming, and this battle will be finished tonight. His power is at its peak, but it's no match for what we have, and we're gonna damn well show him. Tonight will be the final battle for our people, and we will be victorious," I cried, thrusting my fist in the air, and everyone roared their agreement, dragons included.

Thirty-Two

Cassarah

Hunched low on Vasin's back, we flew as fast as his wings could carry us while Jade had us hidden from sight. The world of gray just added to the tone of those around me. It was time for this to end. I would destroy the heart and then if Henry managed to survive that, I'd free him from the life he hated so much.

The ground below us sped by, but I trusted Vasin to follow the pull of the cursed object, taking us in the right direction. I could feel it tugging at me, but my magic cloaked me in a shield of power, fending it off the best it could. Everyone was asleep, the town only visible from the few flickering lantern lights outside a tavern where a man stumbled out of, heading home. No one would know what was about to happen, but the fate of our world as we know it hung in the balance.

"Cass, trust in the fates. They knew this day would come and gave you everything you need to be able to right things. Trust your heart, not your head. The Lost King can't manipulate that part of you."

"He has no heart. He tore it out alongside his dragon's. A man can't live like that, so I will set him free."

"We will set the world free."

"That is my hope. With all this manipulation and lies, no one knows who to trust anymore. Soon, we will show them there is a different way. I just hope they will accept it."

"One battle at a time, dear Cass."

"Wise advice as always, my dearest friend."

Breaking away from the town, we found the church and the graveyard not far off. Headstones in orderly rows represented the lives that have been lost over the years. Further in the back were small stone huts—the mausoleums we were searching for. It wasn't hard to guess which one it might be, with an army of men surrounding it and a handful of dragons circling above. It seemed the Lost King hadn't lost his whole mind yet, but it didn't matter what fight he put up, I wasn't going to let him win.

"Fly directly over it, and I'm going to drop in. Jade still has us hidden, so when he drops the shadows, they will be more focused on what's happening out here than what I'm doing."

"You know they will hate that plan."

"Then I will beg their forgiveness when this is over."

Vasin let out an irritated growl, but he did as I asked, dropping low and slowing enough for me to drop with ease. My wings flared, letting me float safely down, landing right in front of the mausoleum's doorway. Then the world was once more filled with color, just as I let my wings disperse.

"They're here!" someone cried out.

Glancing over my shoulder, I spotted the horde of dragons appear out of thin air, flames bursting from their mouths, taking out the front lines. The enemy dragons dove into the fight from above, but my people were skilled fighters, having spent their entire life training for this moment—the moment the mercenaries leave their mark on the world.

The mausoleum door was made of thick, heavy stone, and I wasn't sure how to get through it. Then I remembered the time when I freed Vasin from the roost so long ago. This time, instead of using an arrow, I manifested a dagger and poured power into the tip of it before slamming it into the stone. It exploded, sending me flying back into the fray of the battle.

"One got inside! Keep your eyes open... they blasted through the door!"

A man reached down and helped me up, clearly thinking I was on his side. Before he could yell as he noticed my arm glowing the mark of my Birthright bright in the darkness, I slipped the knife between his ribs.

"May your mind and spirit be set free," I whispered in his ear before guiding him to the ground where he died.

The chaos of bodies around me tossed me in all directions as I tried to get back to the mausoleum. Dragon riders dropped out of the sky, leaving their dragons to fight while they handled things on the ground. One landed in front of me, and I realized it was Dayson, his ax flashing in the moonlight as he cleared the space around me.

"Cassy-bear, I don't know what you're up to, but you're not doing it alone," he snapped, using the handle of his ax to shove people back.

"I need to get to the mausoleum," I shouted as I drew my sword, fending off an attacker. "I blew the door open, but it sent me flying, and I got swept up in the fighting."

With another powerful stroke of his double-bladed ax, people fell away. "Then let's get going."

I grabbed onto his belt, using him as a shield while he cleared us a path. The sound of swords clashing had me spinning around to find Izel with his dual blades blocking a huge man with a double-handed broadsword. With a swift move, Izel kicked the giant man in the balls and dropped him to his knees, where his head was quickly lopped from his neck.

"I've got your back. Keep going, Day!" Izel shouted.

"HOLD ON, CASS, TAHIR IS COMING TO AID YOU."

"Stop!" I yelled, pulling on Dayson's belt. "Tahir is coming."

The red dragon let out a roar announcing his presence before a stream of fire burst from his mouth. The heat of the dragon fire was intense, but it wasn't close enough to burn us, just enough to clear a path straight to our goal.

"Run!" I ordered, shoving Dayson into movement.

"Goddammit, woman. You're lucky I love you bossing me around like that in the middle of a battle!" Dayson hollered over his shoulder as he grabbed me and tucked me under one arm before charging ahead.

Abbott appeared, fending off those who noticed what we were trying to do.

"Stop them!" someone bellowed.

Arrows zinged through the air, but more dragons darted in and out of the fray, tossing the archers into trees or stomping on them, crushing them to death. Everything was utter chaos, nothing made sense, and no matter where you looked, people fought tooth and nail.

"Cassy-bear, can you sprout those wings of yours when you need to?" Dayson asked.

I didn't understand why he was asking, but I answered all the same. "Yes. Yes, I can."

"Fuck, they're going to be so pissed at me for doing this," Dayson muttered. "Hold on, you're going to be faster without us holding you back."

The next thing I knew, Dayson spun in a circle before launching me into the air. I let out a short scream before clenching my jaw shut so I didn't draw attention. My wings burst forth, carrying me higher above the fray. All of the Lost King's army was doing everything they could to keep the entrance blocked with their massive numbers, but they were going to need more than that to stop me.

Darting forward, I created a shield that I held out front as I hit the wave of people, tossing them to the wayside as I used my wings to propel me forward. I could tell I was getting close as the magic kept trying to repel me like it knew if I made it inside, everything would come to an end. Sweat poured down my face as I used everything I had to keep pushing forward.

Then I was through.

It was as if the bubble burst, and I landed inside with a *thud*. Scrambling to my feet, I wiped my face off with my sleeve, giving my eyes a moment to adjust. The platform where a body would be placed in its coffin was empty, but the ground under it was dug up with a ladder peeking out. Carefully, I ventured forward and peered down the hole. An eerie glow emanated from within, and I knew it was the object I was looking for. The shaft was too narrow to use my wings, meaning I had to climb down like anyone else would.

As silently as I could, I made my way until I was about halfway and could see the bottom. Letting my feet rest on the outside of the ladder, I dropped. Just before I hit the ground, I twisted and rolled, setting me in the perfect motion to pop up to my feet. Bow in hand, I crouched, taking in what was around me. Under this mausoleum was a tunnel that fed into the church's tunnels. It would seem, at one point, someone must have practiced dark magic in this place. An altar sat in the middle of this open room with a metal box etched with symbols I didn't recognize resting on top of it. That is what I'd come for—the heart of a dragon tainted by dark magic, rotting with evil.

"So, you managed to break the curse's hold on you," Henry said as he slowly clapped his hands, entering the altar room. "Foolish girl, did you really think coming in here was the smart thing to do? The power is stronger the closer you are to it. Now it will rip everything it can from you, leaving a husk for your loved ones to find."

I watched him for a moment, wondering how those women thought he was handsome. The dark magic he was using took from him as much as he thought he was getting. His skin clung to his bones, his eyes still that same blue color as his father's stood out hauntingly. They were bloodshot and wild with madness, and whatever part of him that had been human was gone.

"Look how lost you are," I said, shaking my head. "How can you not see that this curse is doing the same thing to you? It's killing you, stripping you of every ounce of humanity."

"Who needs humanity? Hmm? What good has it done us? Humanity is what threw me away and left me to live a lie! I was to be a king, but he tossed me out like the trash he thought I was," Henry raged, spit flying from his mouth as he snarled his words. "No, I will be a god. Once my humanity has been obliterated, I. Will. Be. A. God! Nothing will stop me, not even you!"

Power collected in his hand, the same sickly green color I'd seen around him in my nightmare. When it grew large enough, he hurled it at me. I lifted my hand palm facing forward and stopped it in its tracks. Enraged, Henry hurled bolt after bolt of power at me, only to be deflected.

"You are not more powerful than me! I gave up *everything*!" he screeched.

Using my power, I sent out a rope of it, twining it around his body, keeping him restrained. He tried to fight it, but I knew my magic would hold. Pulling my attention from him, I approached the box as it pulsed with power. Tendrils of wild magic seeped out of it, trying to siphon off my magic, but I waved them aside.

"There is nothing you can do. If you touch it, then the curse will shift to you. It will take your dragon's life and grant you the same thing it gave me. This is what you wanted all along, isn't it? The power of eternal life, serving the dark magic as its slave so you can keep the magic all for yourself!" Henry seethed as he started to claw at himself to get free.

Blocking him and his words out of my mind, I looked at the box. Something in me told me what needed to be done. I reached out to my bond with Vasin, pulling him so that he was with me, bolstering me as I sliced my hand, letting my life's blood flow over the box. It started to shiver and shake, the magic inside it going crazy as it drank up my offering.

"It's all right, Cass. I'm right here."

Taking a deep breath, I closed my eyes, reaching out to the connection with my consorts, then adding in Becka and May. The power that surged through my body almost made me buckle, but I stood strong. Then, I felt two new bonds reaching out to me, sharing their essence with me. Tears pooled in my eyes as I knew it was from the life growing inside me. With the addition of their offering, I knew I had what I needed.

"I love you all," I whispered as I slammed my hand to the box.

The evil crashed into me, clawing at the power I'd collected, desperate for it to fill the void it felt. So, I did exactly that. Everything that I was, that I am, and that I will be, I surrendered it all. Flashes of every happy moment in my life flit by as it was forced into this creature's need.

At one point, whoever created this did so from their own pain and suffering. They needed, like Henry, to have the power to make those who hurt them pay. When that wasn't enough, it needed to find others like them, forcing them to do what it couldn't. That's where I was different—I'd healed my wounds with the love I received from others. Instead of needing revenge, I chose to be better than them. My children will have a mother who loves them endlessly and will tell them that every day. The people in my life will share my burdens as we walk through life together. Revenge is fleeting, but rising above to change a generation or even maybe a nation was far more satisfying.

As the fates said, I was chosen because I was nothing like the others.

Pure blue light exploded, filling the room, casting all shadows from the corners and exposing everything to the light. The darkness couldn't hide anymore—the light had driven it out, cleansing the space from the pain and agony that had been festering for so long. The box under my hand started to glow red and then melted, coating the altar in a sheen of polished silver so brilliant you could see yourself in it.

The blue light started to fade, but wisps of it danced around the space as if the spirit that had been trapped was now free and happy for the first time. When I turned to Henry, he'd vanished—nothing but soot on the ground gave any sign that he'd ever been there. The angry soul had taken far too much from him to survive its final death.

My hands dropped to the altar, and tears rolled off my cheeks to splatter below. My heart ached for those who'd lost themselves to this curse, the belief that the only way they could heal was to harm others. I prayed the fates saw fit to release them from that bondage, to finally find peace and learn another way. I crumpled to the ground, my legs no longer able to hold me up. As I wiped the tears from my face, I spotted a flickering image I thought I recognized.

"Miranda?"

"*Well-done, Dragon Queen,*" she answered, giving me a bright smile.

Another person appeared next to her, wrapping her arms around Miranda's waist. "*See, Mom, I knew she could do it. The others might have doubted a noble woman could pull this off, but they forgot one thing. You were always born with the heart of a mercenary."*

They smiled and waved, dispersing into glowing blue dust as Jade burst through their image. "Little bird!"

"It's over," I croaked, my emotions thick in my throat. "It's finally over."

Jade crouched down, letting me wrap my arms around his neck as he lifted me from the ground. "You did it, little bird. You saved everyone."

"No, it wasn't just me," I corrected, resting my head on his shoulder. "We all did it together because love and hope will always win out in the end."

THIRTY-THREE

CASSARAH

"Are you sure you need to head back to Sheca?" Queen Catharine asked me for the tenth time.

I took her hands in mine and clasped them tightly. "While I would love to spend more time here, I think a week of relaxing and doing nothing is all I can handle. If I don't get these men something to do so they stop driving me crazy, who knows what will happen."

Catharine chuckled at that. "They do seem the intense sort, don't they?"

"You don't mind that I steal King Thomas for a bit, do you? We need to go over our plans with Phillip before he returns to Norden and begins to pick up the pieces."

She waved off my question. "Goodness no. Thanks to your prodding, I found where Harriet's been staying, and I plan to go see her. As you said, if we really love each other, we will find a way to work past what's happened. Thank you for explaining what really happened to me. I felt like a doddering old fool. How could I just up and forget three years of my life?"

"I'm so sorry it happened, but all of that is in the past, and the future is so bright for all of our kingdoms. We need to do better for ourselves and our children," I pointed out as I lovingly brushed a hand over my stomach.

The queen's eyes welled up with tears, but she sniffled and regained her composure. "You come see me any time. I know you lost your mother, but don't forget we are family now too. Off you go now before I change my mind and beg your men to let me keep you longer."

That threat was enough to get me moving. The queen and I had grown incredibly close over the past week, but she was still a lot to handle. Skipping down the steps of the summer castle, I found my men ready to go, their dragons packed up and waiting.

"I thought she was going to change her mind and lock you away," Gavin teased as I passed him.

Ignoring him, I headed right for Vasin, who had his wings out sunning, warming his body up for me. He'd become just as bad as the other men in my life, worrying about the silliest things.

"Cass," Vasin warned, catching wind of my thoughts. *"Just get up here so we can go home. Our time here was needed, but there is still so much for us to do."*

"Bossy, bossy, bossy," I said as I climbed up. *"All right, you grumpy old man, let's go home."*

The flight was what I needed. We kept the pace efficient but did not push us harder than we needed since we still had half our army with us. Once I'd taken care of the heart and Henry died, anyone who'd been influenced by either was freed. Many people awoke to find themselves in the middle of a battle they didn't know they were fighting. Of course, there were those who were fully aware and kept up to the bitter end, but we outnumbered them. It was a swift ending to a war that took generations to build.

King Thomas came out immediately with Prince Phillip to deal with things and help assist those displaced from their home kingdom. The three of us came up with a plan for the future—well, most of one, that is. After the battle, I slept for two days, drained from using so much magic, and this sent the guys into a frenzy. When I woke, they treated me like I'd almost died or something. That is why

I requested them to join me in Sheca, where everyone will feel much more comfortable.

Our dreams for our kingdoms' future were big dreams, but I really believed they could happen. Right now, everything was in shambles—Errit had no ruler, Utros was reeling from the impact of those under Henry's influence recovering, and Norden was going to be under Prince Phillip's rule when he returned.

Queen Mary still refused to speak to any of her family, but Catharine decided it might be best if she took care of her. Being in Creisal wouldn't remind her of what happened, and it would be best for her not to be in Sheca any longer.

That first sight of Sheca as we crossed over the mountain range was one I loved. It was a beacon of green in the harsh terrain, a haven for those who needed it, and a land who put their people first. Dragons came and went freely, choosing those they wished to find friendship with, an occurrence we hoped might start to happen in other kingdoms. Vasin circled the valley, letting me take it all in. I might have been gone for only two weeks, but so much has happened, it felt like a lifetime since I was home.

"You're back," Helena cried as she pulled me into a hug. "Oh dear girl, I've missed you terribly."

"I'm not sure if I should be offended. You're never that excited to see me, and I'm your own grandson," Cole pouted as he walked up behind me.

Helena smacked him upside the head before pulling him into a hug. "Foolish boy, you're all I have left besides your grandfather. Of course you matter."

"Yeah, well, that won't be true for long. Someone is adding to the family," Cole whispered loudly.

Helena whipped around to look at me, hands covering her mouth as her eyes grew wide. "Is it true?"

Smiling, I nodded, causing her to let out a shriek as she wrapped me up in another hug. "Oh, this is the most wonderful news! Just wait until I tell Ballard. Oh, who am I kidding... I'm telling everyone."

With that announcement, she released me and hurried off into the castle.

"You did that on purpose," I said, glaring at Cole.

"Now, little mouse, would I do a thing like that?" he asked, grinning at me.

Arms wrapped around me, pulling me away from the face I wanted to punch. "Whoa there, spitfire. I know how good your right hook is, and I don't think you want to give him a black eye just yet. We have a feast to go to tonight. You want to keep him looking pretty, right?"

"I suppose," I muttered.

"Isn't being pregnant supposed to make you sweeter?" Jade asked as we all gathered in our sitting room.

Abbott smacked him. "Don't believe everything you hear. Cassarah is already sweet. It makes sense it would make her feistier."

"That's it, none of you are sleeping with me tonight," I announced.

They paused a moment then shrugged, clearly not at all worried.

"Bet you a gold coin she'll be worming her way into our beds looking for some lovin' before the night is over. Normal Cassarah is energetic, but pregnant spitfire is relentless," Paxton said as he flopped into a chair. "I mean, I really shouldn't be complaining. Who taught her the tongue trick?"

Grabbing a pillow, I hurled it at his face, smacking him right in the nose. "No more tongue trick for you, and you'll also be at the end of my list of people's beds I crawl into. Keep talking, and I'm sure I can come up with some other punishments."

The guys backed away from him, leaving him to his own demise.

"Nice, assholes... real nice," Pax muttered, clutching the pillow to his chest.

As the world changed, so did I. My belly grew bigger, ankles swelled up, and I craved pudding all the time. I would wake up in the middle of the night and need to eat pudding. The guys were amazing dealing with my mood swings that I knew made me more challenging to live with. They loved the high sex drive, and I used it to make up for everything I did during the day. They always knew if I felt guilty about my behavior when an afternoon delight happened in the planning hall between meetings.

Becka was my saving grace as she acted as my external brain, helping me to remember what I was doing with my life. Carrying two babies left me waddling around the castle, continuing to do all I could, but I was slowing down. Once I was on the castle's first floor, that's where I would spend the day until going up for bedtime. The guys argued, but we all agreed I would continue to rule as normal as long as I could manage.

"Cassy-bear, don't bite my head off when I say this, but I'm not sure you should hold an audience hall session today. We've kept you to the second floor, and I'm not sure we could get you back up to our rooms later," Dayson explained, watching me warily that I wasn't going to throw anything at him.

"Day, I hear you," I answered. "The problem with that is, this is so important to the new way we want to have all our kingdoms running, and Sheca has been doing this the longest. Everyone from Errit, Utros, Norden, and Creisal are here to see how I conduct this session."

"Love of my life, I fully understand that and wouldn't ask you not to if I didn't have a reason," Day countered.

Frowning, I looked at him. "What reason is that?" A wave of pain hit me, and I clutched my stomach, groaning.

"That is my reason. The pain is happening more often, and it seems to be getting worse," he pointed out. "What if you end up giving birth right there in the throne room?"

"Well, that would certainly be a story to tell." I chuckled as I pushed on the table for leverage and moved my massive belly in the right direction. Standing, I took a deep breath and smiled. "See, I'm fine."

Taking a step, I gasped as fluid poured out of me, splashing onto the floor.

"That's it, you're done. It's not gonna happen, and I'm calling Alto once I get you in bed," Dayson muttered as he hauled my round body up in his arms and hurried me to our room.

Becka spotted us, and her eyes went wide. "Alto?"

"Yes, go now... her water broke," Day answered, marching right past her. "Make sure the others know."

"How do you know my water broke? Maybe I just peed myself?" I countered.

He just gave me a look that told me I was walking on thin ice, so I shut my mouth and hung on. Another wave of pain hit me, and I crunched myself in his arms.

"Oh God, that one was awful," I cried, trying to rub the tight skin of my belly to make it feel better. "Could you two try not to kill me before you're born?"

Faster than I would have thought, Dayson had me in my room and sitting on the edge of the bed. "How are we doing?"

"It feels like my children are trying to claw their way out of me, but other than that, I am great," I snapped.

"Hang in there. We don't call you Dragon Queen for nothing," Day offered, trying to be encouraging.

I grabbed him by the front of his shirt and dragged him down to my level. "Go find someone else who is going to be more helpful."

His eyes went wide, and he nodded, backing away slowly. Then another wave of pain hit, and I was screaming, which had him moving into high gear.

"Please tell me Alto is coming!" I heard him yell at someone.

"Goodness, you certainly aren't taking this well. Go on, find the others. I'll sit with her while you do that," Helena soothed, then appeared in my room moments later. "What did you do to that poor man? He looked like he was going to cry."

Groaning, I rocked forward, grabbing my stomach as my whole body seemed to contract on itself. "He wasn't being helpful, blathering on about stupid things."

"Ah, I see," Helena commented as she kneeled before me, brushing a cool rag over my face. "Let's see if we can't get you out of these clothes. It will be much easier to deal with this whole thing without so many layers."

It was a struggle, but we managed to get me down to my shift. The damn thing was wet and sticking to my legs, and I had a feeling it wasn't going to survive this birthing.

"Do you feel like you can get up and walk around a bit?" Helena asked.

I shook my head. "No, the pain is too bad and coming faster."

"Believe it or not, that is a very good sign. It means your little ones are eager to get out and meet you."

"The feeling isn't so mutual at the moment," I said, glaring at her.

Helena laughed and patted my arm. "Trust me, when those little ones are in your arms, you won't care a lick about what you just went through. They will be worth it."

When this wave of pain hit, I felt the urge to push, but there was no way I was going to be doing that without Alto here. Then, I heard the crash of a door and male voices growing nearer.

"Hold up," a female voice called. "Absolutely not. There is no way I am going to let all of you in there while this is happening. You're going to drive her mad."

May the fates bless you for the rest of your life, Alto. She was right. If they thought they were going to be in here talking to me, I might stab one of them. There was a heated discussion, but it was cut off when my guttural cry cut through the air.

"There is no discussing this. I've told you what's happening, and your wife needs me. Are you going to listen, or do I have to stand out here, leaving her alone to make sure you do as you're told?" Alto challenged. There was some sort of answer, and then Alto was striding in, arms full of things. "Oh, Helena, good, I'm glad you're here. It's nice to have someone who knows what's going on with a level head."

Alto moved about the room gathering things, placing them where they were needed, and finally came to stand in front of me.

"Have you reached the point where you want to push?" Alto asked.

I nodded, unable to talk as I tried to control my breathing through the pain. When the next contraction hit, I could feel a shift, and something was coming whether we were ready or not.

"Something happened," I gasped, standing. "It's coming... it's coming fast."

Both women moved into action, grabbing my arms and walking me to the foot of the bed where two ropes had been tied. We'd gone over what to expect so I leaned my back against the wood, grabbed onto the ropes, and squatted. Helena came to the side, cloths in hand while Alto was right in front of me, lifting my dress over my knees so she could catch the baby as I pushed.

"You are doing amazing, Cassarah. This is the worst part, but we are nearly there," Alto coached, gripping my knees and looking me right in the eye. "When the next contraction comes, I want you to push like you've never pushed before and don't stop until I tell you, understood?"

Biting my lip, I nodded, feeling the tightening in my lower back, signaling the start of a contraction. I screamed, my hands turning white with how tightly I held the ropes and pushed.

"That's it!" Alto praised. "I see the head. You can do it... keep pushing!"

Then the air was filled with cries of a new life entering the world and mad as hell about it. Alto handed the baby off to Helena, who wrapped her and handed Alto a knife. The cord was cut, and Helena bustled off to clean up the baby while I did this all over again.

"You did great, Cassarah," Alto murmured as she moved her hands over my belly. "I'm just checking to make sure this second baby is just as ready to leave as its sibling."

Quickly, another contraction happened, but it was shorter and seemed to shove the next baby in position.

"Ah, that's lovely, just lovely," Alto said with a smile, meeting my gaze. "Are you ready to be a mother of two?"

"I just want them to be all right and preferably out of me," I answered, sobbing as I laughed, the stress making my emotions all over the map.

The next contraction moved in, and I was bearing down, pushing this baby out like it was my only purpose in life.

"There it is, you got this," Alto cheered. "Come on, one more big, big push."

"I'll fucking push you!" I screamed as I did what I was told, pain lancing through my body telling me this baby was bigger than the last. "Oh God, tell me I'm close!"

"A bit more... the shoulders are broad on this baby. Let me see if I can assist," Alto explained. "Push again, and I promise this will be over."

"If you're lying, I'm going to stab you," I panted, gathering all my strength and pushed.

A literal *pop* could be heard, and the baby was out and in Alto's hands. I could tell that the baby was indeed bigger than its sibling. Helena hurried over with more cloths to swaddle the baby while Alto cut the other cord.

"Is he all right? He's not crying," I asked, my breath coming quickly as I tried to fend off panic.

Helena smiled down at the baby. "Oh, this little man is just fine... wide awake and alert. Just seems like he doesn't need to share his thoughts with the world yet unlike his sister."

I sobbed, letting go of the ropes and sliding to the mess-covered floor. "A boy and a girl?"

"Yes, Cassarah, a beautiful baby girl with her father's seafoam green eyes, and this little boy is the spitting image of Abbott. There's no denying who their daddies are," Helena cooed as she cleaned up my son.

Alto cupped my cheek, drawing my attention. "I'm going to need one of your men to help me get you to the bathing chamber to get you cleaned up. Then you can hold your babies."

Weeping, I nodded, unable to control the joy exploding from my heart. They were fine—everything I went through and survived didn't affect them in the slightest. Relief washed over me as Abbott came to carry me off.

"You have a son," I whispered. "What are we going to name him?"

Abbott looked down at me with so much love and joy and kissed my forehead. "How do you feel about Christof? It's a family name. I had a little brother who only lived a week who'd been given it."

"I think that's a wonderful name, and I love it's part of your heritage," I shared as he helped me into the water.

Too tired to complain, I let him wash me from head to toe. He brushed and braided my hair and carried me back to the room, where the bed was turned down, and Helena and Alto waited, holding my children.

"We didn't let them see yet. It seems only right that you should first," Alto said with a grin. "You did all the work, after all."

Helena offered me one child. Her skin was darker than mine but not as deep as her father's. The curls came from both of us, though, along with the dark coloring. Her stunning eyes gazed up at me, almost as if we were both shocked to see each other. "Hello, my little flower," I whispered, nuzzling my nose against her cheek. She gurgled her joy, waving and kicking her arms and legs.

Then Alto placed my son in the crook of my other arm. He was just as beautiful as his sister, with creamy skin, light blue eyes, and a bald head. He was absolutely stockier than his sister, but it fit him perfectly. He would be a brave warrior like his father, protecting our lands with his sister right at his side because I could tell these two would be inseparable.

"Can the others come in now?" I asked, not lifting my gaze from these stunning miracles.

Someone chuckled, causing me to look up, and there, standing around the bed, were my men. I gave them a watery smile and motioned with my head for them to join me on the bed.

"Don't get shy on me now," I teased. Jade crawled over to my left side, peering down at our daughter. "She's perfect, isn't she?"

He nodded, completely at a loss for words as tears welled up in his eyes. "What are you calling her?"

"I have an idea, but only if you like it," I said. "There was someone through this whole ordeal who taught me so much through her life experiences. She lost so much yet through her sacrifice, we all survived."

Jade frowned. "Who?"

"Miranda, the Raven Queen," I answered. "Our daughter is going to do so many amazing things. I just feel it."

"Then it sounds like the perfect name to me. Both of our children have some big shoes to fill. Considering who their mother is, I think it's best we give them all the help we can," Jade agreed, kissing her forehead.

"That's where you're wrong, my love. We are only the ones who have set the plan in motion. It will be their job to change the world for good," I explained.

"Good thing they have one of the best role models as a mother to learn from," Abbott shared, stroking a hand over our son's head. "We will do our best to add to that and teach them everything you've taught us."

"Hope and love... it can change the world," Cole said, smiling.

This is just the beginning.

Of what?

Of everything.

~The End~

About Author

Elizabeth is an International Best Seller, originally from Illinois but now living in sunny Phoenix, AZ. Elizabeth has been writing for nine years and started out in YA Fiction but recently found herself loving the Reverse Harem genre. Like her favorite books, Elizabeth loves to write about strong women of all varieties. Not all strength is flashy or apparent at first glance—some lies just under the surface.

Don't Miss Out!
Be the first to know what is coming next by following Elizabeth's social media! You never know when or what will be coming next!
Website: ElizabethKnightBooks.com
Facebook: Elizabeth Knight's Unicorn Queens
Instagram: elizabethknightauthor
TikToc: elizabethknightauthor
Newsletter: https://landing.mailerlite.com/webforms/landing/i0m1g8

Also By

Mercenary Queen Series - Complete series
Birthright
Dragon Queen
Forgotten Throne
The Final Battle

Sunshine & Rainbows Omegaverse
Bailey-Rose Duet: Clouds & Daydreams + Petals & Promises

Knot All Is Omegaverse
Knot All Is Lost Duet
Knot All Is Ruined Duet

Caprioni Queen Complete Series
Glitter & Guns
Blood & Heartache
Revenge & Truth
Love & Power

Hidden Empire Complete Series
Two Tricks
Three Tricks
Four Tricks

More Tricks
Our Tricks

<u>Hidden Empire Novel</u>
Harper's Renegades

<u>Omega Assassin</u>
Dual Nature
Hidden Nature
Perfect Nature

www.ingramcontent.com/pod-product-compliance
Lightning Source LLC
Chambersburg PA
CBHW070441300726
48975CB00007B/1996